RAY GRIGGS

Published in the United States by RG Entertainment, Ltd.
Through IngramSpark and Amazon.

ISBN 978-1-7348489-0-8

Printed in the United States of America on acid-free paper.

www.rgentertainment.com
www.jacksterlingadventures.com

First Edition

Book design by Ray Griggs
Book Illustration by Didier Konings

Dedication

To my lovely wife Krissy, who puts up with my Peter Pan syndrome and the need to look at things through a different lens, along with my four enchanting children: Angelina, Gabrielle, Benjamin, and Abigail. As they are my artistic muse, my only regret is that I can't freeze time and keep them young. For them, I dedicate 90% of my time, while working the other 90%. Yes, the math is correct. I like to multitask.

Additionally, to my fellow directors Steven Spielberg, George Lucas, and Richard Donner. They inspired me as a child while showing me an archeologist who carries a whip, a legacy that takes place "a long time ago in a galaxy far, far away..." and proof that a man can fly.

Acknowledgments

Like to thank Didier Konings, with the book cover and trailer. Anyone who has worked on *Wonder Woman, Ghostbusters: Afterlife, Tomb Raider,* and *Stranger Things,* then willing to put up working with me—my hat is off to you.

Also, a special thank you goes to my friend Adam Baratta and Advantage Gold; as one of my commercial clients, their influence in the world of gold only helps make my stories shine.

And a recognition to the REAL Joe Lorenzo, a casting director who not only cast all my projects, but whom I had to base one of my characters after. He has always had an ear to bounce one of my crazy ideas around, which one day would make a great story.

Gratefulness to Sir Richard Taylor; you're a true artisan and friend who always believed in me and inspired me to be a better artist.

I want to express my heartfelt gratitude to Jerry Molin, one of the legendary producers, who has a significant heart and has encouraged me to never give up, despite Hollywood's struggles.

Acknowledgment to Triton Submarines and Patrick Lahey. Their imagination and engineering allows us to explore a new world that exists just under the ocean, new depths for personal submersibles that never seemed possible except in science fiction, and which let my character to have a craft to maneuver around.

And a blessing to YOU, the person who purchased my book and was willing to open your wallet to buy my work. Thank you, for, without you, none of this would be possible, and I genuinely hope I fulfill or exceed your expectations in the adventure that lies ahead.

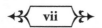

Continue the Adventure

UnderWaterBookSeries
JackSterlingAdventures
Jacks_DeepDives

To sign up for *Jack Sterling* Fan Club:
visit www.jacksterlingadventures.com

Contents

Chapter I

The Discovery

World aquatic life cycle. Similar to a flying saucer descending from the heavens, the blue light source illuminating the water is attached to a small submarine, the Triton. Shaped like a bubble, a transparent pressure hull is attached to the engine, allowing the operator to have an unsurpassed field of vision. Meanwhile, gazing out from the inside of the bubble and controlling the mini-submarine is none other than Jack Sterling—a rambunctious young man in his early 30s, who runs a small salvage and boat recovery service called Cast Away Towing.

Jack's clientele—which primarily consists of insurance agencies—inspired this name. They hire Cast Away Towing's services to search for, find, and recover recently reported capsized boats. Marine insurance fraud is the most common occurrence with respect to insurance claims, as ship-owners willfully cast away vessels, which are inevitably grossly over-insured.

From a wannabe ship owner's perspective, it all starts with the itch for freedom. To go out on the ocean whenever they like. Instead of subscribing to a financially minimalist lifestyle, and due to the fact that they are unsavvy investors, whether it be a fishing or sailing boat, they do not realize the upkeep until it's too late. From paying for registration, docking fees, insurance premiums, and regular maintenance to winter storage, the vessel ends up being like a second mortgage, forcing them to work longer, with no time to enjoy boat on the ocean. Discovering that the resale values are not as high, nor are used boats quick to sell, owners are left with few options to avoid getting behind on their payments. However, most boats carry *All Risk* policies, which provide coverage for a broad array of calamities, from theft, vandalism, lightning, fire, grounding, sinking, or even loss to the seas.

Now for most of those options, it would be too hard to get away with the fraudulence, but with the reality that the world is covered in water, the vast ocean allows for a limited ability to recover one of these vessels, presenting a quick way out of debt.

The next step that usually follows is looking for that right opportunity to cast it away to the bottom of the ocean, never to be seen again, in the hopes of receiving a sizable check.

For native Floridians, tsunami season happens to be one of those opportune times. Every year during tsunami season, Jack sees increased revenue, as multiple reports come through of boats sinking to the briny deep, despite whether or not a storm actually accosts the coast.

Perhaps Jack does this because he likes the thrill of the hunt and the mystery of figuring out what really happened. Are lost items truly lost? Or maybe it's the sense of unfinished business sitting on his shoulder.

One of the drawbacks of this job is that he makes more enemies than friends. However, Jack Sterling's work is not all dealing with insurance companies and con artists within the deep ocean. On occasion, he finds himself in more of a humanitarian role, responding to calls from those who are in need of rescue—whether they are lost at sea or are facing mechanical issues that require a tow. A part of his talent comes from his almost obsessive interest in marine archeology.

Others insist that he is just an underwater treasure hunter, finding sunken history from long ago, but these excursions take time and usually require

extensive funding. Like a knife through melted butter, the Triton maneuvers through the ocean water, focusing on the task at hand: gallantly searching for something that was lost in the ocean a short time ago.

Through the pit of darkness, the external mini-sub lights come across a silver reflection, bouncing light back on the right side of the hull while catching Jack's attention. With a yaw rotation, Jack banks right and begins a gradual descent. Being 3,000 feet below the water surface, a fiber optical cable tethered to the Triton secures his position.

A live, high-resolution video feed broadcasts his excursion and can be transmitted up to the surface station. The video screen records what he sees through his transparent hub of a bubble. The lights of the mini-sub come to rest on the propeller of the stern of a yacht that is turned upside down. While it has recently been resting on the surface, signs of the ocean beginning its process of engulfment are evident.

Just as Jack's eyes open wide, a crackle, followed by squeals, comes across the transmitter like a digital two-way radio.

On the other end of this underwater communication device is Dymitry. *"Come on, Jack. Tell me, how awesome am I right now? We found the shipwreck, didn't we?"*

"We?" Jack quips.

Dymitry quickly jumps back on the radio. *"Aw, Man! Don't go there. You know it was my algorithm that calculated this location. You are not getting all the credit for this one. Come on. What do you think? It's the Fly 460, isn't it?"*

Jack pauses. "Well…you could always swim down here and see for yourself."

"Ha. Ha," Dymitry laughs out sarcastically. "You know how that would end. So, tell me, Jack, exactly how many sunken 2018, forty-six-foot luxury yachts made by Sea Ray happen to be sunken in this area?"

Jack chimes in, and without a doubt responds, "Statistically speaking, there are over three million sunken ships, and—"

Dymitry cuts off Jack in frustration. *"Okay, now you're just screwing with me. I'm telling you, we found her. Do you realize how much I will be able to sell this software for? You know, you just might be looking at the next Zuckerberg. So don't mess with me."*

Jack rolls his eyes and smiles. "Yeah, scratch that last request of coming down here. I don't think the ocean is big enough for your head."

"I know what you mean. No amount of space can contain my awesomeness." Dymitry shrugs and stares into the video monitor, looking at the vessel. *"Hey, I know it's a fiberglass body, but I'm pretty impressed with the lack of corrosion on that ship."*

"We are crossing over from the twilight to the midnight zone, the land of the sand and silt. Basically, it's a desert down here." Jack moves his head back and forth, trying to get a good look at the back of the ship. "Hey, Dymitry, with the ship being upside down, I can't seem to make out the name. It appears to be buried in the sediment. I'm going to maneuver the Triton up to starboard and see if I can find the hull identification number."

"You got it."

"Oh, and Dymitry?"

"Yeah?"

"Great job on the software. I do think you've really gotten something there."

Dymitry smiles to himself. *"Thanks, man."*

Jack maneuvers the joystick and propels the Triton forward. "Now, why it took two years, I will never know."

"You could have done it yourself... oh wait...you need me," Dymitry mutters.

Dymitry is right. Jack has only one employee, his best friend Dymitry Jones, who has always been great with computers. They met as kids back in

the summer of 1996. Jack had once again been shipped off to camp, as his father had gone on a long fishing expedition. Sometimes Jack resented his father for forcing him to interact with other kids. Emotions were never his strong suit, but now that he explores the seas, it helps him to understand his father's ambitions.

Camp Little Bear. Jack cringes at the memory. The camp is located in Osceola National Forest in Florida, and is best known for its hardwood forests, swamps, and black bears.

Keep in mind, though, no one had ever seen a black bear at the camp, especially during the daytime. However, one could tell they had been around, as campers would occasionally wake up to ransacked garbage cans, most likely due to bears rummaging through them in the middle of the night. For the most part, the bears would stay away from camp. Now, there would be some disgruntled counselors who would often say this was on account of having monstrous ten-year-olds running around, hopping and hollering enough to scare the bears away.

Every year, they would see a rise in parents sending their hyperactive kids, accompanied by their prescriptions for Ritalin. Jack had fun watching the freaks, although he was certain they all had the same opinion about *him*. The year Jack and Dymitry met, it was an unusual summer, and a group of unsupervised kids snuck out of camp activities to go zip-lining across the lake. The zip line, a pulley suspended on a rope that was mounted around a tree which grew on the edge of a cliff, then sloped down to another across the lake, was a daring and fun experience for the campers.

For some ten-year-olds it was the height on the cliff that was the thrill. For others, it was being suspended twenty-four feet above the water. It was the kind of height that could cause heads to spin. Jack lost all sense of balance, just before the two of them vomited the remains of their lunches.

Nonetheless, the kids could not help but want to have a little bit of adventure when the counselors were not looking. With the camp's issues with staffing, it was easy to get away from observing eyes. Jack was among those stowaways. He was actually quite an intelligent and mature boy for his age, since he had gone on far more adventures with his father in his short ten-year lifespan than his peers could have ever imagined.

Unfortunately, having been forced to come to summer camp, Jack thought he would make the most of it and take a stroll with the others up to the zip line versus participating in the scheduled bug collecting that the counselors and the other campers were off doing. Patiently waiting his turn, Jack couldn't help noticing Dymitry, a beanpole African-American kid, often teased in school for being a nerd and his love for video games.

Dymitry was there on a dare to be the first one to go down the zip line. Everyone knew he was afraid of water, since he had a reputation for skipping swim class in school whenever he got the chance. Now, while Dymitry was the type who did not really care what the others thought, he was experiencing his own feelings of vertigo, but they did not have anything to do with heights. No, his issue lay with the presence of a ten-year-old girl named Jasmine—Jasmine Pinkerton to be exact. In fact, if it were not for her daring him to jump on the zip line, he probably would not have even come.

Dymitry had reached that age where puberty was kicking in. He began taking notice of girls, and, especially when it came to Jasmine, he could not refuse the chance to grab her attention. No one thought he would actually go through with it on account of his fear of water.

Being a video game junkie and having his own flair for adventure, Dymitry wanted to prove to Jasmine that he was not afraid. In his mind, this was no different than his new video game, *Crash Bandicoot*. He had confidence with a controller in his hands, imagining that if he just gained three Aku Aku masks he could achieve invincibility, allowing him to dash across the zip line to avoid a bottomless pit and attain his Wumpa Fruit. However, in the real world, as he grabbed the zip line, ready to jump, he momentarily glanced down. He just stood there at the edge of the cliff, frozen in time, staring at the water. At that moment, he realized that, unlike a video game, he only

had one life.

Jasmine, standing with her arms crossed, cried out impatiently, "Well, are you going to go or not?"

Just then, the sweet sound of her voice filled the air, quickly soothing his fears, and brought him back to his blithesome self. Holding on to the zip line with one hand, Dymitry smiled, and with one hearty push of his feet, he kicked off the edge and went sliding down, feeling no regret. He still looked back at Jasmine in the hope of catching a twinkle in her eyes, reflecting admiration for this profound act of courage. Not five seconds down the zip line, as he turned back from looking at her, he caught a glimpse, not of the water below, but the fear-wrenching sight of what was at the other end of the zip line awaiting him.

He gazed onward, holding on to the pulley for dear life, yelling, "Oh, crap! A bear?"

The other kids looked up quickly and saw a black bear, which just happened to roam out of the forest two feet from the other end of the zip line. Out of sudden fear, the kids start to scream, and the noise vibrated across the lake, causing the bear to look over and see Dymitry heading right toward it. Lurching into defensive mode, the black bear raised up on his hind legs and roared out a sound that curdled in everyone's ears. Dymitry was only getting closer as the zip line was closing in straight for the bear and what appeared to a ten-year-old boy's jaws of death. He was quick to realize his invincibility game mode was about to end. The bear used his front paws to come down on the tree, shaking the entire zip line and jostling him back and forth as he continued to approach the bear.

While he was still only halfway across the lake, fear seemed to have struck the bear, as he saw the human was not slowing down and was only getting closer. Out of a sense of fight or flight, the bear jumped off the tree and hotfooted back into the forest. In doing so, the bear's claw unintentionally caught on and slashed the end of the rope tied around the tree, causing the rope, zip line, and Dymitry to plummet into the water. Tears coursed down the children's faces.

The children were all paralyzed in horror and focusing in on the water, like a deer gazing into headlights. They were afraid and unsure of what to do.

Jasmine turned to the other kids and yelled, "Someone, go and get help."

One of the children took off running toward camp, while the others who remained would forever remember the longest thirty seconds of their lives. The water appeared motionless, as there did not appear to be any sign of Dymitry. Knowing he could not swim, they all feared the worst. All of a sudden, they saw ripples of water and someone rising to the surface, gasping for air. However, it was not him.

During the chaos, no one had seen that Jack Sterling had jumped off the twenty-four-foot cliff and swam underwater toward where Dymitry had fallen. Jack often had good foresight, which he had developed from previous excursions with his father, and having a quick intuition for knowing when things were about to go south.

It was actually during the roaring of the bear when Jack had jumped. Cradled in his arms, he held Dimitry's head above water, above where he had rescued him from the bottom of the lake. Dymitry had bumped his head when he fell, rendering him temporarily unconscious. Jack pulled him ashore, and, akin to an experienced paramedic, he began to give Dymitry mouth-to-mouth resuscitation while the children made their way to the other side and looked on.

Jasmine crouched down toward Dymitry.

"Is he dead?" Jasmine asks worriedly.

"No," said Jack.

Expressions of fear transformed to relief as Dymitry lurched forward, coughing fervently and regurgitating water. While he lay there, dazed and confused, Jasmine ran over and hugged him.

"I'm sorry, Dymitry. I will never ask you to do that again."

Dymitry looked toward Jack, seeing his grin. Dymitry just smiled back and gave him the thumbs up, realizing his act of courage for Jasmine had paid off. Unknown to him that day, he would grow up and never be content in a long-lasting relationship, always wanting the next girl who came along—even if that girl was Jack's long-term girlfriend, even though that was an attempt bound for failure. However, the one person he always remained loyal to was Jack.

With a bump on his head to prove it, Dymitry would always remember that Jack Sterling had saved his life that day, leading them to become the best of friends. As such, they remain so today. A beacon illuminates in the dark as the Triton glides up the starboard bow. The lights finally arrive on the HIN identification. The last number is covered with sediment and mud.

Jacks pulls out two smaller joysticks that control two mechanical arms, which protrude from the mini-sub and wipe the residue from the side of the ship. "Hey, Dymitry. It's upside down, but looks like the hull identification number, and says…4…6…0…F…L…Y…5...0...4."

"Yahoo?" The radio breaks into a musical number as Dymitry sings, *"Money, money, money, money, MONEY?"*

Jack looks at his clipboard with his work orders on it and then tosses it behind him. "Damn, it's a match?"

Dymitry says, *"What are you so negative about? We struck gold. The software works, and we are going to be rich, my friend."*

Jack, engaged in his expedition, ignores Dymitry and makes his way to the vessel's hull. As Jack moves past the outside windows of the bridge, the Triton's lights shine upon the single sideband radio, which had been turned into a home by a group of red sea crabs—as they scurry out of the light like cockroaches running over a kitchen floor, more of the unit is revealed. Jack is suddenly reminded of hearing the call that came through that day.

"Mayday, mayday?" The captain was anxiously crying his lungs out as his vessel went down.

He was aboard the *Fly 460*, made by Sea Ray. It was a forty-six-foot luxury yacht that had been caught in a vortex of winds that engulfed it from all sides. The captain could not tell his exact location, except that they were fifteen miles off the coast of Florida. He had expressed that the hull and navigation were severely damaged, and that water was continuing to gush in.

The coast guard responded that they were currently searching for him, and encouraged him to stay in contact with them as long as possible. It was also reported that all the passengers on board the *Fly 460* had been evacuated, due to the heroics of its captain, Andrew Gibbons. He gave the phrase 'the captain goes down with the ship' a whole new meaning.

As he stayed on board to give the last life jacket to a remaining passenger, the courageous captain was left with no option for escape. Jack listened to the horror unfold across his sideband radio. It was early September 2017, and Jack and Dymitry were heading back to shore. They happened to be on the same frequency when the transmission came through, and had just saved a couple of storm chasers who had ignored the warning signs and ended up getting trapped in their sailboat. Hurricane Irma was in full swing, and all boats and divers were prohibited from going near the water. But, for Jack, the sea was his spiritual abode. Hearing the captain's call and knowing it was devouring his ship with no chance of helping him was too much for him to bear.

The captain had called out his HIN number as 460FLY504, so they would know they had the right ship, should it ever be discovered. The *Fly 460* sent out one last horn call for help—one not unlike that of a lion, the king of the jungle, who gives out one last glorious cry after getting shot by a hunter. A few moments later, the *Fly 460* and Captain Gibbons sank to the depths of the ocean, leaving nothing in its wake.

The mystery remains, because none of the passengers were ever found,

and their identities still remain unknown. The coast guard searched for days, but came up emptyhanded, almost as if Captain Gibbons and the *Fly 460* were nothing but mere ghosts trapped in a radio transmission. Captain Gibbons had left behind a six-year-old daughter and a wife, who had assumed he was at work, and had no idea he had even been out in the ocean, and thus no idea whom he had taken with him. As the story goes, none of the boat's passengers or captain was ever seen again, and the ship was thought to be lost forever, until now.

Coming out of a dream state, Jack's radio breaks the silence once again.

"Hello?" Dymitry asks. *"Was it something I said?"*

"Dymitry, *Fly 460* is Captain Gibbon's ship."

"Who?"

"I didn't connect the dots either. You remember during Hurricane Irma, that ghost call that came across the radio, that had all those passengers and a captain who went down with the ship?"

"Captain Andrew Gibbons? No way," Dymitry responds on the radio with excitement. *"Wait, I thought that boat was seriously damaged. I remember that dude was screwed. He had no clue where he was, except somewhere off the coast of Florida."*

"And yet here we are, currently off the coast of the Yucatán Peninsula," Jack says. "Aside from some pre-corrosion setting in, this boat lacks any real wave damage in the hull. Heck—the navigation system looks like it was probably working before it sank."

"No, you must have the wrong HIN, and the work order doesn't say anything about Mr. Gibbons. This belongs to a woman named Susan Rice," Dymitry explains, perplexed.

"I'm pretty sure the hull identification number is correct. I can't forget a thing like that. As for the name, maybe his wife went back to her maiden name." Jack is silent, then speaks out, "The strangest part is all the cabin windows are open. Why, considering the vessel was traveling through a heavy storm?"

Dymitry pauses. *"So, another case of marine insurance fraud? That would explain why the underwater locator beacon wasn't working."*

"Maybe, but every fraud case we ever dealt with in the past, the owner was still alive to try to collect the insurance money, not missing with his boat. Nor did they have any passengers, especially in this case, when the insurance is valued at over a million dollars," Jack answers.

Jack continues to maneuver the Triton around, searching the sunken vessel and looking for clues. "I would like to add that this fiberglass bottom is flawless. So how and why did it sink?"

Dymitry responds, *"See, there you go. You just went way above our pay grade. It is not our responsibility or concern. We found the ship like the insurance company asked us to. I say let's bag it, tag it, and let* The Falcon *reel it in. It is eMarine's problem now."*

"You're right, Dymitry. Let's just get paid for once. Turn on the towing wrench and drop the line. I'll find cable clips to strap it to. And stop calling my tug boat *The Falcon*, it's degrading to her."

"'Degrading?' You have me all wrong. It is the toughest hunk of junk on the sea," Dymitry laughs as he types away behind his Mac laptop that also has a *Millennium Falcon* sticker on the front case.

Succumbing to the reality of things, Jack shrugs. "Let's just get some money, alright?"

Outside, walking on the deck of a rusted old tugboat that belongs to Cast Away Towing, Dymitry talks into his Bluetooth headset, which he rigged to the communication device to broadcast wirelessly. He pumps his fist into the air. "All right, that's what I'm talking about, MY MAN JACK!"

Dymitry turns on the tow wrench as a loud sputtering sound starts to knock around. He grabs a hammer and bangs on the top of the motor, caus-

ing it to clear up suddenly.

The Bluetooth headset is interrupted by the sound of Jack's voice from many fathoms below. *"Dymitry, be gentle with her. She's all I've got."*

Dymitry chimed in, "Don't let your girlfriend hear you say that, or you might find that statement to be true."

"Alice isn't the jealous type—"

"Probably because you lack emotions and there's—how would you say it—zero probability of being interested in anyone?"

Jack rolls his eyes and continues, "She is the only one who understands the love that I have for both my vessel and her. She would never put any pressure on me to choose."

Dymitry fake stabs himself in the chest and grabs the line from a massive, rolled-up metal spool. He wheels off the wire and drops it over the back of the stern while continuing to banter with Jack.

"Maybe that's why you've been together for like…four, no, wait, five years, and you have yet to ask the big question…"

Jack was shocked at Dymitry's response.

"I know you think you know Alice, but you don't. Not like I do. She doesn't want any of that. She just likes it the way it is. Simple…kind of like my tugboat."

Dymitry gawks. *"The Falcon* is not simple. It's in constant need of attention. She's going to shock you one day, just like Alice, and leave you stranded out in the middle of the ocean."

Cast Away Towing's operations consist of a fifty-five-foot 1981 tugboat vessel, and the fancy, one person Triton mini-submarine that Jack is currently maneuvering. The boat seems to be a natural habitat for rust collections. It's painted lime green, with a row of tires that hang off both sides of the vessel. These are used as bumpers to protect other boats when towing.

Inside, however, one can notice Dymitry's handiwork, as the tugboat is decked out with fancy equipment, from 4k video monitors to Wi-Fi, sonars, and ultrasonic transmitters. There are even a couple of laptops and monitors, along with dozens of loose wires hanging everywhere. One would think it was a high-tech rat's nest. Dymitry's personal favorite is the gold dice that hangs from the bridge's front window. A lifting crane on the outside has been jerry rigged to the deck of the ship, which allows the Triton to be lifted in and out of the ocean. The mini-sub and lift look out of place when considering the newness and the financial value of them both. Naturally, one struggles to afford such a high-tech piece of marine equipment as the Triton. Jack got some inheritance money from his father after his mysterious disappearance, and it only felt right to put it toward something both of them would have appreciated.

Having a passion for underwater deep-sea diving, and considering the insurance companies' demand for people who can find lost vessels, Jack took the gamble and spent it all on the Triton, leaving nothing for a rainy day. While advised against it, he rigged the mini-sub lift to work on his tugboat. *The Falcon*, as Dymitry likes to call it, as he saw it akin to the *Millennium Falcon* ship, was the fastest hunk of junk in the marina. It was also the toughest hunk of junk in the sea.

Like the *Millennium Falcon*, Jack's tugboat is also in constant need of repair, but he continues to hang onto it for several reasons. No matter what they pull or raise from the ocean, his vessel always comes through for him. Despite the severe weather the ship has seen in its lifetime, it continues to stay afloat and survive the toughest of storms. One time, Jack caught himself accidentally calling the boat after his father. While the discovery of what happened to his father may go unsolved, he cannot part with what he has left of him, especially while he feels his father is lost, not gone.

Down below, the *Fly 460* now has the towlines wrapped through cable clips on the back of the stern, and Jack is using the Triton's robotic arms to secure the last of the line.

"Ok, Dymitry, she's all strapped in. Go ahead and lift her up slowly."

"Roger that."

With the press of an industrial button, the tow wrench gives a metal knocking noise back and forth as the old gears start to spin. The massive spool starts to turn slowly, rolling up the wire from the depth below. As the wrench gets warmer, featherlike clouds of steam begin to develop, slowly evaporating off the engine. Under the ocean, like a boot stuck in the mud, it takes that initial yank to free the vessel from its surroundings. It's jerked out as the sediment shifts, allowing the stirring of any clinging sand and silt.

The vessel is lifted from the rear while slowly being pulled up to the surface in a vertical position. Jack knows this is probably not the best way to handle raising ships from the ocean, but most of these vessels recovered are considered dead boats anyway. The insurance company would rather leave them in the ocean if it were not for the need to physically have them for legal purposes in an attempt to prevent paying the hefty insurance claims. The issue of what to do with these end-of-life boats is that there is no money to be made in recycling or scrapping old boats.

Most of these recovered vessels or end-of-life boats end up being cut up and buried deep within the soil of a landfill. Jack knows, no doubt, despite the one-million-dollar price tag only eight months ago, the *Fly 460* will join the ranks of tens of millions of other end-of-life boats headed for the dump over the next several years, potentially contributing to the global problem of toxic chemicals leaking into the ground. The *Fly 460* was once thought to be lost forever, but now it has successfully left the scene, headed on a free elevator ride to the top. The sediment of sand and silt begins to slowly drift back into place. With little visibility, it is hard to tell what parts might have fallen off.

Jack maneuvers the Triton once more to skim the surface of where this vessel had once sat. As a watchtower, he searches for an escaped convict. The mini-sub's lights peruse the bottom of the ocean floor, casting light on anything that might be of interest. Nothing of importance seems to be left behind, but a twinkle of a reflection is thrown back, catching Jack's attention once more. Small bits of chrome and metal parts seem to still be scattered about. He continues his search until he crosses over it again.

This twinkle seems to hit him differently, as it reflects back with sharper light that seems to glow. It appears to be symmetrical. Out of curiosity, he decides to use the robotic arms attached to the sub and reach out for it, slowly grasping at it. The glow appears so small. He raises the arm toward his transparent bubble to get a better look. With the object in the robotic arm's fingers, with it practically touching the acrylic bubble, he leans in. Sand falls off it, revealing a glistening gold coin.

"Are you seeing this? Dymitry?" Jack shouts.

With the tow wrench engine so loud, Dymitry decided to put on some even louder music while he continued to raise the *Fly 460*. Not paying attention to the video monitor, nor hearing Jack's comment, he did not see the image. Down below, Jack is in amazement, as this gold coin shows more aging than the vessel that laid atop it. It was clearly not only any gold coin, but also a numismatic, a 1944 coin to be exact.

Jack's father had a coin collection he often showed off. He was missing most coins from the 40s, but Jack knew exactly what each looked like from listening to his father describe them.

This coin is undoubtedly from 1944. The giveaway is the inscription around the edges: *CITTA DEL VATICANO.* Resting in the center is a beveled image of the coat of arms of the Holy See and Vatican City State.

This religious symbol combines two crossed keys in the same position as the cross of St. Andrew. Traditionally, the gold one on the right alludes to power in the kingdom of the heavens, while the key on the left, which is normally silver when not on a gold coin, represents the spiritual authority on earth.

The cotters of the keys are pointed upward, as if they were a representation of being in the hands of Christ. This is the official insignia of the Holy See, a representation that comes from the Gospel, when the Apostle Peter was given the keys to the kingdom of heaven by Christ. It has long been a Christian belief that the Vatican Church is the eternal church of authority, as it was established in the 1st Century A.D. by Peter and the rest of the twelve Apostles.

Curious as to who is on the back, without hesitation, Jack grabs a spinner dial on the dashboard that controls the outside robotic arms. With just a flick of his fingers, he uses the mechanical armatures to spin the coin around, as if he were touching it with his fingers. As the coin flips around, time slows down as it comes into the light, and Jack is caught off guard.

The room spins, causing tingling to travel up his arms. Heavy emotional weight is put on his muscles. He can feel them weakening as the decompression sickness worsens. Yet none of these things are actually happening, as Jack is in a pressure-controlled mini-sub, but his mind is in such disbelief that it can't grasp what he is looking at on the back of that coin.

He flips a switch on the Triton to turn on an additional external bright light to double-check the image. While this light uses unnecessary power and he is already getting warning lights of needing to surface, none of that matters at this moment, as he might have just found the discovery of the century. This would rewrite history.

If Dymitry's new software could find lost ships based on last known locations, it would make the front page of *Time* magazine. The success of this news would throw his story to page fifteen and bury it among the obituaries. The only success Jack had ever seen in the past as a treasure hunter was on *The Today Show* for discovering a part of the Spanish San Miguel treasure. Jack never made any money from it, as he ended up donating the findings to his local museum. He always felt lost treasures should be shared with the world, versus kept in one man's vault.

To Jack, everything is lost until found. This treasure, now found, left him pondering what to do or who to tell.

Inscribed on the back of the gold coin is not the image of an honored human silhouette he is traditionally used to seeing, but is instead an image so terrible and so vile that it still represents evil and induces nightmares even today. It's as large as the back of the gold coin itself, a symbolic representative of everything wrong in the world—the image of the German Swastika Logo.

Throughout the years, there have always been rumors of Pope Pius XII at the Vatican not only being a supporter, but also helping Adolf Hitler rise to power during World War II as his financial backer. In return, Hitler had agreed to destroy the German Catholic political oppositions while betraying the Jews in Europe. This coin could prove it to be true.

Treating the coin like a glass egg, Jack controls the arms and puts the gold coin into an external basket that he is able to lock, making sure not to lose it as he flips some more switches and grabs the joystick to the Triton to begin the ascent to the ocean's surface.

Chapter II

Lorenzo's Bar

B ack in St. Augustine Florida, sitting on a wooden pier is a warehouse owned by eMarine, who is one of the largest insurers of pleasure boats in the country. Inside rests the recently recovered Sea Ray *Fly 460*. Seawater is still dripping from her pale fiberglass body, leaving algae residue behind that is slowly infesting the vessel, as if a mystery has just been awoken.

A specialized team of insurance field inspectors from eMarine shows up to the location, who could easily be mistaken for FBI agents, with their dark navy jackets, Oxford white button-up shirts, and tan khakis. Treated as a murder investigation, the field inspectors scavenge through the boat, taking pictures and grabbing any evidence they can find.

Each item that turns up becomes part of a larger puzzle that has its own story to tell regarding what had happened to both the crew and ship that frightful day. Jack and Dymitry are filling out all the necessary paperwork so they can be compensated for delivering the yacht unscathed. Jack can't help but notice an iconic-looking detective standing nearby. His origins are of Latino descent, but he is wearing a beige fedora with a matching trench coat. Underneath his coat he's wearing black Italian pants, with a white Oxford button-up shirt. The recommended burgundy police tie—which is a psychological color to help build trust—drops down from his collar. A shine emitted from a glistening golden badge also hangs around his neck that is labeled *Detective Hernandez*. His black shoes cast a reflection that they are as new as the agent himself.

"So, they're sending newbie detectives over now?" asks Jack.

"How did you…?" Hernandez hesitates. "Never mind." Shaking his head, he turns and continues making notes in his small black leather notebook.

"Well, do you have much experience with marine mysteries? I can tell you personally the stress level sometimes can be quite high," says Jack.

Hernandez feels forced to indulge Jack in the conversation. "No, you're right. There are not too many lakes in Boise." Hernandez leans into Jack. "Spending ten years in narcotics where I was getting shot at on a daily basis makes a guy look for a change of scenery." Hernandez reaches out and pats Jack's shoulder, giving him affirmation. "However, transferring to a job where yuppies lose their yachts and corporate insurance companies refuse to pay them, I'm pretty sure the stress level of this job will be just fine." Hernandez smiles, turns, and walks to the ship.

"I see. Being an experienced detective, I'm sure you already have an idea how she might have sunk?" Jack adds.

Not looking back, Hernandez continues to walk toward the vessel. "All boats will sink if you leave them out at sea long enough, Mr. Sterling."

Dymitry smirks, as he knows this detective has underestimated Jack. "Sure, along with thirty other maintenance mistakes that can be made to send a boat drowning to the bottom of the abyss, but that is not what happened here, Hernandez."

Hernandez stops in his tracks and looks back at Jack, who has a smirk about him, as if he knows something the detective does not. "Look, thank you for your help, Mr. Sterling, with finding the boat and all, but it's a pretty

open-and-shut case. Captain Andrew Gibbons went down with his ship and drowned, due to an electrical malfunction."

"What kind of electrical malfunction?" asks Jack.

"According to the electrician earlier, he found a breaker shortage, which caused the bilge pumps to quit working," says Hernandez after a pause, folding his arms. "Without the pumps, Captain Gibbons lost the ability to drain any water. Considering the mayday call came in when he was traveling through Hurricane Irma, the hull had collected enough water to cause it to sink du to the overweight of the vessel. Then, it capsized."

"And what about the missing crew?"

"As far as we can tell from our investigation, there never was any crew."

"Never any crew?" Jack hesitates, turns, walks toward the yacht, and climbs on board.

Hernandez shouts out, "Hey, you can't be up there. That's an investigation scene."

Jack ignores the detective. "I won't be long, just give me a minute." Jack says, "You were saying there was never any crew?"

Hernandez's fingers scratch the five o'clock shadow on his pale face, realizing there is no harm in hearing Jack out.

"Yes, no one ever showed up on a missing person's report, and we found all the original life jackets tucked in their original storage containers. There was no evidence anyone was ever on board. Well, except for Andrew Gibbons, the Captain, of course. He was no doubt real." Hernandez pauses for a moment. "I take it you didn't find his body?"

Jack is preoccupied, looking around the boat. Hernandez then walks over, climbs up on the yacht, and walks to where Jack is.

Hernandez resumes, "I didn't think you did. We just figured Captain Gibbons dead corpse probably got carried off as a meal ticket for some shark."

Jack opens a wooden door and looks inside the cabin. "Did you notice the inside wall of the cabin is warped?"

Hernandez puts his hands on the wall to feel the damage. "Probably water damage from being submerged."

"So, why didn't the captain use a life jacket?" Jack resumes his examination of the boat.

Hernandez crosses his arms as he gets the sense that Jack does not believe him. "Well, there is more to that story. You see, Captain Gibbons at the time was going through some financial issues, and his wife had just filed for divorce. It's possible he just felt his life had no meaning. Knowing the coast guard wouldn't arrive on time, maybe he saw an opportunity with the electrical malfunction to go out like a hero?" Hernandez thinks for a beat and then gets excited in his thoughts. "In fact, I bet that is why he decided to make up the story about the crew. Maybe, some last act of goodwill, hoping to be immortalized and remembered as something better than he really was. This leaves us to debate whether we tell the world the truth or let his legacy remain as a hero."

"He is no hero," says Jack as he looks at the electric breaker up and down.

"Well, no." Hernandez scratches his head. "However, people on the streets of St. Augustine looked up to him, they think he sacrificed his life during that hurricane. You really think we should tell people that he committed suicide?"

"No, because he didn't commit suicide," Jack says as he rubs his hands across the side rails of the boat.

"So, you're saying he drowned?" Hernandez, copying Jack's motions, trying to figure out what Jack is looking for.

"No, I am saying he is still alive," Jack interrupts.

As if the sound of the warehouse suddenly got silent.

Hernandez mutters, "What…how do you know that?"

"Occam's Razor."

"Come again?"

"A theory that if there exist two explanations for an occurrence, the simplest one is often your answer," argues Jack. "It sounds like he suffered a lot of misfortunes, only to travel through a dangerous hurricane, only to have an electrical shortage happen at that very instance."

Hernandez looks exasperated. "Come on, you have seen *Gravity* with Sandra Bullock? Some people just have terrible days. When people are gone, they are gone. The cap is dead."

Jack makes his way over to the inside cabin. He understands where Hernandez is coming from, but they just have different beliefs about treasure and history. Jack isn't going to accept the captain is dead until he sees it in the flesh. He's simply…missing. Until then, the hunger of wanting to know will keep him searching for the truth.

"The chronology is an issue too, if you count from the point in time when the distress call was made to the moment the coast guard arrived at the scene. The boat had already sunk out of sight, deeper than they could have dived in less than thirty minutes. Not to mention all the cabin windows were wide open when I found her at the bottom of the ocean. Pretty unusual during a storm, don't you think?"

"Not if he opened all the windows to help bring in more water to sink faster."

"Why all the work of trying to sink a boat and drown at sea when you could just as easily jump off into the ocean?"

"As I said, he wanted to go down as a hero, so knew he had less than thirty minutes and needed the coast guard to believe everyone had drowned or was lost at sea, so he had to sink the evidence," Hernandez replies dismissively.

"Well, you're right about sinking the evidence," says Jack. "As you said, not many lakes in Boise, Idaho, so what you don't know is that Sea Ray prides themselves on building these with a large amount of flotation inside the hull. They get the bragging rights of being an unsinkable legend." Jack leans over the yacht and knocks on the side of the hull with his fists. "A yacht this size would have to have taken in thousands of gallons of water to weigh her down. Considering there was no damage to the hull, it would take weeks for her to sink, even with heavy rains, giving coast guard ample time to find her."

"And yet it happened," says Hernandez.

"So, tell me, Detective Hernandez, how does one sink the unsinkable in under thirty minutes?" asks Jack.

Hernandez is looking at Jack, who is down on to the floor, crawling around the deck as if he lost something. "Well, if I had to guess, Captain Gibbons must have known about the pump problem for some time. He came up with a plan, and then went out to sea with the ship already filled with water."

"No-o-o," Jack grumbles.

"Why?" Hernandez asks with all the authority he can muster.

"Oh, I can answer this one," Dymitry interjects, standing beside the yacht.

Jack nods. "Go ahead, Dymitry."

"That theory is not likely, Detective, as this yacht is equipped with an EPIRB."

"Pardon?" Hernandez's eyebrows shoot up in question.

Dymitry continues, "An Emergency Position Indicating Radio Beacon. Think of it like how you use 911 GPS locations on cell phones, only EPIRBs work off satellites. Basically, it is how the coast guard was able to find the ship's exact location. Had Captain Gibbons had any water in his vessel, the coast guard would have been notified a lot sooner, as it goes off whenever it

comes into contact with any water."

Jack exclaims, "The distressed radio call, the lying about having any crew and the sinking of the boat, it was all made to look like the ship went down in the storm, when in fact he didn't commit suicide. He just faked his own death."

Hernandez is at a loss for words.

Jack rubs his hand on the deck near the entrance of the cabin. "Here you go. Come look at this."

Hernandez physically gets down on the floor and sees Jack rubbing his hands over some large scratches. "Okay? So there are some scratches."

"No, scratches are created by something heavy being dragged across the floor. These jitter markings are from something heavy that shifted due to weight movement or vibration," says Jack. "I believe you will find that the diameter of these markings will match to a metal clamp around a hose that was hooked to an external pump on another ship."

"An external pump?"

Jack continues, "Captain Gibbons tampered with the breakers to stop the binge pumps from working. Another ship was parked nearby that had a massive external pump. You will see the hose was dragged across the yacht and laid right there, filling the main cabin with water. Those inner cabin markings were created from massive pressure hitting one spot. Keep in mind these external pumps can move a thousand gallons of water a minute, especially with an endless supply of water. Thus causing the yacht to be bow heavy. At which point, when the opened windows reached sea level, it allowed all the ocean water to rush in and carry her down."

Hernandez replies, "Then what about setting off the EPIRB before the coast guard could arrive?"

Jack walks into the cabin and looks on the side of the cabinet. He notices sticky residue stuck to the wood next to where the EPIRB is mounted. "Captain Gibbons must have had scuba gear. This is the edge of where duct tape was applied, suggesting he had some airtight bag tapped around the EPIRB. When the Sea Ray was finally submerged, he cut away at the bag underwater, setting off the EPIRB, so it wouldn't be made to look like sabotage."

Dymitry chimes in, "With the boat sinking in fifteen minutes, he made a distress mayday call, but not from his yacht as it was already submerged, but from the other vessel while they were getting away. This would allow enough time for the coast guard to arrive at the last EPIRB pinged location, and the Sea Ray to be lost to the sea forever. By making the distress call from the other boat, Captain Gibbons and his accomplice had more than enough time to get away."

Jack nods in agreement. "Then!—the storm shielded them from being seen and succeeding in faking his death. Despite any rumors of divorce, there is a good chance Mrs. Gibbons is probably in on it, as she would be the only one to have access to both the life and boat insurance money."

Dymitry claps his hands together. "Ha! So, it *is* another case of marine insurance fraud."

Hernandez takes out his cell phone. "I've got to get on the phone with the department. You should have been a detective, Mr. Sterling."

Jack smirks. "You mean the long hours of undercover work, with the possibility of being beat up, stabbed, punched or shot at? I think I'll stick to marine archeology."

Hernandez smiles. "You're a treasure hunter. And here I thought you just found lost ships for rich yuppies."

Jack responds, "No Mr. Hernandez, treasure hunters are modern-day pirates who salvage, even sometimes destroy artifacts, all for quick profit, with disregard for any cultural heritage. I like to be bounded by a deontological code of ethics."

"Then why work for eMarine?" asks Hernandez.

Dymitry walks over with a paycheck from eMarine in his hand. "Unlike vessels today, where we have more data and information to help find their exact whereabouts, searching for ancient shipwrecks is full of disappointments. They are extremely expensive endeavors that require patience and perseverance. Now, let's say you happen to get lucky and find that white whale. Then what? Not too many investors looking to take on that risk for underwater answers to our past."

Jack smiles. "Soon we won't need them. Dymitry has been developing something pretty amazing to make those searches easier."

Hernandez nods and tips his hat to the both of them. "I wish you the best, and thanks for your help. Now let me do my job, and see if I can find this guy."

Dymitry is still holding on to the paycheck as if it was cash. "All right, come on, Jack, let's go celebrate at Lorenzo's."

Usually, Jack is the type who likes to stay and continue to help out, but Jack's impatience is starting to show. Lying in his pocket is the gold coin that he found on the bottom of the ocean floor. His fingers occasionally reach in and stroke the round object to make sure it is still there, brooding over the possibilities of how it ended up where it did. He knows it did not belong to Captain Gibbons. A man who would go to such great lengths to fake his own death would unlikely be so reckless as to leave such a relic behind. Nonetheless, it had been a long day. His girlfriend was taking night classes at the community center, and she was not scheduled to be home until later. Jack figured the enigma of the gold coin could wait till morning, and he could have a few drinks.

They bid Hernandez good night, but the detective is already talking on his phone with his department to issue a warrant to search Mrs. Gibbon's property. Night has fallen upon the quaint city of St. Augustine. The majestic wharf contains quays and piers, which serve the city's fish market for the locals and tourists alike.

At night it looks abandoned, even though it was bursting with fishmongers only a few hours ago. As a scent of butchered fish still lingers the air, the twilight stars are concealed by the full moon, illuminating the ebb and flow of the ocean tides that continue to rock the docked boats back and forth. All that remains visible is several lampposts that glow a lighted path up to the north end, where you will find an upscale bar known as Lorenzo's. The music isn't loud, but the noise from the patrons can be heard overshadowing the break in the waves. Aside from the spectacular ocean view, Lorenzo's offers open boat slips. They spawn off the main dock, which sea patrons use as parking spaces to stop in for a few drinks.

Pulling in to the harbor, Jack and Dymitry manage to luck out and find an open pier in front of the main entrance of the bar. Dropping anchor, they tie up their tugboat, making sure everything is locked down for the night. The Gollum obsession kicks in one more time. Jack double checks his pocket and feels relief, as the gold coin is still there. After disembarking, they start walking up to the bistro, when Dimitry's cell phone rings.

Jack looks puzzled. "It is kind of late for a distress call, isn't it?"

"The number is registering unknown." As Dymitry answers, he places the call on speakerphone. "Hello?"

Hesitant to answer at first, the strange voice on the other end comes through. *"Is this Cast Away Towing?"*

"Yes, I'm sorry. We are off the clock right now. However, if this is an emergency, I have a number you can call."

The unnerving voice responds after a beat of silence. *"Where is Jack?"*

Dymitry looks at Jack, who shrugs his shoulders. Dymitry bellows out, "Jack's..." Dymitry takes a beat. "I'm sorry, but who is this?"

The cold sound of his voice echoes across the speaker. *"How did you find the…the…?"*

"Fly 460?" Jack interrupts, *"The Fly 460?"* He grabs the phone. "Who is

this? Hello? This is Jack."

Male breathing is heard on the other end, only to be cut short by dead air.

Jack looks perplexed. They look at the phone only for a brief moment of hesitation. "He hung up, Dymitry."

"How could he know? It had to be someone from eMarine, right?" Dymitry asks.

"Let's just see if he calls back." Jack grins. "Come on, forget about it for now. Let's go inside. Drinks are on me."

Joseph Lorenzo, better known as Joe, is the owner of the establishment, known for his exquisite taste and his excellent Italian seafood appetizers, like clam bacon peppers, a vinegary red bell pepper clam mixture combined with the richness of the bacon to create an appetizer that is salty, smoky, and sweet, and smells like heaven. The customers find them intoxicating.

Part of Joe's secret is his daily delivery of fresh clams. Enough people owe him favors. They make sure he gets the best pick of the bunch. Many find Joe to be the *Casablanca,* Rick Blaine type, from his clean-cut sharp Italian clothes, to the way he runs his joint as if it is a place of freedom from all worries outside that door, be it political or personal.

Lorenzo's name derives from the Latin *laurel,* which means wisdom. Joe has worked hard for his reputation. He has built quite a contact list, always knowing a guy to help fix any situation, from politicians, local law enforcement, to even members of the Cuban mafia.

The bar has an unusual atmosphere that not only attracts sailors, fisherman, and Waverley drifters who are usually looking for something, but also its own set of local regulars who make this their home away from the sea. Jack is one of those regulars, as Lorenzo and he have known each other for quite some time, being that Lorenzo was friends with his father. Joe would know about the Vatican Nazi gold coin conspiracies. Who better to show than someone who is from Italy? Jack thought it would finally be nice to have proof of what Joe believed was only a myth.

Once inside, Jack and Dymitry notice two empty seats next to the bar. Recognizing both of them, the bartender proceeds to make their drinks and place them in front of them.

"There you go, Dymitry, with your regular Mojito, and Jack, a Macallan 18 neat," says the bartender.

"Thanks. Have you seen Joe?" asks Jack.

"He is in the kitchen, should be up shortly," the bartender replies.

As if light descended down from the heavens, Dymitry is suddenly caught off-guard and mesmerized by a glimmering light glowing off a lady sitting at the other end of the bar. He gives Jack a nudge.

"Whoa, take a glance at the girl over there. She is absolutely gorgeous, and she is all alone. This could be the one, Jack."

Jack looks over at her and shakes his head. "I think you will want to pass on her. She is not your type." Jack wanted to continue and say something along the lines of, *no girl is your type, that's why you have five girlfriends at a time...*

Suddenly, as if time slows down, she gently looks up at Dymitry with her bright green eyes, leading him into temptation as he becomes locked in on her high cheekbones, dark skin, and the golden trail from her neckline that leads down to her bosom. Being coy, she reaches up and begins to twirl her chestnut colored hair, radiating a smile with her glossy red lips that could melt the coldest of hearts. Dymitry looks back at Sterling.

"Okay, well, clearly you don't know me, Jack."

Jack looks amused as he taps Dimitry's glass. As smooth as a fox in the hen house, Dymitry gets up from his chair and drifts over to the other side of the bar, hunting his prey. Jack knows Dymitry will be preoccupied for the rest of the night.

An older gentleman sitting next to Jack is a perfect representation of the typecast senior citizens who retire in Florida for its warm winters and tropical climates. The man is thin and gaunt except for a protruding potbelly covered by an oversized bright blue Hawaiian shirt, with a red flower printed pattern, resort collar, and button placket in the front. He is wearing tan colored shorts along with black socks under his sandals. The bar lights illuminate his tired face, with deep wrinkles embedded in his forehead. On top of his head rests frizzled white hair that is as pure as snow and shines like snow, too.

His twinkling eyes sat under his thick, peppered eyebrows, a well-groomed, signature Tom Selleck mustache and stubble chin making the girls quiver. He has an unlit cigar in his pocket, yet his body does not radiate any traditional smell of smoke or tobacco, but whiskey and overdosed aftershave. He is reading the local Floridian paper when he couldn't help but notice Jack and Dymitry.

The elderly fellow says in his raspy voice that soon vibrates out loud with power and command, "So you're a single malt guy. Let me buy you a drink."

He lifts his empty whiskey glass and shakes it back and forth, calling attention to the bartender. "Two Macallan 30's on me."

Jack is quick to interrupt the bartender. "I'm sorry, can you just keep mine the 18 years."

"But there is no comparison to the 30-year-old malt."

Jack listens and nods. "That's what I have heard, along with the struggle of trying to go back and drink an 18 after you have a 30. I mean no disrespect, but it's an expensive habit as it is. The way I look at it is if I never taste it, I don't know what I'm missing."

The man expresses friendliness. "Fair enough. Give the man what he wants, but unfortunately, I know what I'm missing, so keep mine the usual."

Jack extends his hand. "Jackson, but you can call me Jack. Thanks for the drink, and pleasure meeting you."

"Likewise. They call me Bob."

Jack utters back, "Well, that's pretty simple."

"Great. I'm a simple kind of guy," Bob replies, "So what brings you into Lorenzo's, besides trying to score your friend a date?"

Jack grins. "Dymitry isn't going anywhere with that girl."

Bob looks over at Dymitry, who is flirting with the girl. She is smiling back. "They look like they are hitting it off."

Jack leans into Bob, pointing his whiskey glass at the romantic couple. "Body language. Look at her eyes. They are the secret to her soul. They keep wandering around the bar. She is only being entertained until something better comes along. Her arms and legs are crossed as her body leans away from Dymitry, when it would be leaning toward him. Additionally, there is no mirror effect."

"Mirror effect?" Bob's face appears lost in a thick fog.

Jack sees an educational moment, then proceeds to go on. "That's right. If a girl is really attracted to a man, she is going to choose to mimic his body language. It is really a subconscious action. Her body is trying to make a connection with whom she is aroused, without actually touching him. In essence, if he picks up his glass to take a drink, she would subconsciously follow. That's the mirror effect. If you watch, Dymitry keeps picking up his drink, yet she barely touches hers."

"Wow, are you some kind of shrink?" Bob exclaims.

"It's science. Action and reaction. You can find your soulmate through science. And no, I'm a marine archeologist." Jack freezes and thinks for a beat. "Or at least that's my hobby. Dymitry and I own a search and rescue operation where we make our bread and butter by finding lost ships at sea."

Bob chugs back his whiskey. "So why the fascination with human psy-chology?"

"It is more psycho-anthropology."

Bob looks discombobulated. "Okay?"

"As an archeologist, it's not enough to study human history and the analysis of physical remains. You also have to study the psychology of the last known person in contact with that artifact. Kind of like detective work. If you understand what he was thinking, you may have a better understanding of how to find whatever it is you're searching for." Jack nudges Bob in the elbow. "Not to mention it also helps you stay one step ahead of your competition when you have to ward off looters and grave robbers looking to make a buck or build up their personal collections."

Bob chokes on his drink.

Jack, in fear, says, "I'm sorry, Bob, are you ok?"

Bob clears his throat. "Yes"—he coughs— "thanks, sorry. It just went down the wrong pipe." Bob coughs once more. "So you knew the girl at the other end of the bar would never go out with your friend all through psycho...anthropology? It's just fact. No emotions?"

"Well, that, and when she found out he didn't have any money..."

"How can you determine that?"

"Again, it has to do with her body language and..."

"Does Dymitry know he is talking to an escort?" Lorenzo utters as he walks up to the bar.

"And there is that." Jack turns around and smiles at Lorenzo, "Hey, Joe. No, I'm just messing with him, curious to see how long it takes Dymitry to figure it out."

Bob shakes his head and laughs. "Too cruel."

"You see, Bob, sometimes it's not about psychological deductions, but just having some pre-existing knowledge." Jack beams from ear to ear.

Expressing tenderness, Lorenzo leans in and hugs Jack. "How are you, my friend?"

"I'm good, Joe. Dymitry's good. Cast Away is starting to see some profits."

Lorenzo looks at Bob, blowing off Jack's words. "'Cast Away'? I tell him he's special, not like his father. Great things for this one's future."

"Lorenzo?" says Jack.

Lorenzo looks over to Jack. "What? I can't help it...I've been looking after you as if you were my own since your father ditched you."

Jack looks disgruntled. "He didn't *ditch* me, he disappeared." He had been declared dead, but those idiots didn't know what they were talking about.

Lorenzo let his shoulders drop. "I'm sorry, you're right, let's not fight." Lorenzo looks at Bob. "You are keeping good company with this one." He points to Jack. "You know, last year he found part of the Spanish San Miguel treasure. Nearly 20 million dollars in old relics just laying off the Florida coast."

"Really?" says Bob.

"Yes, but being the Boy Scout he is, he donated it all to the museum." Lorenzo smiles.

"That's because it belongs in the museum," Jack responds.

Lorenzo looks confused. "I'm just saying, you couldn't just keep a million dollars' worth...."

Jack smirks. "What do I need with a million dollars, Joe?"

Lorenzo shakes his head at Bob and gives off a smile. "You believe this guy?" He turns to Jack. "Okay, you called me earlier and said you found something unbelievable...Well, what do you have?"

Jack looks around to make sure no one is eyeing him. "You know what, Bob?" Jack says, his voice unusually low. "I think you will appreciate this too."

As if the room gets silent and all eyes are on Jack, he reaches in his pocket and takes out a blue microfiber cloth. Unwrapping it ever so slowly, the light starts to reflect off the golden coin that lies inside. When he slowly puts the coin on the top of the bar slate, a single metal clank is heard as it settles. The polished metal object appears luminous. The eyes of everyone are upon the glowing item. Pupils widen and skin becomes flushed as fear starts to run down their faces.

"Is that what I think it is?" Bob says, rubbing his finger along the symbol engraved on the coin.

"Swastika?" Lorenzo says.

"I know," says Jack. "It is Raubgold, just like we talked about."

"Raubgold?" asks Bob.

"Stolen gold," Jack says, his smile undeniably wide.

"Hitler ransacked Europe," murmurs Bob.

"After Hitler transferred and laundered the stolen gold aboard to fund the Second World War," continued Jack.

"He had a little help, of course," Bob utters, and Jack looks sharply at him.

"Where…how…?" Lorenzo asks.

"It was just lying there on the bottom of the ocean, during my last deep-sea dive," Jack answers.

"I remember hearing about these gold coins when I was little, but I've never seen one," Bob says. "How did he get the backing to mint his own coins?"

"And that's where the conspiracy theory comes from." A thick Italian boisterous accent is heard next to them by the bar. "The coin is fake."

In their excitement about the discovery, nobody noticed the newcomer standing just a little way away, obviously listening in on the conversation taking place at the table.

Jack and the others turn their heads toward the intruder in disbelief and indignation. Jack asks the question reverberating in everyone's mind: "Fake? What makes you so positive?"

"I have seen these before. They have been sold by gypsies all around Italy and Paris. You're lucky your finger doesn't turn green just holding it. Nothing more than a tourist scam, Mr. Sterling," boasted the Italian stranger.

Lorenzo replies, "I'm from Bologna, I don't ever recall seeing these over there…"

"Sometimes we see only what we want to see?" the Italian stranger replies. "But don't take my word for it. Take it to a jeweler. He may laugh at you, but I'm sure he will show you it is nothing but fool's gold."

Joe and Bob have a look of disappointment.

Jack is holding up his coin and looking at it with intensity. "So, you're saying this is fake?"

The stranger nods his head.

"Excuse me, Bob." Jack takes the doubloon coin between his thumb and index finger. Like a game of quarters, he slams the coin on the bar top in a forty-five-degree angle. Light cascades across the spinning coin as it bounces like a smooth stone skipping across a pond, hitting the counter only to bounce back up and inside Bob's glass of whiskey.

"HEY?" Bob bellows out, as drops of Macallan splash out of the glass and onto Bob's Hawaiian shirt.

Everyone watches in slow motion as the golden coin slowly sinks to the bottom of the whiskey glass.

Bob, now agitated, yelps, "What did you do that for?"

"Float test, gentlemen. Real gold is 19.3 times heavier than water, and will always sink due to its density. However, fake gold floats. Isn't that right

Mr.—" Jack hesitated. "You know, I never did get your name, and yet you know mine?"

Everyone turns and, like a shadow in the night, the Italian stranger who so strongly wanted them to believe the coin was fake has now vanished.

With a look of confusion, Lorenzo says, "Well, that was weird."

"Very peculiar, indeed." Jack looks around for any signs or clues. Here they are, just admiring a possible artifact among like-minded people they can trust, only to be interrupted by some creep. The lightness of the mood darkens.

Bob scoops up the gold coin out of the bottom of his whiskey glass. "So, I guess he is the one that didn't want to look like a fool? There's no doubt now that it's real?"

Jack comments back, "Straight off the U-boat herself."

"Wait, these came off an *actual* U-Boat…but then…do you mean?" Lorenzo can't talk any slower. Jack could tell he was trying to keep his excitement level down. "That it exists?"

"What exists? Am I missing something?" Bob queries.

"It is what both my father and I have been searching for," exults Jack. "The Spear of Destiny."

Chapter III

The Spear of Destiny

What's the Spear of Destiny?" Bob asks as Jack takes the coin from him, and wipes it down with his shirt.

"It's the lost ark of the sea, Melville's White Whale," Jack replies.

Bob grins. "Oh, I can tell this is going to be a good, Lorenzo. How about another Macallan 30?"

"On the house," Lorenzo offers gleefully as he refills his drink.

Jack starts flipping the coin through his fingers flawlessly, as if he were dodging traffic on a motorcycle during rush hour on the 405. He leans back and begins to tell an elaborate story.

Tales untold and treasures mysteriously perished have a way of resurfacing, for truth always prevails. Mankind often believes the fabricated truth presented before them, but the verification long bolted and buried eventually comes forth.

To be able to relive such a fantasy, a myth long lost, had been unfathomable for Jack. But, now, as he sits in the bar, surrounded by privy eyes and eager ears, he knows the words rolling off his tongue are more than just a fable.

For centuries, it has been known that humanity is driven by power. Authority is akin to lust. People crave and seek it endlessly, and at any cost. It's a disease powered by envy, an illness that seeps like a poison into the system and lures the brain to commence acts of absolute horror. Superficial needs and greed fuel envy. To watch another soul blossom leaves the others seeking the same. Fame and prestige are what people adorn themselves with, even if it diminishes the light of honesty from their blackening hearts.

Such a traditional practice had sprawled over the Roman hearts as well, leading them to conclude Jesus Christ's life. Accusations against him had arisen like a testament, only never fully accredited. The day had come when Jesus was mercilessly hung on a cross on the outskirts of Jerusalem, on account of a hoax. He was claimed to be anti-Judaic, to be creating an illusion of being the Son of God. Alas, the words of the antagonist had to succeed. His resentment conquered the dull senses of the land.

Recalling how the women had wept and all the followers had beseeched the powers that be for mercy and pardon, soon they all went silent. The event had surely altered the future. Even the Governor, Pontius Pilate, having failed to find the requisite reasons to deem Jesus guilty, and fearing the outrage of the people, had gone with the decision. The events thereafter left a lasting impact on the generations to follow. It showed how once non-believers could turn to the faith, given that they witnessed a miracle themselves.

Jack recounted the story just as his father had once told him before. He continued with Pilate not wanting to have Jesus and the other bodies left on the cross the next day, which was the Sabbath. He had asked his top centurion solider, named Longinus, to find a few men and cut off the legs of all those crucified to hasten their death. Longinus, whose age was catching up with him, was nearly blind, but wore many battle scars on his sleeve. He took the long trail up the hill with two of his finest Roman solders to Golgotha. Crowds, along with Mary and the disciples were still gathered around, lying still in sadness. By late afternoon the soldiers had approached the enormous cross on which Jesus was nailed, but they found him to be already dead. All of his breaths had long been seized, leaving Longinus and the soldiers in a state of disbelief. While the other victims were still heaving their last breaths, why was Jesus not alive?

Longinus stepped forward, looking at the man who claimed to be the Son of God. He now lay there as a mere mortal, powerless and weak. Gasps suddenly erupted all around, as Longinus pierced Jesus' limp body with a slash of his rusty spear. The blade, slicing the skin, tempered the side of Jesus, letting blood flow profusely. To the onlookers' disbelief, clear water also appeared to cascade out of his flesh. Legend has it that at that precise moment, the clouds rolled in and skies turned dark. Thunder clapped as lightning struck across an impending skyline, as if reprimanding a disgusting act. But its intensity had struck the hill of the three Crucified, as if commanding an apology of all those who had been blind to their actions. By then, it was too late for the sinners to ask forgiveness.

"It is here where the story of the spear really begins," Jack states.

His friends before him are captivated, and he continues to recount the history, where the blood and water of Christ seemed to splatter across Longinus's eyes. The stream of blood eliminated any further reasons for people to doubt Jesus' death, but his blood seemed to have miraculously restored Longinus' barren sight. It was if rainbows of color poured into a desaturated world. Scripture states, "They shall look on him whom they pierced."

Longinus shouted aloud, "Indeed, this was the son of God!" Jack's lips tremble as he silently utters the words from scripture.

However, with Longinus' new vision, his eyes were quick to gaze on a blue, glowing light that now radiated from his hands. The blood of Jesus Christ had not only bestowed Longinus with sight, but it had also seeped enchantment within the spear. Legend says that what appeared to be water pouring out of Christ was really God's essence, which had then fused within the spear.

Having witnessed a miracle, and seeking forgiveness for himself, Longi-

nus had then embarked on a journey to uncover the truth for himself. He traveled to the ends of Caesarea of Cappadocia, where he surrendered to the lifestyle of that like a monk, and lived isolated from the rest of the world. Having placed himself in the hands of the deity and being self-proclaimed protector of the Spear, he found himself aging more slowly than everyone else. No longer did he find himself becoming ill or experiencing natural physical harm. His physical strength only grew stronger, and his mind remained sharp. Years turned into decades, and decades into centuries, as he outlived all those around him. Kings would rise and fall as his tales became that of legend.

His dedication to his faith had the power to shed light on the guilt and injustice of what he had done. Never feeling that he would ever be forgiven, his new sense of immortality had led to his anger and depression. His regret at what he had done to Christ only continued to grow stronger, along with the spear's effect on him, and soon he would be tempted to use the spear for self-interest, to acquire worldly possessions. He sent the cathedral a letter detailing his life, along with giving them the Holy Relic, to protect like the Holy Grail, knowing in the wrong hands the user could wield God's unbounded power. Shortly after the Spear was in safe hands, he felt the loss of the power from within; he embarked on a journey to the highest mountaintop. Longinus was met with the harshest of weathers, but after standing strong through it all, he shouted up to the heavens, "I can no longer burden this cross to bear, and only ask for your forgiveness for all of my sins, my Lord." Then, he plunged his simple, rusty blade into his heart, taking his own life.

After the incident, the Spear was preserved within the sanctuary of Holy grounds. Later known as the "Holy Lance" or the "Spear of Destiny," it was safeguarded as instructed and hidden away as a religious relic. Despite Longinus' past, the Church would eventually recognize him as a Saint and protector of the Holy Lance. You can find a statue of him beneath the dome in Saint Peter's Basilica.

Sadly, the Church was ineffective at keeping the secrets of the Spear and the legend of St. Longinus from the world. Many Roman Emperors had sought out and come into possession of the Holy Relic of God, shaping their destiny. From Constantine the Great into the dark ages of Theodosius the Great, King Alaric, to Aetius, even falling into the hands for a brief time of Attila the Hun. In 768 AD, the Holy Lance eventually found its way into the hands of Charlamagne, never allowing it to leave his side; as Emperor of the West, he became the greatest ruler in history, known as the founder of the First German Reich. Charlamagne felt the Spear gave him that divine right to rule all of Europe. Strangely enough, with the Spear by his side and despite the odds, he had won over eighteen battles throughout his reign, conquering all of the Germanic Saxons and converting them to Christianity.

Until one day, when coming home from winning another glorious battle, Charlamagne was riding along the side of a mountain edge when an extremely bright comets appeared out of nowhere, lighting up the sky, causing exotic outbursts of meteor showers to appear, as if it was raining down from the heavens. His horse reared up, as it was instantly frighted, throwing Charlemagne off and losing the Spear of Destiny over the side of the cliff. He ordered his men to scour the mountainside to find it, but came to no avail. A week later, Charlemagne fell ill with a fever and died, following the same legend as before. Each one of them, driven by greed, had been a victim of losing the Spear mystically, leading to their own annihilation. However, before all that the Holy Lance had an ability to pass on victory in battle to any of its holders. Each time a new emperor ventured to conquer a country within Europe, the Lance traveled too. That is, until it would be lost, and the empire would fall immediately to another. Like a baton, that fate passed on from one ruler to another. Perhaps it was a trial by the Lord above or a punishment for the lands that had crucified Jesus. The Spear of Destiny was a contrivance essential to winning against all odds.

The Spear was eventually found on the mountainside. While no surprise came with Charlemagne's life ceasing, the next rulers had banished the Holy

Lance. It was to be buried where no one would ever find it. After all, the emperors were relishing in the sacrifices made by the rulers before. Having witnessed their deaths with the disappearance of the Lance, the other rulers wished for a more serene life.

From there, it would lay dormant from the world for years, until June 1098, when a drunken peasant named Peter Bartholomew started having visions from the apostle Andrew. His dreams told him he would have the power to allow the First Crusaders to have victory in sieging Antioch against the Muslims, despite the colossal odds. Bartholomew's ongoing visions lead him to the Cathedral of St. Peter, where his dreams had him take an iron candle stand from the altar and smash it onto the cathedral floor. With the sound of stone cracks echoing off the walls, and the dust and debris clearing in the air, lying underneath the new broken tile next to Bartholomew shone a green, glowing light, revealing the most priceless of Holy treasures, the Spear of Destiny. After giving the Lance to the Knight of the Crusaders, Raymond the IV, they acquired their victory just as Saint Andrew had promised them. Dreams continued to haunt Bartholomew, cautioning him that by not placing the Spear of Destiny back into its resting place, the Holy Relic's occupancy would cause tremendous devastation, and result in the holder's demise. Raymond refused to listen to Bartholomew's warnings, as the Spear of Destiny became a valuable relic again, this time among the First Crusaders. Raymond would lead his troops to Jerusalem, and eventually captured Tripoli and built his castle. Time would pass to the spring of 1105. He felt his new dwelling was the ultimate symbol of strength and that he no longer required the rusty blade of a Holy Lance. He cast it aside to a local merchant. Then, like the rulers before him, Raymond IV of Count Toulouse mysteriously died a week later. The cause of death on record is unknown.

Jack takes a breath and looks on in silence before raising his glass. He can see that he has a captive audience.

"So, what did the merchant do with the Holy Lance?" Bob says, perplexed, as he downs another drink.

"Relax, Bob. Can you let the kid finish?" replies Lorenzo.

Jack comments back, "No one knows for sure. There is a legend that it was given to the guardians of the Holy Grail, the Knights Templar. I've never been able to find out. We just know that the Spear of Destiny vanished from the world, and wouldn't resurface till eight hundred and three years later."

Chapter IV

Hitler's Reign

J ack knew the story well. The Spear of Destiny had earned a reputation of harboring powers. *Ye who wields it can conquer the world, but should it fall out of your hands, all you have gained shall be lost, and ultimately you will be met with your own demise.* Of course, this knowledge came along after bearing witness to the downfall of endless dynasties. Long after the disappears of the Lance from Batu Khan, the world was at peace again from any powerful religious relics. Leaving people muddled as to whether it was really a weapon of mass destruction, or a Holy Grail? Over time, the history of the spear became that of an urban legend. The legends circled into fables, and fables weaved into myths. Even today, it is a story that very few are familiar with. Except there was someone shrouded in darkness who truly believed in this myth of the Holy Lance that can shape destiny, and he would stop at nothing to acquire it. The seedling for evil seemed to have planted itself deep within the soul of a young boy born in Germany.

Adolf felt he had a greater purpose in life, maybe as a man of the cloth. More than that, he knew his destiny was never to be reached if he was to follow in his father's footsteps of being a customs bureau officer.

His escapade came to a conclusion after his brother—and biggest supporter—Edmund was struck with the measles, and died. No longer was there someone to believe in him or encourage him, or even lift his spirits with a simple smile. Unable to deal with the death of his son, Hitler's father did penance by punishing Adolf. He had stopped him from wanting to pursue a path to be a priest, along with cutting off all of his creative endeavors. He put Adolf on a train and sent him off to join academic schooling in Linz.

Jack Sterling can't help but take a moment from telling the story, as memories of his own childhood struggles start to flood in. From being forced to do all that he was told as a child, despite Jacks own passions, leading up to the tragedy that happened to both of his parents. In spite of Jack's brief silence, neither Bob nor Lorenzo dwell on the reason. Instead, each of them is still a captive audience member, listening to how the story will unfold.

Jack calls on the strength of his father to finish the tale of the spear. A force passes through him, and he takes a deep breath.

Adolf Hitler defied all that he was taught in Linz. His only escape at his new school became the sessions of caroling praises of his nation amongst his friends. As a young man, he continued to falter academically while excelling in his chosen art. His spiraling nationalist thoughts consumed his spirit, only to be darkened each time his family rebuked him. This was the pattern he became used to, until the sudden news of his father's demise came through.

Henceforth, Adolf was called back by his mother, who was against him being forced to pursue a future he did not seek. He was enrolled in Steyr for a year, where his performance improved until another tragedy struck him. With the aid of a program meant for orphans and his mother's guidance, he made it far, until he reached the Vienna art school. The school became the very reason his dreams were buried. His application to enroll for the fine arts program was rejected twice, suggesting he take up the path for architecture. Although, that was a suggestion entailing mockery, as his academic grades were insufficient.

His dreams that were once so vivid were now crippled into dust, and he

couldn't help feel utterly alone in the world. For everyone around him, he seemed to be a subject of rejection. He was born for a reason, yet robbed of his destiny.

Due to the inner turmoil Adolf was going through, his seeds of darkness were growing, leaving him with mixed emotions. All of this came to a halt the day his eyes landed on the very item known to captivate a person into its trance.

It was in September, 1908 at the Hofburg Museum in Vienna. They had opened their doors to showcase some of their most prized relics to the public. Walter Stein a close friend of Adolf's, and, hoping it might cheer his spirits, invited him to come along. Long after the Second War, Stein talked about his experience he had that day. Saying Hitler was distracted, as the museum was closing and they were in the middle of looking at a painting, Adolf said he was hearing voices, almost calling out to him.

Stein followed Adolf as he searched through the museum, seeking out the voices which lead him to a tucked away back room. The small room was forbidden to the public, but there was not a guard on site. Adolf helped himself in, only to find his footsteps navigating him toward the case, like a powerful force that compelled him to be lost in its sight. Incased in the glass laid was a powerful Holy relic.

Bob blurts out, "The Spear of Destiny?"

Jack smiles as he takes another drink.

Sitting within the locked glass case was the Spear of Destiny, radiating a glow that was so bright, anyone looking into it would be transfixed. Later, Hitler would tell this story in *Mein Kampf.* The magical relic gave him an everlasting bond. The priest had come in, alarmed that someone had intruded where they were not wanted, and had asked them to leave, as the museum had closed. Adolf paid him no mind, as he still was unable to lift his eyes off the spear. Each reflection of light against the blunt blade darkened his eyes. Like a talisman, he felt he must have possessed this relic in a previous life.

The words seemed to roll out from his tongue subconsciously. Adolf had now become clear of his Destiny, and why the Spear was calling out to him. With this lance he could feel the power that would allow him to hold the fate of the world in his hands. Adolf walked out the door with Stein, but turned around and looked at the priest and gave him a stern warning.

"I will be coming back for this someday."

If only the priest knew back then that Adolf uttered a solemn vow, he probably would have concealed or even destroyed the spear. Adolf was so obsessed, his dreams were haunted by its image of the tool that was used to stab the Son of God, compelling him to study and decipher its true power. Each new legend he discovered about the lance only bewildered him. He realized this was his prophesy to fulfill.

With time, as the political situation increased between that of the Christians and the Jews, Adolf Hitler's resentment only escalated with a specific race in particular. With the loss Germany suffered in World War I, Adolf desired to serve people of his own kind. To safeguard the interests of Christians rather than let the Jews who were invading his country relish in abundance. He finally saw his destiny just as the great Charlemagne had done with the first Reich a millennium ago. Just as the great William Ludwig had attempted with the Second Reich during the Prussian War. Now it was Hitler's time for a third. Only this time, it would be one that would last for a thousand years, ruled by an emperor with the perfect race, like all German emperors who surround themselves in jewels. Adolf Hitler believed that the world belonged to those who held power within the palm of their hands. To take it, they needed an emblem of war, and he knew exactly where to get it.

Jack's eyes traveled to his own palm holding the Swastika gold coin. *Power, altered by ego and fueled by rejection, was what led countless seekers to the Spear of Destiny. If the coin was within reach of the Holy Lance, do I risk a similar fate, or worse yet, risk tampering with the safety of the world?*

He can't help but let his mind plummet into wonder as he continues on

with the story.

Adolf's inner dark seed that took over his heart had affected his mind. With each conquest, Hitler felt he was thinning out the herd and making way for his perfect German Aryan race, who was loyal to their Führer, all to fullfill his destiny of becoming a great and powerful Emperor. His soul wasn't possessed by a demon, but by Satan himself. Little did Hitler know, there was someone else rooted in darkness living in Italy at the time, whose destiny would eventually align with Hitler's. This man believed in absolute leadership, and together with Adolf, they would form a bond and a common goal of creating the new order. Only this man came didn't come from a military background, but the cloth, and his very essence is one of infallibility, presumed to be preserved from the possibility of error. The aura of holiness belonged to none other than Pope Pius XI.

In 1938, two days after Hitler took over Austria, causing humanity to slide into the ongoing slaughter of World War II, he felt it was now time to take destiny into the palm of his own hands. He sought to fullfill a promise that he made to a clergyman thirty years ago. He traveled with his army onto the main street of Vienna, only to find the Pope was waiting for him. It was no secret what Hitler wanted, and the Pope knew while the new Führer was building his ultimate Nazi regime, he was deep in debt and suffering from what fuels all great wars, money. Fortunately, the Vatican was sitting on lots of it.

Pope Pius XI had goals of his own: to increase and centralize the power of the papacy, to eradicate all Catholic political oppositions, to total recognition and acceptance of the Vatican's law by the German state, thereby forcing absolute-leadership. Instead of Hitler taking the Spear of Destiny by force, the Pope offered it to him in good faith as part of the treaty agreement. With that came an understating that the Vatican would secretly fund Hitler's War, using the Vatican's gold as reserves against lending institutions. As a revenue stream, Hitler would continue to loot any gold and collect a church tax from newly occupied European territories. The gold would be re-melted into a new coin that would bear two symbols: one of the Swastika logo, the Holy See crest on the other. This unique gold coin would symbolize the bond between them for a new world order.

From Hitler's perspective, besides backing his war, it showed that a tremendous moral authority trusted his word, and enhanced his respectability with the loyal German Catholics, opening up the floodgates to millions joining the Nazi Party. Now with the Spear of Destiny in his possession, and the financial backing of the Vatican, he could feel the tables turning. The war would go on for years, and he became known for "lightning in war," better known as the Blitzkrieg: breaking through enemy lines with overwhelming force and speed, allowing him to conquer all of Western Europe.

By 1943 the Allies were making some progress in driving back Hitler's forces in Italy, where a particular Army unit, nicknamed "Monuments Men," composed of art historians, architects, curators, were put together by President Roosevelt to steal back some of the treasures and stolen art to return to their rightful owners. President Roosevelt felt American victory in Europe would have little meaning if the relics and history of the country were lost. With several successes through various mines, castles, and secret vaults, the Monuments Men were making a great strides in stealing back some of the artifacts, even gold Hilter and his army were taking for their own collection. But they had yet to find the Führer's most prized possession. There was someone else hunting it down, who would stop at nothing until he found it. General George S. Patton, also known as "Blood and Guts." The General saw himself as a Christian warrior, and ever since he was a child, he too obsessed over the story of the Holy Lance, and the power it posed in war. He was devastated when he heard Hitler had taken it from the Vatican.

Hitler found out he was searching for it. He couldn't risk more of his treasures falling into his enemy's hands. The Catholic Church was also was getting nervous the Americans would discover the Pope's dirty hands had been funding Hitler's war machine. With the threat of cutting off his funding, Hitler was forced to take creative action. One of the most famous captains in

the navy of Nazi Germany, better known as the Kriegsmarine, was Günther Prien.

The most significant amount of wealth transferred in human history took place during Word War II, and it was called Operation Fish. There was fear of the Nazis taking over England, so the British government moved over three hundred billion dollars' worth of gold across the North Atlantic sea to Canada. The plan was for Winston Churchill to run the Commonwealth from Montreal. Through massive convoys, they managed to transport the thirty thousand tons of Gold across the North Atlantic Ocean, but not without suffering some casualties and heavy financial losses.

Captain Prien became one of the most successful Nazi officers due to his combat record, having helped sink more than forty-one percent of the British ships, with him only losing one of his German U-Boats. Churchill made it his mission, with his entire British fleet, to hunt down Captain Prien. This happened in March of 1941. Captain Prien was marked for dead after a bloody battle out at sea, west of Ireland. A British destroyer, the *HMS Wolverine,* confronted him in battle and came out victorious after several successful explosive depth charges left fiery wreckage. Captain Prien was blown out of the sub, with some injuries, and washed up on the shore of Faroe Islands. Healing from his own wounds, he ended up blending in with the Norwegians until two years later, when he managed to make it back to Germany.

Hitler knew he would have bigger plans for Captain Günther Prien, and chose to keep his existence classified. Over the years, Hitler had set up several underground bunkers in secret locations around the globe. One in particular, with its alpine-style architecture and European culture, was the Patagonian city of Bariloche in Argentina. What made this location so perfect was that the local President, Juan Perón, was a Nazi sympathizer, and he allowed safe passage into his country. Even after the war, there would be these organized escape routes.

Bob's transfixed on the story, but can't help but chime in: "Ratlines, isn't that what they were called?"

Jack nods his head in agreement.

That's right, the Vatican helped create these routes from Europe to Argentina for highly decorated German soldiers, looking to use these paths to avoid the risk of being captured and tried on any war crimes. Hitler knew that should he and his forces be taken over in Berlin, so long as he had a footing in Argentina and the financial backing of the Vatican, the Third Reich would not be defeated, only temporarily held back. It was now Captain Günther Prien's turn to transport a wealth of gold across the North Atlantic, for his Führer, so that he could continue his reign. Only the captain had help, with a unique submarine that Hitler designed and purposely left off the books, listing it has a non-commissioned vessel in the Kriegsmarine. Marked as *U-Boat 2553,* this submarine was intended to be operated primarily as a submerged vessel that ran on an electric diesel engine. A unique engine that was so quiet that US battleships could only hear the ocean water's rumbling until the U-Boat was right underneath them, by which point it would have been too late. The US sailors might be lucky enough to see a hint of bubbles before instantly revealing a black twenty-four-foot long metal torpedo barreling toward them, only to rip their vessel apart, sending them into a watery flamed hell on the sea. The ability to wipe out an entire Navy with a single submarine.

Jack can't help but think back to when he was a child, listening to the wild tales of Captain Nemo.

Inside this specially designed U-Boat was everything one needed for the long underwater sea voyage. However, there was one special room on this particular submarine that was engineered as one of a kind for these U-Boats. The room was a massive vault that took up a quarter of the entire vessel, and was located in the stern. Constructed all out of iron, but covered in an outer shell of stainless steel to prevent rust, the high-tech self-sustaining room was built with an air-tight chamber. The vault had its own backup generator, dehumidifier, and pressure control sensors. The only entrance to this magnificent strong room was a steel door that was ten feet wide by eight feet tall and

three feet thick. It contained a sophisticated twenty-seven-numbered combination that only the Fuhrer and Captain Prien possessed. The crew was quick to realize they were carrying their Fuhrer's rare cargo, and he'd taken all the precautions to minimize the risk of losing anything. It was reported that if any seamen were caught even messing with the door, Captain Prien was ordered to shoot them on sight. Loaded with the Vatican's gold and many of Hitler's other treasures, to prevent capture from Allied forces, Captain Prien and his 35 seamen set sail for Bariloche, Argentina, on March 6th, 1945.

Jack's face falls as he takes a swig of his drink. He witnesses the single ice-cube that lies sunken on the bottom of his glass. "This next part of the story is what information I have managed to compile throughout the years, from the actual seamen that traveled on that fateful voyage."

It was Friday, April 20th 1945, oddly enough Hitler's birthday. The crew onboard had been submerged for over fifty-five days, traveling en route to Bariloche. By their calculation, they should have been out of the Atlantic Ocean and entering the Caribbean Sea. However, Captain Prien had woken up to an unusual alert from one of his faithful officers, Lieutenant Klaus Erberger. The heading gauge was just spinning in circles. Captain Prien and the seamen couldn't help notice that the air in the submarine was unusually cold that morning, and charged with massive static electricity. The captain checked his own personal compass; he also found it spinning in disarray. In fact, all the seamen's navigational tools were found to be in chaos. No sense of direction seemed to be working.

Additionally, all the internal submarine clocks seemed to be frozen. No one could tell the direction they were headed, nor how long they were traveling. Captain Prien had his men turn the wheel from port to starboard and back again to try to get a sense of location, only to end up in circles. Grabbing the periscope, Captain Prien thought it best to get a visual of the sea, only to discover what the seamen took to their own grave in disbelief.

From the view of the periscope, there wasn't one single form of life that seem to exist within the ocean—no mammals, fish, or even moving organisms. The ocean bed was also stripped of any color, as it lay bare, with a lack of coral or reefs. The water seemed to be still, as if frozen in time. With each breath, they could see the warm moisture of misty clouds rolling off their breaths. To what the seamen can only explain as the longest day of their lives, they continued to move forward, not knowing how long or in what direction they were heading. They might as well have been blind men, searching in a newly discovered room, reaching out for some wall or door to grab onto, hoping for some hope of origin.

Because of all nautical myths and superstitions, the picture of death, mystery, and fear couldn't help but run through the German seamen's veins, as they all had heard the tales of this happening before. A fleet of planes that would just disappear, only be marked as dead due to the calculation of time that passed and their possible fuel capacity. Coal ships with a crew of 58 men all being swallowed up within an hour. Countless vessels had vanished into thin air, while strange lights appeared in the middle of the ocean. If this was true, and their calculations were off, they were still in the North Atlantic Ocean, trying to pass through the Bermuda Triangle.

The irony was that Captain Prien was determined not to be another mysterious casualty, lost at sea forever, despite that was how the history was written. Now, these submarines were designed that they only needed to surface to periscope depth for the recharging of the battery cells, which took place via the snorkel, allowing them to stay submerged longer. However, due to them now navigating in the blind, Captain Prien decided it best to come up for a full surface to get perspective of his surroundings. This would allow him to go the old fashion route of looking up to the celestial stars to find his true north. Who knew this small action would lead to his demise?

The navigations and clocks were not the only instruments to be crippled, but their passive sonar, which received sounds coming from other vessels, also appeared to be damaged. As the black hulk of a U-Boat slowly surfaced out of the water, revealing the proud white German swastika and the U-Boat identifier *2553*, it was met unexpectedly by a US Navy battleship that hap-

pened to be sitting less than one hundred feet away. Both forces were caught off guard. The battleship needed to take advantage of the element of surprise. With acceleration, they attempted to seize the surfaced submarine before it could dive, quick to fire off a torpedo as a warning shot. However, the Nazi sub was not the only one experiencing trouble in the Bermuda Triangle. The US torpedo, which was only supposed to graze the German U-Boat, instead registered a miscalculated direct hit along the stern. With the U-Boat catching ablaze and struggling to dive, and the crew was quick to jump off the German submarine and into the ocean, raising their hands in surrender, even United States captivity being a better option than being lost in limbo on a sinking ship.

As the US Navy collected the survivors, the German *U-Boat 2553* slowly sank as more wreckage started to drift from below to what we know as its final resting place. The only two passengers who remained unaccounted for were Captain Prien and Lieutenant Erberger. They were in the stern when the torpedo hit, so they may have died upon contact, or they were Nazi officers who were loyal to the end, and were proud to go down with the ship. In any event, all the remains of the Vatican gold and Hitler's most prized possessions were now gone.

On this same day, Hitler was relocated to a secrete bunker in Berlin, as the United States forces had been fighting a massive battle the past four days in Nuremberg. Through heavy bombing and massive hand to hand combat, many lives were lost, but on that morning, as if destiny was intervening, the German forces lost their foothold and began to falter. The city was gray and dismal; a pillow of smoke brimmed over all of Nuremberg. The ground lay blanketed in the dead, which blended in with the rubble. Embers cascaded into the horizons, as if the souls of those who were loved and lost from a vicious war were ascending into heaven. The devastation was created by a mentally ill dictator, driven by his selfish desire for what he thought was his destiny. On the other side of the city, General Patton was overseeing the 3rd command overtaking Nuremberg Castle. He had gotten wind through his intelligence report that the Spear of Destiny was being stored in a secret bunker underneath the Nuremberg castle. Monuments Men arrived on location and, along with General Patton, through a series of underground tunnels, they found the secret shelter that was a renovated beer cellar. After finding a vast amount of Europe's treasures inside, and realizing how much the Nazis had taken, in the corner of the room, inside a small wooden crate was the Spear of Destiny. General Patton had finally gotten what he was after: the Holy relic of God. It flet best that the Spear of Destiny should be in the hands of the United States, and who better to preserve it then Patton himself?

Back in Jacksonville, Florida, the German prisoners were taken to Naval Air Station, where they were interrogated, before sending them off to Leavenworth penitentiary to await their trial. Agreeing on a reduced sentence for their cooperation, each of the crew members told what they knew, which was very little. They weren't on any war assignment or torpedo strike. They were simply on a transport mission, carrying some of Hitler's personal treasures he had stolen from various museums to Argentina. They couldn't even begin to list the contents, as they been unknown to them, except for one. They could not have known, as this cover-up was too big to keep secret. They were, of course, carrying the infamous Spear of Destiny. The Real One.

Bob bursts out, "Wait! I'm confused? There's a second one?"

"Oh, this is the good part. Please Bob, let Jack finish. He is almost done. I have heard this story several times from his father," Joe replies.

Jack smiles and continues on. "With Hitler knowing General Patton would never give up searching for it, he wanted to make sure the one in Argentina would be safe, and he created an exact replica of the Holy Lance, storing the second one under the castle in Nuremberg, leaving Patton to believe he had captured the real Spear of Destiny."

Jack recalls that the US Naval fleet went back out to find any possible remains, but the search was futile. No trace of Captain Prien or Lieutenant

Erberger or any additional wreckage could be seen from *U-Boat 2553*. It was declared that the submarine had bedded itself deep within the pits of the Bermuda Triangle. The real Spear of Destiny was once again lost to the world, and peace would now follow. The news of *U-Boat 2553* still managed to make its way back to Germany, and was utterly devastating to Hitler, in addition to the loss of Nuremberg. The very means of him acquiring discrete power, the very source of his relentless success, had drowned. Previous revelations of all the emperors who had gained the Lance, only to lose it, filled Adolf's senses. He knew what his near future now entailed—bleak damnation. Petrified of inevitable loss, the man grew berserk. All he was able to to do was reminisce about the power he felt resonate within his fingertips since the very first time he had held it, the magical relic that was supposed to have an everlasting bond now gone, and his 1,000-year Reich sure to follow.

Ten days later, on April 30th, 1945, locked and burrowed away in his quarters of a refurbished air-raid shelter in Berlin. Hitler and his wife Eva Braun finished dining on a substantial amount of food. Decked out in their most elegant attire, they finished the night off by consuming a couple of hydrogen cyanide capsules with their wine. Hitler would not allow himself to be caught and be tried for crimes against humanity, for death was better than dishonor. He watched as Eva, whose eyes were pooled with tears, collapsed slowly in his arms. With Hitler's capsule for some reason taking longer to have an effect, he grabbed a pistol and shot himself beneath his chin. They both were found dead on the sofa. Six years of war were now over.

With the gold coins sunken to the bottom of the ocean, all that remained were rumors of the Vatican's involvement with Hitler. Pope Pius XII then went on to make a public condemnation of the actions of the Nazis and against their persecution of the Jews. With the lost relic treasures not being on a high priority list in the US Navy, General Patton's office didn't learn there was another Holy Lance until later that same year. However, the information was too late, as Patton had died shortly after in a horrific auto accident. One could argue that had he owned the real Spear of Destiny, with all its holy powers and mystery, Patton may have survived, but by that same logic had Hitler kept the Holy Lance physically on him, he may have not lost the War or had taken his own life. With the museum in Vienna laying claims to the artifact that was in Patton's possession, not knowing of the one lost at sea, the United States returned the Spear back to them, keeping the story of the mysterious *U-Boat 2553* and the other lance classified. "You can still see the Holy Lance in Vienna, on display today. Who knows if the museum knows it's phony, so long as the public believes it? I guess that is all that matters to them."

Jack looks at the gold coin with the Holy See logo on one side and the Swastika logo on the other. He places it down on the bar ledge in front of him.

Jack sighs. "Pope Pius XII had traded his belief in God to make a deal with the 20th century Devil in giving Adolf Hitler what he required the most. Then, like so many conquerors before him, Adolf lost the real Spear of Destiny to the world. This coin maybe be the key to its finding it."

Just as Jack's thoughts were mustering a voice, time itself for that brief second slowed down to a dead stop. All the sound that made up the existence of life in the room seemed to be sucked out of reality. A piercing eruption quivered the ambiance and the bar, like a tremor that shook the vicinity. Shivers shot up Jack's spine, radiating out his entire body as the glass of the bar shattered before bellows of panic and frantic scurrying from the other patrons followed. With bloodshot red eyes and shivering temples, he turned to locate the source of the blast, until his eyes reflected the sight just outside.

Raging streaks of red and orange flames seemed to have engulfed his boat in their wake, giving birth to hate and confusion within him.

Jack's tugboat, known only to Dymitry as *The Falcon*, lay motionless on the ocean's pier, while the uncontrollable flames engulfed the wooden vessel like an oversized bonfire, burning away any physical connection Jack had with his father. His whole livelihood was on that boat, and at rapid speed it

was all transforming into smoldering remains. He stood in disbelief as he was submerged in pillars of black smoke, seeing only tiny embers managing to break through and scurry away to the night sky. Like a Viking being buried at sea, Jack could only imagine that if the tugboat had a soul, each of these smoking remnants represented different memories and moments of the life the tugboat had procured.

Chapter V

The Aftermath

ll the events passed in a blur, and Jack, lost in a horrendous daze, overlooks the blaring sirens in the distance. The audience he had held captive with the intriguing story was now dispersed. Some had given their condolences and bid their farewell, while some, like Bob, Lorenzo and Dymitry, lingered around. The red and blue lights of the police to that of an ambulance and a fire brigade had engulfed the area in their safety. Jack, on the other hand, remains by the foot, watching his *Falcon* lose its breath as it is eaten by the fire.

Jack stares ominously into the fire onboard the ship. "Wait, where's my Triton?" as Jack runs over to where the firefighters are extinguishing the last of the fire.

Dymitry runs around the dock. "I don't see anything."

Jack notices that the cables have been snapped off the mounting bolts. "The force of the blast must have propelled it into the water."

This is one of those somber moments in life where no one really knows what to say. Dymitry stands there with his hands on his head, speechless in disbelief, continuing to stare into the abyss of the ship as the flames start to

slow down, leaving a charred vessel, barely adrift on the sea, anchored to the pier. Jack's whole livelihood is being destroyed right before his eyes. However, he feels the needs to console Dymitry and give him hope, as this too was a life shared by him.

"It's ok. At least we know the software works. We'll just sell it to the highest bidder and get us a new boat. We'll be back at sea in no time. Besides, you always made fun of this hunk of junk. I know your laptop is probably a pile of smoldering ash, but you made a backup, right?" Jack asks, unsure of himself or what's to come next.

Dymitry pauses, but then replies, "Of course I did."

Jack gives a smile puts his hands on Dymitry's shoulders "See, all is not lost."

Dymitry knows his friend better, and he can tell that Jack is bottling his emotions like he always does. "Well, the backup was on the *Falcon*."

Jack becomes very still. "I see. Any cloud backup of that backup?"

Dymitry shakes his head.

"Any code stored *anywhere* else?"

Dymitry shakes his head, again.

"How could you not backup your backup, Dymitry—"

Dymitry isn't the only one to blame here. "You freelance for a marine insurance company. You happen to take out any insurance, *Jack*?"

Jack shakes his head and stares into the flames. "Alice is going to kill me."

Not knowing what to say next, Dymitry just walks off. "Well, goodnight, Jack."

Jack just rolls his eyes while the Triton lies sunken somewhere in the inlet. Jack knows deep within his heart that no paramedic, no amount of water, would be able to put out the destruction *The Falcon* has already incurred.

Each second that was wasted had inched the vessel closer to its demise. Just as the black smog intensified, the night sky grew glum, suffocating all the restless hearts underneath it, instead of caressing the tormented heart with its subtle breeze.

Jack's emotions take a further plunge as the fire brigade that once stood mighty by the pier is now reversing. The Deputy Fire Marshall approaches Jack. "I gather you are Mr. Jack Sterling, the owner of the vessel."

"I highly doubt you'd be approaching me if I was just a bystander." Jack crosses his forearms over his chest, his eyebrows knit in confusion as he anticipates the questions he knows all too well.

The investigation to follow was simply a mundane procession for Jack. After all, he had been the brain behind Cast Away Towing. Would it too be another in a long line of startups that smolders to ashes? The mere thought of being unemployed for whoever knows how long started gnawing at his already palpitating heart.

Jack's long-term girlfriend, Alice, was a full-time student, and he knew she couldn't support the both of them. That wouldn't be fair. Jack knew that Lorenzo, being a longtime family friend, would probably find an opportunity at the bar till Jack got back on his feet. But where was Jack to find solace when his heart belonged to the sea? His eyes drift back to the now diminishing blisters of orange—all the memories he had made of endless adventures with Dymitry, Alice, and his father. The investigation that was to follow already left him dreading it. Sighing, he turns to face the inspector once more, only this time he drops his vexed demeanor. He is not the man to blame, yet the conversation to come forth was irking him already.

Deputy Fire Marshall JD is a stocky man from Waco, Texas, a small town, where you find some of the friendliest and most spiritual people. The Fire Marshall extends his hand in understanding, and Jack grasps it for a firm handshake.

Jack replies, "Marshall."

In that deep southern Texas voice, JD replies back, "Please just call me JD. Gosh, Mr. Sterling, I feel reel bad for what happened here tonight, I really do. We tried to get the fire out, but it was just too far gone."

Jack continues to look out at the burning vessel. "What's your thoughts on the cause?"

"Well, sir, we won't have the full report till the fire is completely out, and there will be a diving crew that can help search through the wreckage in the morning."

"Maybe they will find the Triton?"

"What's that?"

"A mini-sub."

"Oh, okay. Yes sir, I'll have them keep an eye out for it. However, back to your other question: it still too early to say for sure, but it seems like there might have been a DC electrical fault."

"DC electric fault?"

"Sadly the wood floor is dated, not really up to today's code, in addition—"

Jack interrupts, "My father built that floor with his own two hands; we never had any kind of issues."

"I can understand that, but you see, it looks like you guys had some fancy equipment, and that mini-sub?"

Jack rebuts, "Triton."

JD replies, "Anyway, way too much power for this little tugboat. All those fancy computers, what were those for anyway?"

Jack answers back, "It helped us find things."

"Isn't that what Google is for? No matter, with the condition the vessel was in, and that kind of amperage you were pulling, the heat coming from that fuse box and through those copper wires, the floor was just like dry timber waiting to be lit."

Jack snaps back, "Well, JD, let me tell you one thing: this boat has never had a faulty wire, because I kept it well maintained."

"There's no need for you to get your britches in a bunch. I'm just telling you how the accident happened."

Jack replies, "This was no accident."

"Well, you seem to know so much, why don't you delight me with what conclusions you have made, Mr. Sterling?" JD's voice grows loud, causing a circle to form around the two men. "Do you think the fire was deliberate? According to your partner, you were the last one on the boat."

The Marshall seems to have turned the tables on Jack. Was he not the one always highlighting a case of insurance fraud? His bottled-up emotions were wanting to emerge to the top. His jaw tightens at the faint taunt and allegation. He immediately picks up his guard to defend himself, but before words could have rolled off his tongue, Bob intervenes. For a split moment, Jack flinches, swearing to himself internally not to have seen the old man walk near the two.

Bob interrupts, "JD, please pardon the man; he just needs a fresh perspective and some rest. He just lost his boat."

Bob leans over, "Jack, not now. Let me help you sort all this out. I have a boat with a winch and some divers that can be out here in the hour. We will find the Triton and whatever remains, and keep it safe for you."

"I don't mean to sound ungrateful, but why would you do that?" Jack pondered. "I should probably stay."

"Nonsense," Bob demands. "This is a lot to take in, and honestly, there is not much you can do, as it will be a late night of clean up."

The Fire Marshall can't help but interrupt. "Golly, sir, I don't even know

you, and I want to give you a hug. That's mighty nice of you." He looks over to Jack, realizing his stress. "Mr. Sterling, if it's any consolation to you, we plan on being be out here, and will work with your buddy. We will call you if anything comes up."

Jack scratches his head, looks at the clean-up mess of his boat in flames, then looks back at Bob. "You would really do that for me? Why?"

"I'm just an old man that was taken by your story tonight. I see a talented individual who has just fallen on some bad luck. I have a couple bucks, I'm very familiar with marine equipment, and I like to help. If you'll let me?" Bob pleads.

For the first time in a while, Jack feels like he has a father figure in his life, someone with a bit more wisdom, and the financial clout to get him out of a sticky situation. The reality is that Jack is financially strapped. Everything he had was in *The Falcon*, so he's open to the idea of this new stranger willing to give a helping hand. Not to mention the emotional stress of it all. Surely he can have a clear head in the morning. "Well, yes, I guess. Only if you're sure," said Jack, rubbing his fingers through his own hair.

Bob starts walking with Jack toward his vehicle. "Don't worry about a thing. We will figure all this out in the morning. Go home and get some rest. I think you said you had a girlfriend waiting for you?"

Bob is right. Alice is probably starting to worry, and he has a lot of news to share. "You're right, Bob. Sorry, JD. Let's just talk about this in the morning."

"Understand, Mr. Sterling. Just know in Texas we have a saying: 'When God closes one door, another one opens.' But I think you see that tonight with this nice gentlemen. If anything comes up, we will give you a call."

Bob smiles at JD. "Thank You, Marshall. I will be back." Then the two walk off in unison. "Jack, listen, I know you are distressed at the moment, but finding that gold coin will—"

Jack's stunned, then starts to fish in his pocket. His eyes bulge out of their sockets, interrupting Bob. "Where is the coin?"

"You had it? Oh God, Jack, did you leave it back in the bar?"

Bob and Jack run back into the bar. Lorenzo is already cleaning up when they burst in asking about the coin, but Lorenzo has not seen it, suggesting that maybe it fell off the counter during the blast. The three of them search across the entire restaurant, yet the glistening of gold is already gone. The coin Jack was holding an hour ago is nowhere in sight.

Jack's shoulders drop as he paces in frustration. The throbbing headache now threatens to explode his sanity, causing him to cup his head in his hand. "Dymitry picked it up—he must have?" Jack said as he waited for his friend to call and let him know that the coin was safe. Yet that didn't happen, either. Painful memories started to rush over him with each passing minute. Bob places his palm over Jack's shoulder.

"What will you do now?"

Sterling, unsure of the answer, shakes his head in despair.

Bob's low voice only met with Jack's sigh. "Look, I know this is not the right time for you to be thinking all of this. Let me get you a ride. You just go home and have a good rest. I will take care of this tonight." Bob writes his number on a napkin. Jack stuffs it in the pocket that once held the missing golden gem. "I promise we will figure this out."

Before Jack can even stutter anything in response, Bob walks out, only to return a few minutes later. A long dark Denali is parked out front. Bob helps Jack in. "Jack, James is my driver. He will take you home safely. Don't worry about a thing. We will talk in the morning."

Jack nods.

By now, the night is too far gone in silence and desolation. Jack's steps, growing as heavy as his heart, settle in the SUV before accepting his new reality. Passing isolated roads on the way to the buildings appearing in his sight, the car comes to a halt in the driveway of his apartment. A sigh escapes

his lips.

The driver, looking in the back seat of the car through his rear view mirror, says, "We are here, sir."

Jack is not quite ready to get out of the vehicle. "You know I just met him tonight. I never got his last name."

"Who, sir?"

"Your boss, Bob? What kind of man is he?"

The driver turns around and looks back at Jack and smiles. "It appears he likes you, so let's just call him a friend."

"That he does, James. Good night." Jack walks out toward the light of his apartment as the driver nods and drives off. The apprehension of divulging the horrors of the night to Alice crosses his mind before he tucks it at the back. He will break the havoc to her, but not tonight, he promises as his hand reaches for the key in his wallet.

With a slight tuck, the door gives way for the light to spill out, before Jack swiftly traps it once more within the apartment. The distinct yet muted scent of vanilla and cinnamon hits his nostrils, telling him she is home. Scrunching his nose, he crosses the gray vinyl flooring and walks straight before turning left to enter the living room, where, as expected, Alice is sprawled over the white chesterfield, where college books and essay papers are scattered across the floor. She is passed out from studying.

His footsteps grow softer as he approaches her slouched figure, her eyes closed. He pats her forehead and is about to escape to the bedroom.

She shuffles. "Sweetie, you're back?"

"You're studying too hard." Jack sits by her, and she places her head on his knee.

"I was waiting for you. What took you so long?"

"Sorry to have kept you waiting."

Leaning back, Alice fully opens her eyes to notice Jack's sweat-drenched shirt and disheveled appearence. The smell of char and petroleum overwhelm her senses, causing her concern. By now, he knows that holding the truth from her until dawn will only be an invitation for an unwanted argument, yet he pleads.

"Can I explain tomorrow?"

"Jack..." the forced reprimanding in her voice leaves Jack groaning.

How hard he had been battling with anger and his own distresses, struggling to keep his pain at bay. The last thing he wants is to be reminded of having lost his greatest asset. He feels as if his total existence is hanging in the balance. Despite his intent to withhold his emotions, his frustration outpours in a torrent that he will later regret.

"You want to know what happened, Alice?"

She gives an affirmative nod and folds her arms while giving an expectant expression.

"Well, *The Falcon* exploded while I was sitting at the bar enjoying a moment of normalcy."

"What? The boat... the boat blew up?" Horror is evident in her voice.

Not wanting to show weakness, he watches her hands tremble. "I'll get another one, it's okay." It wasn't okay, and it never would be. From finding the coin, to losing the coin, and his boat exploding...it was too much.

Her eyes widen. "Are we going to be okay in terms of money? I can pick up a part-time shift—"

"I can't think about that now, Alice. I'm going to take a shower and go to bed." His words didn't reflect any doubt, but it was strongly felt in his heart. He isn't sure if they'll be okay. However, he does know that he isn't going to put any additional stress on Alice. He'll find a way.

Jack stands and tries to remove his shirt.

"Why do I feel like you're pushing me away, Jack?"

He turns to face her, and her face is blanketed with emotion. Emotion he feels, but cannot show. "There's nothing else to say, Alice. What do you want from me?"

"I don't know, some type of emotion? You just lost the one thing that matters to you most."

"I know."

Alice's jaw drops, as if Jack insulted her, like she meant nothing to him. "I'm glad we're both on the same page in terms of where I stand on your list of priorities."

"Why do you always do that, Alice? You're searching for verification and validation that you come first. We live together. Isn't that enough?"

She waves him off, and he takes it as his permission to go take a shower.

The worry she had for him is growing into concern. They had been friends since high school, and even though they have been a couple for years, it still feels like *just* a friendship. He only has the capacity to love one thing wholeheartedly, and that is his love for his work. Each word exchanged in the argument tore through her wounded heart like a bullet, rather then words. And each wound was made worse by accusations of disloyalty, and the relationship having withered with time. She stands there waiting secretly to be held in his arms, only to see it isn't happening.

The door then slams shut as she storms out of the living room and up the stairs to the bedroom. His grip tightens at his shirt as he pulls it back on, then he collapses on the sofa, not caring about anything at the moment. His raging emotions left him depleted of all strength, and soon lull him into a perturbed sleep.

When morning rolls in, Jack's eyes flutter to an eerie silence, as if the day was observing mourning for his loss. He drags his feet across his house, only to find the missing presence of Alice. The reason for her disappearance is discovered when he draws himself to the kitchen. Before him on the gray surface of his refrigerator is a white paper. Its purity is corrupted with ink, and words tarnish all that stood until now. His eyes scanning each letter, leaving his foundation uprooted. If the events of last night had crumpled his life, the truth now abolished his existence.

Jack, I think after all that happened last night, we both need time and space to clear our heads. I still don't even know everything, because you're pushing me away, and I desperately want to know. I just need more from you, and I feel like I'm not able to give you what you need. When you're ready, please let me know how I can be enough for you, and we'll get through this.

T.C, Al

Alice had left. Or did she? Women were so confusing. Why did she have to give him options like that? There was never just one right answer. In Jack's head, the possibilities were endless. He did know that he wanted to be with her, but digging into his emotions, he struggled to let her in. Realizing this only lead to him driving her away.

Feelings of irritability soar as he drags his feet back to the living room. Needing time to think, he jumps onto his Peloton bike, hoping a little excercise might clear his head. The workout proves futile. Jack sits on the couch running his hands through his hair, when lying on the table, a flashing red light on his phone catches his attention. He proceeds to press the button.

Jack, this is Dymitry. Where are you, man? And why didn't you call me last night? Well, I hope you're still alive and this message doesn't reach your ghost. I'll keep this short. Why don't you head to the docks? I'm trying to go through whatever there is left of The Falcon. *Meet me as soon as you hear this.*

His heart plummets to his feet. He's worried about Alice, and he wants to make sure she's safe, but there are bigger things at hand right now. Alice will be back. Pushing all aching developments up till now away, his feet maneuver on their own, and he storms out of his house.

His thoughts travel from one loss to another, each seeming irrecoverable. Jack keys his white Nissan Sentra. Soon the car gains its momentum, making its way toward *The Falcon's* resting place. Each time his car is forced to decelerate, his knuckles turn white as their grip tightens around the steering wheel.

Jack heaves a sigh of relief once the ride comes to a stop. Without plucking the key out of his car, he sprints toward the pier. The sight that stood before him was devastating. The once glorious lime green streaked with rust was now all charred. The garland of wheels had all melted, including the rope. His body started to grow cold.

Dymitry places his hand on Jack's shoulder. "I'm sorry, man."

The two men walk toward where Dymitry had placed two white picnic chairs. He handed a beer over to Jack from the cooler.

"Seems like you have been here for too long, Dymitry."

"Since morning."

Jack pauses. "Alice left."

Dymitry gawks. "…And?"

"I don't think it's a permanent thing. She just needs time."

Dymitry doesn't want to pry. If Jack wants to share more, he will. But he doesn't.

Jack tells Dymitry everything, from the conversation with Bob to the incident at the bar, and how Jack's life had sunken by midnight. As much as he loathes having to relive the memories, his mind is content to have the support of Dymitry. His friend, who shared a similar look of dismay and disapproval, was his only family now.

Jack closes his eyes and takes a sharp breath, letting the dampness of the air around the dock comfort him. Slowly, he lets go of all the horrid memories of destruction, letting his senses calm.

"Did you find the Triton?" Dymitry asks.

Jack stares out to where the ocean meets the pier, lost in his thoughts. "Bob said he had some people that can try to rescue it."

"I'm sorry, who are you?" Dymitry's confused voice startles Jack.

His eyes trailed in Dymitry's direction, landing on the Floridan-looking old man from last night. Only this time holding a vintage dark brown leather briefcase bag.

A smile breaks across Jack's face. "Bob? I was just talking about you."

Jack places the beer down. Bob's hand rests on his knee as he pants, taming his breath.

"Oh, he's Bob?" Dymitry asks.

Jack only nods at his friend and patiently waits for Bob to speak. The silence is broken after minutes. "Any luck?"

Dymitry, sensing Bob's lack of strength, offers him his chair, which the old man graciously accepts. Soon he indulges both young men regarding his visit.

"Yes, we found it," Bob replies, pleased with his results.

Still wishing for a miracle, Dymitry can't help but ask if they found his laptop. Bob then begins to pull out of his bag an oversized airtight bag, the contents of which contained a chard black melted Mac Book Pro that is still dripping water from inside. Bob offers his regrets. "Sorry. Not sure what good it's going to do?"

Disappointed Dymitry grabs the laptop from Bob. "Wow! Worse than I thought. Thanks anyway."

Jack, looking over at the Mac computer, only confirms to himself all hope is gone. "Is the Triton in any decent condition?"

Bob beams back with excitement, "Amazingly enough, while it was blown

off your vessel and thrown into the pier, she suffered no real physical damage from the impact. My guy even started it up, and everything seems to be working."

Jack nods in response. "Thanks, Bob. I really appreciate what you have done, but I should think about selling it."

Both Bob and Dymitry are shocked to hear the news. "What!" Bob gasped. To simply have Jack admit defeat stunned them. Bob had foreseen a future where the truth might be revealed. "You cannot just quit now, Jack. "This is absurd. I mean, I saw the passion burning in your eyes earlier." Bob asks him to reconsider, as this is an opportunity of a lifetime. Whereas for Jack, this is another reason for him to begin anew.

Dymitry listens keenly to each word, wondering just how true the legend is. Jack seems to be the only one capable of extracting a fortune from the bed of the ocean. The task was not ordinary, and hence needed the complex program Dymitry designed. Nonetheless, the burden of pain only left Jack denying the offer.

"You can't remain in the slump forever. Now what will you do?" Bob pesters, looking toward Dymitry for support.

Jack shrugs. "I simply don't have the money, Bob."

"That you don't have to worry about. I am arranging a boat for you. In fact,…" Bob sheepishly scratches his head, causing Dymitry to furrow his eyebrows together.

Jack is still unfazed. Bob breaks down the news of how he is acquainted with the CEO of Adler Enterprises. The name alone is enough to leave Dymitry choking on his drink, and this time Jack's interest sparks. This explains how Bob had the resources to rescue the Triton. Adler Enterprise is more than a brand name. It is a vortex of opportunities, as it contains the largest fleet of marine vessels in the country, handling everything from marine construction to transpiration to shipyard services. While Jack's dream to find worldly treasures that time has forgotten seems to have sunken beyond his reach, fate might have other plans.

"How will I repay them? Have you thought of that too?"

"Well, yes…"

Jack, not wanting to have to come up with another excuse, was taken aback. "Why not find someone else for your scavenger hunt, then?"

Each second, Bob grows exasperated, rubbing his forehead in annoyance. "Jack, hear me out. After this, if you say no, then I won't bother you anymore. You are blessed with a gift, kid. Having spent a lifetime, I think I know what I'm doing here. Trust me, I did not gray my hair skinny dipping in my youth. Importantly, you know this is not a scavenger hunt. You have seen for yourself what lies under these waters."

"Tell me one thing, Bob. Why are you behind *me* achieving this?"

"It's odd how you only see my motive. Well, if it makes you feel any better and secure, then it's simple. I am an adventurous soul who lacks the essential ingredient to this—youth. And you lack the resources for it that I can provide. To me, it's a perfect match. Not only is there a thrill that will come with this, but you can also say in a way that I might be keen on exposing the truth behind Pope Pius. Don't think too much about this, Jack. This is not only an opportunity for you and me, but also for your friend. If you can pull this off based on your friend's program, you know it will be a win. If you still don't believe me, then come with me. I will show you something."

Bob beckons for Dymitry and Jack to walk out of the dock and trail after him to his Ford F-250. Once all of them are strapped, Bob's car skids and darts toward the other end of the dock. As soon as Bob hits the brake, Dymitry hastily jumps from his seat, while Jack only sits there.

As promised, before them, Adler Enterprise's ocean class tugboat is over 146ft. Like *The Falcon,* it's propulsion powered by two Tier II Caterpillar diesel engines, allowing for the toughest open sea voyages. In addition, it's

fitted with a remote fixed boom deck crane. Its base is tainted with nightfall, and the white on top gleams like a blank canvas, waiting to be painted with endless adventures. Bob signals for both Dymitry and Jack to check the vessel. The latter only stands while his friend wastes no breath running over to the ship.

Bob steps out of the truck and pleads to Jack one more time.

"Look, she's straight off the shipyard. They're even allowing me to give her a name. Would you check her out for me?"

Jack's interests start to spark. "That is some relationship you have with them, Bob; do you have a name you're tossing around?"

Bob scratches his head, looking at the ship, then turns and looks back to Jack. "I always like the name *Calypso.*"

Jack gives a smile. "The Greek goddess? Why, because of her gift of immortality, or her rescuing of a shipwrecked hero?"

"Whichever one inspires you to come on board," Bob smirks as he starts to walk onto the vessel.

Jack follows Bob's gaze on board the ship, taking note of an excited Dymitry dashing out of the vessel. Dymitry's outburst that follows leaves Jack with little choice than to shun his friend. As promised, *Calypso* came equipped with a tech-room, or as Dymitry declares it: "the dungeon of technocracy."

Jack couldn't help but notice a familiar large shaped spherical object sitting on the deck wrapped in a tarp, underneath the lifting crane.

"As promised, in working condition." Bob pulls away the plastic cover, revealing the bright yellow Triton that Jack spends most of his time in, bringing back a feeling of belonging. While Dymitry runs around the ship like a kid in a candy store, Bob puts his arm around Jack. "Adler Enterprises is loaning me the boat. Don't worry, it's of no cost to you. I'll take care of it. I have some work I have to attend to here, but take her out for a couple of days, see if you get any closer to finding that U-Boat." Bob pauses to get a read on Jack's response, then continues. "You said it yourself that your software gave you a general location. Take the next couple of days and see if it pans out before you decide to hang up the towel." Almost trying to make Jack feel guilty: "Would you do that for an old man who rescued your Triton?"

Dymitry sees this as an excellent opportunity to test it out. "Come on Jack, he's just trying to help."

Jack is deliberating. How was he to face the sea without *The Falcon*? How was he to pick up his broken pieces without having his own soul bleed? How was he to leave without mending things with Alice first? Then it dawned upon him that life did not freeze. The path only changed.

For years, after spending his time in the shadow of his father, Jack had given life a chance, and then was gifted with Alice. To him, she was his saving grace. But apparently, he had a funny way of showing it. He always felt complacent, half-hearted, and inconsiderate around her. Not that she ever said those words, but he saw it in her face, and in the constant need for recognition around him. He saw her. He really saw her for everything she was worth. Everything he did on a bigger scale was for her. Maybe that wasn't good enough. *He* wasn't good enough—not for exploration, and not for Alice. Now it seemed as if life was giving him a chance to redeem himself—his father's face flashed before him.

All that Jack thought was to live his life by the wave. His father had left him in the hopes of an unforeseen adventure. Ever since the disappearance of his father, he grew inclined to *The Falcon* in the hopes of finding a thread worthy of reason to understand why his father took off despite knowing how the odds were lined up against him?

If the love Jack nurtured for the ocean was inherited, then how could he deny his lineage? Alice might have left, but he still had his life before him. He had spent his life unlocking doors and recovering sunken mysteries. But the biggest mystery of all remained hidden.

Today, Jack knew the moment not only offered him what he desired the

most, but also his friend. How can Jack be selfish now, when Bob has been so gracious in helping him with the Triton, and with Dymitry, who always put Jack's interest over his?

Now, everything could change. Jack was being handed a key, harboring the power to twist his fate and alter his course while giving answers to the unknown. The smallest flicker of a beam of hope rekindles within his soul, as Jack turns to face the expectant faces of Bob and Dymitry, and gives a wink.

"What are you standing around for, Dymitry? Let's go find us a U-Boat."

Dymitry has look of delight as he runs inside the bridge, dropping off his laptop and gearing up to set sail.

"You boys have this? Because I can get you more crew," Bob asks.

Jack confirms that he wouldn't have it any other way than just the two of them hitting the high seas, letting Bob know they'll be just fine. As Bob leaves the Calypso, he looks back at Jack. "Let me know how it goes on your return. 'Fair winds, and following seas.'"

Chapter VI

Bruce or Gustavo

"Where are we now?"

"Off the Florida Keys... there's a place called Kokomo..." Dymitry lifts his head from ship's computer screen.

"Dymitry." Jack's warning remains unheard.

"That's where you want to go to get away from it all. Come on, you know this is classic, Jack." Dymitry breaks into a song and cheesy dance to try to cheer Jack up. "Aruba, Jamaica, ooo I want to take ya to Bermuda, Bahama, come on pretty mama."

Jack scoffs. "You're an idiot. Augh, what am I doing here? We have been cruising endlessly for the past five days, diving back and forth, only to surface as a failure." Jack's irritability is on full display. "Are you sure these are the last known coordinates your software was spitting out?"

"I could double-check if it wasn't melted to a crisp, but yeah, it was around this area. Even narrowing down this region, it is still a lot of ocean to cover. Besides, don't you think you're being a little harsh on yourself?" Dymitry drops his shoulders and nears his friend, who is perched by the glass gallery overlooking the vacant waves before them.

"I'm going to take some fresh air." Announcing that more to himself than anyone else, Jack storms out from the bridge, leaving Dymitry to brood over his state and watch helplessly as Jack descends the ladders and makes his way toward the main deck.

It had been five days since the mishap at the bar. His mind wonders, but gives up trying to solve who would have tampered with his boat; all that remains left of his father is the childhood memories and the Triton. Also it has been five days since Jack ran away from his problems with Alice. To him, the time apart was only adding to his anxiety, but he wasn't about to let anyone know that Alice had that power over him. As per Dymitry, Jack needed to make the most of the time apart—so that's what he would do.

All that fills Jack's senses now is the free ocean breeze. Strong, yet letting the current beneath domineer the boat's movement. A peal of bitter laughter that erupts recalls the night of dooms Each blistering flame still resonates with his mind. The brilliance of nature was there within his grasp, yet he did not savor the moment. The sea ambiance is disturbed by the holler of Dymitry.

"Jack, you better get in here!"

Jack shakes his head before retreating to the bridge room.

"What's wrong?"

"Come check it out for yourself." Dymitry beckons Jack's attention toward the larger screen perched on the table in the middle of the room.

While the looming dot on the navigation screen on the right goes unnoticed, the active sonar reflects some metal from below.

"Dymitry, I need you to activate all these screens." Jack examines the monitor meticulously.

"Did we hit something?" Dymitry's voice brims with excitement and expectation. Little does he know that the disoriented thoughts of his friend are bound to leave him dispirited.

"It seems that way. And if I still find nothing, we will go back to Bob and return his expensive gift."

"Jack. Will you still not give this a chance?" Dymitry, hurriedly readjusting, shifts on his screen and looks over his shoulder for reassurance from his friend.

"I am sorry to disappoint you, but it seems we are on a wild goose chase out here. You'll soon be able to see for yourself. How far does the fiber optic cable go?"

"There is a little over eight thousand feet of cable attached to the Triton."

"Good, the depth finder is reading the foreign object to be less than a mile down, so we should be fine."

Moments later, Dymitry locks the outside of the latch on the Triton and begins to lower Jack into the water using the hydraulic winch on the *Calypso*. The sun retreats, as the water soon engulfs the Triton as he descends into the abyss. Strapping himself in the middle seat, Jack watches the traditional power flicker as he turns on the instrument panel. Dymitry's voice sparks on across the acoustic speaker.

"Testing, testing can you hear me, Jack?"

"Loud and clear. I will be activating the cameras so that you can view as well. But keep your eyes trained on the navigation for me, please."

"Sure, you get to have all the fun..."

"Hey, by all means, you are welcome to take this plastic bubble while I sit in the room and track your movements."

Dimitry shakes his head no, realizing quickly he has the better end of the deal. Their conversation halts as Jack's view transitions from the clear sky with fleeting clouds to opaque green waves encompassing around him. From light blue hues, the water soon shifts color like a chameleon as the Triton continues with its descent rhythmically. Now Jack is accustomed to the snor-

keling site of Key West.

In this secluded part of the ocean, while Jack is still able to make out the brief and distorted coral reefs, he feels the eerie silence seep within his heart. No longer is there an array of blue and red fish's careless swimming. Here, Jack witnesses the muffled swaying of the sultry reefs embellished in groups. The hollow vacuum only dips him further toward the ocean bed, alarming his senses toward a concealed peril.

Jack isn't more then 200 feet below yet, but with each space Jack's eyes seem to be glossy, with a shade of longing and tranquility. The light grains of sand give a clear way. His calculative maneuvering leads him further around the boulders and rocks adorned with reefs, while some are adorned with algae. He continues his hovering; the glistening sunrays only giving way to what lies idle beneath the aqua green after he enters an opening amidst the coral boulders. Here the rippling of the water is insignificant, hence shadowing the gleaming metal sprawled across the light sand.

The spark within Jack rekindles as his fingers cause the remote to extend the metal manipulator arms on the side of his vessel and gingerly grasp the 10-inch wide metal embedded within the sea bed. Rather effortlessly, he pulls in close to inspect the rusting metal through the acrylic bubble of the Triton. His eyes widen. His voice stutters as he calls out for Dymitry to acknowledge the truth.

"Do you see this, Dymitry?" Jack asks.

Dymitry replies through the sound system. *"Is this what the sonar was picking up? Doesn't look that big."*

"Agreed. It looks like some scrap metal that got blown off of something big, possibly our U-Boat. Do you see the additional debris down there? She was defiantly hit by something."

"If it was our U-Boat, that means she can't be that far away."

"Only one way to find out. I'm going down for a deeper dive," Jack replies.

Excited, Dymitry bellows out the underwater acoustic communication system. *"Ladies and gentlemen, Mr. Sterling is back; you feel like singing now?"*

"NO!" Jack makes his way down to ocean ledge, where the metal that was once a part of a story to something more prominent lies motionless, rusting way.

The Triton's arms once again reach out, grabbing the metal wreckage as the mini-sub's lights bring the foreign object into the light. Jack gets his confirmation, as it reveals a partially painted swastika flag, yet no excitement comes through the underwater acoustic communication system.

Once and then twice, when Dymitry's surmised excitement fails to fill Jack's ear, he diverts his attention back and enters the hollow opening further. The robotic arms of the mini sub are thrust back, swiveling left to right, combing the sand, until the metal resonates upon making contact. Jack simultaneously scurries the sand away like a dog digging in the ground to bury its prized bone. Only he is unearthing what lies beneath. Continuing to use the robotic arms as a shovel, in one swift movement, he plows the flat surface before pulling out any foreign objects.

Like a gold miner, Jack gently removes the excess sand, now revealing the once priceless treasure. He has discovered more of the swastika coins scattered about, lying around the metal wreckage. Jack is once again filled with excitement; all his worries seem to have instantaneously vanished.

"Dymitry, you're right, we are getting closer. You're not going to believe this, but I'm no longer worried about that coin I lost," beams Jack.

He continues to open a collection box attached underneath the Triton. Using the robotic arm, he starts collecting all the gold coins he can gather. He even starts to mutter a familiar song under his breath as he is working.

"We'll get there fast and then we'll take it slow, that's where we want to go…Oh, come on Dymitry, don't be mad at me, talk to me. Look, you even got the song stuck in my head!"

Once satisfied, having collected enough of the lost treasure, he safely mounts and locks the tin lid underneath.

"Dymitry, I have been calling out to you. Is that new equipment even working?...That's it, I'm coming up," Jack says through the underwater acoustic communication system secured around his head. Looking out the right side of the bubble window, he notices something extraordinary, and is soon filled with excitement.

"Oh, Dymitry is going to want to see this," Jack exclaims.

Suddenly the mini sub makes a large thud sound that echoes inside the pressure hull.

As the Triton is making its way to the surface, the vessel lurches forward, sending Jack flying, collapsing against the acrylic bubble. Panic grips his senses, making him scramble to his feet to take note of the sudden assault. The sight, however, only leaves profanities escaping from his lips. His attacker, seemingly adamant, pulls itself back before crashing against the back of the submarine again.

"Dymitry, Dymitry, I think I'm being attacked by something. Is the cable broke? Why don't you respond?" Jack's voice continues to grow an octave higher as he bellows in the microphone and erratically navigates the submarine to crawl out like a crab from a hole.

Despite his triumphant clambering, once the mini-sub emerges in the open, Jack's eyes glance upon what he feared. This image reminds him that death takes many forms, and this one prowls these waters in the shape of a blunt torpedo, with pale grey back skin and a white underbelly. With three hundred razor-sharp triangular teeth designed for only two things, to kill and eat its prey, this natural-born killer has found its next victim. Appearing twenty feet long, this great white shark swims around the Triton, analyzing what he thinks is his sitting target.

"Oh, hello, Bruce, my name is Jack...I'm not the food you are looking for,"

Jack states as he and the shark stare at each other.

"So, you can go about your business; just move along…. OR NOT!" Jack yells.

With a quick jerk, the jaws of death open once more as it storms toward the vessel at full throttle. This time, as the sheer weight of the shark rolls on top of the mini-sub, Jack is forced to the seabed with a less then gracious landing. Dust settles as the lights start to flicker. Jack's attention is averted to a deep scratch that lies on the outer layer of the acrylic. Being blown off *The Falcon*, the Triton might have been knocked around one too many times. From out of the shadows, the mini-sub is hit once more, only this time the great white's teeth have latched on, trying to bite into the fluorescent yellow bubble as if he intends to pop it. Even though Jack knows the shark doesn't have the jaw strength to bust the acrylic glass, as Triton designed them to withstand thousands of pounds of pressure, fear consumes his body just the same. In a frenzy, Jack lurches the mini-sub further away, clutching on corals for support to thrust himself away from the clutches of his assailant. But the large critter overshadows the vessel, arching his back, flexing his cartilage and revealing its mighty jiggered rows of teeth, leaving his body limp, clamping on tighter. The shark is close enough now that Jack can look his aggressor in the eyes, for what he hopes not to be his last memory. Jack sees the shark's dark blue beady killer eyes roll back in its head, a trait sharks have to protect their eyes when feeding.

"Come on, Bruce! Why can't we be friends?" Jack whimpers.

Blood drains from Jack as the jaws align alongside the holding above the bubble. Each time the shark tries to dig its jaws deeper into the clear aryclic bubble, the submarine resonates with fright and vigor. The added weight of the animal seizes the movement of the submarine, leaving Jack's forehead looming in a pool of sweat. In the hopes of wriggling free from the clutches of death, he drags the submarine toward *Calypso*. However, as he makes the climb upward, the shark jerks the mini-submarine back and forth, causing him to hit his head and wreck against the rocky underwater cliff.

The robotic arm falls limp, hoses dangling freely now and floating with the moving water. Jack turns his attention back to the ferocious shark sprinting in his direction, causing him to pull back the remote of the submarine and swivel past. His eyes continue to sweep the corals adorning the boulders in hopes of securing a safe passage until his eyes scan a ledge further down from the corals. The trailing of the shark was enough to let him know that his chances of a secure escape are thin.

Delving his fingers deeper within the controls, as Jack's senses heighten, he lifts the mini-sub with him and notices the shark reciprocating his gesture. This is his last resort to climb out in one piece. He continues to bring the submarine up until the skyline becomes clear before letting the submarine take a free fall. The barrel roll captivates his target, as each movement is carefully noted and the shark mirrors them. His head starts to pound as the impending doom narrows in on him.

The vessel comes to a halt, facing the shark and the helpless reefs behind it. Each passing second seems to last a lifetime. Jack, backed against the ledge, waits for the bloodlust monster to strike him. Once the nozzle of the shark becomes a point, he takes a deep breath, and jets the Triton upward with full throttle, dodging the shark's speed of attack. A piercing sound erupts from beneath against the reef while the submarine staggers upward. Now, as he glances down, he notices his former robust attacker lying idle by the foot of the ledge.

His hands tremble against the remote, reassuring himself that the tin can of coins is still attached underneath, which it is. Jack collapses in his seat. The bruise on his forehead finally declares its presence, causing the shivering to intensify while his eyes take in the blaring daylight. His eyes flutter as a dip causes a ripple to waver the mini-sub. He looks over and notices the gold is sitting just below the surface. Jack feels comfortable with the fact that people are not going to be diving in shark-infested water, even for gold.

As the gazing of the sun starts to trickle heat along with beads of sweat rolling down his neck, Jack turns his attention back and nears the submarine to the boat, but his movements come to a standstill as he notices another vessel next to *Calypso*. Creases form on his forehead. Deliberating against bringing the gold coin back, he hurriedly scampers from the submarine to land on the main deck of the tugboat.

"What the…" his voice trails as he shelters his eyes from the blazing sun upon noticing five men dressed in the finest three-piece black suits.

All of them have their eyes fixated on Jack, their hands nestled on their gun holsters on their belts. "This boat is now under surveillance…" But before the man standing on the furthest right of the boat could have completed his warning, Jack recognizes a sixth man boarding the boat and makes a swift movement toward him.

Ignoring the rest of the men donned in similar attire, Jack forms fists, ready to lunge, only to be grabbed my several men, twisting Jack's arms behind his back, leaving him defenseless.

In a thick, boisterous Italian accent, all too familiar to Jack, he hears, "Pleasure to see you again, Mr. Sterling. I've heard a lot about you."

"Wish I could say the same about you, except you're that stranger from the bar," Jack replies.

"I presume you do not know my name. Allow me to introduce myself. I am Inspector Gustavo Vincenti. The head of NCB."

Dymitry is confused. "Who's the NCB?"

Jack cringes. "National Centre Bureau. It's Vatican City's own focal point for all international policing activities. Think MI6, only not as polished."

"Now why would the Pope need secret service agents?" asks Dymitry.

"I am here to protect rather confidential information for the Vatican, and it needs to be protected at all cost." Gustavo warns them with his tonality.

Jack turns to face Gustavo with a scowl. "I don't want to hear about the hideous deeds from the world you protect. Who gave you the right to have

climbed onto my boat?" adds Jack.

"Well, we can kick them off just as fast." Dymitry grabs a crow bar, but stops in his tracks as a handgun is placed against his temple, causing him to only gulp. His brown eyes are free from crippling fear.

"Sure, let's point a gun at the only black guy," Dymitry sarcastically insinuated.

Jack is eager to make a move, but his arms are still twisted behind his back. "This is assault. You can't get away with this."

"Sure, I can. I have diplomatic immunity." Gustavo gives a big smile, then continues. "Stop worrying. We have no intention to hurt anyone, Mr. Sterling. We are here only to relay an innocuous warning," Gustavo affirms.

"Innocuous warning, eh? After you blew up my boat outside the bar, and you probably stole my gold coin, too? How dare you show up here?"

Jack's spitting of anger only results in Gustavo pressing Jack's hand at his back further, and a yelp escapes his lips.

"Quiet now, Mr. Sterling. I can assure you that I had no doings in the mishap that took place back at the bar. Well, except for the coin. I did go back in during the explosion and take that. I don't have time to waste on sea looters like you."

"You know I can't just decide?" Jack replies.

Gustavo is thrown off guard to the question. "Can't decide what?"

"Which is worse? Bruce, who is in bad need of a dentist, or the Italian man, standing in front of me, who smells like bad prosciutto," mocks Jack.

Gustavo smiles as he looks at Jack. "He's got moxie, this one. Security protocols. As I said Mr. Sterling, I don't have time to waste on people like you. Tell me, did you even spare a thought when you were busy disclosing those the historical affairs, on what this could do to the image of the church? You most certainly did not. I tried even to tell you the Raubgold was a fake but you wouldn't listen."

"But it's not fake, and you know it," chides Jack as he tries to struggle out of the men's grasp.

Gustavo continues. "Your continued reckless attitude to search for what you think is the truth is what brings me here today! We can't have the world thinking we had a corrupt Pope in office. Just imagine what that would do to people of faith. The words you so carelessly let slip off your tongue, and the physical evidence you seek entail the power to compromise national security. Thus, as a representative of the Vatican, I warn you to be mindful of your behavior. If you are found to ever be meddling in affairs that comprise our nation's safety, your actions will be declared as a terrorist act and will be served a punishment accordingly. Consider this to be your last warning, Sterling. You shall be responsible for your own consequences."

"Man, Jack, I don't know what you did to piss Guido off, but just don't ever talk about anything ever dealing with the Pope again."

Gustavo utters, "It's not his words, it's his evidence."

"What evidence? You have the gold coin now," Jack says.

"That I do!" Gustavo smirks as he observes an unusual movement in the ocean.

Bubbles come to the surface as a man donned in a drenched scuba diving suit surfaces with the rustic tin Jack had hidden beneath the submarine. Panting, he rests his palm on his knees to tame his breath. "Inspector, he had them hidden beneath the Triton."

"Hey, those are mine; if you want some, I suggest you and your buddies dive overboard and look for them yourself. Tell Bruce I said hi!" Jack badgers.

Gustavo pirouettes Jack by his arm, and as soon as his face comes into view, Gustavo curls his fist. Pulling it back, he crashes his fist against the square of Jack's jaw, causing him to collapse on the ground. Gustavo, gripping Jack by his collar and giving the man no time to recover, wrenches him

from the ground. A bruise has already started to form around the corner of Jack's lips. "Is there more?" asks Gustavo.

Jack is quick to counter. "This was all that I found." He spits out some blood.

Gustavo, seemingly uninterested, tightens his grip around Jack's neck to keep his swaying body still. "As I said, these are fake, and being confiscated. Should you ever get the itch to look for more, know the price will be either your friend or your girlfriend's neck. It is in your soul's best interest never to go on such an expedition." Sneering, Gustavo beckons his men to leave.

Dymitry and Jack patiently wait for Gustavo and his entourage to descend the ladders before disappearing. As soon as the other boat dwindles off the radar, the duo embrace each other before hurdling forward and unleashing an array of questions. Jack narrates his ordeal back underwater, while to Dymitry tells of his dilemma of being held hostage. As Dymitry declares that Jack's predicament was momentous, Jack grabs a map and finally confides in Dymitry about the burdening secret he had been hiding.

"While I was down there, I saw a clue that will allow us to find *U-Boat 2553*. It was not the blackend piece of metal that was the clue, but what was left behind. The vessel was no doubt hit, but it did not go down where everyone, even the computer, calculated it to. The remaining crew managed to continue on a course and drive it, until their final resting place, but that couldn't have been more than seven or eight knots if you calculate how fast the hull was taking in water."

"How could you possibly deduce all of this. I know you're good, but not that good," Dymitry utters.

Jack smiles. "When *U-Boat 2553* was struck in the stern, it must have lost the power to submerge, which means it could only propel forward. A metal beam had to be potruding down from the ballast tank, dragging down its backend into the ocean floor, slowly losing debris and filling up the hull until it made its way to the final resting place."

"Are you saying...?"

Only a nod comes from Jack, causing Dymitry to pause mid-gasp. Jack collapses on the couch placed against the wall of the bridge room, and Dymitry loses himself inside the map.

"If what you saw is true, then this trail leads to the rest of the wreckage, rested somewhere along here? Then it now becomes Cuban property."

"I know, Dymitry, I know. But I cannot just pluck out the spear as if it is a rose in a garden. It is truly forbidden in Cuban waters, let alone that fact that we are being watched by the Italian Holy See..." Jack closes his eyes, rubbing his fingers against his temple. "We need to head back and talk to Bob. He may have some connections."

Jack knows deep within his heart that he must defy all odds and battle all the hazardous obstacles placed in his way. If only he could just see Alice one more time.

Chapter VII

Second Chance

Not being able to get ahold of Bob, Jack and Dymitry take up a familiar and safer setting at Lorenzo's. Blaring music and low lights ease the knots along Jack's shoulders. Still, his voice refuses to find strength, leaving Dymitry to bellow their orders at Joe before dodging his way through the crowd. A loud thud causes Jack to snap from his previous sulking demeanor and face Dymitry, along with Joe. The obese man's receding hairline jumps back as he offers a toothy grin to Jack.

"Heard the two of you have been living the dream," Joe declares loudly, causing the neighboring patrons to crane their necks in their direction.

"If by a dream you mean nearly being ripped apart by a shark, then yes."

"Don't sulk, my boy. I come equipped with the remedy to all your wounds. A fine bottle of Macallan, just as you like it."

Having settled the tray on the round wooden table between them, Joe proceeds with filling the 8 oz glasses halfway before sliding them toward Dymitry and Jack. Neither waste time and they just gulp the contents down in a long chug. A sigh escapes their lips as the drink cools the wrecking ache and the humid air around them.

"Don't mind us, Joe. This is just what I needed." Dymitry slips his glass toward Joe with a smug smile on his face.

The older man only raises his eyebrow quizzically before refilling and returning Dymitry his glass. "Why don't you tell me about your adventure, now?"

They begin to tell the details of their adventure to Joe, but hold back the details of the NCB and the path to the wreckage. Dymitry and Jack agreed not to divulge it to anyone, as they don't want to risk someone else cashing in on their potential findings.

Time passes and they have now almost emptied three bottles of whiskey. "Yeah, not really worth wasting life over some glittering coins..." Joe pauses, twirling his glass before him as the lights dance with the drink and a spectrum of color reflects on the table. He looks back up at Jack as his amusement returns. "Was it really the great white?"

"Yes, it was. And no, before you ask if it was anything like *Jaws*." Jack narrows his eyes at his friend, who had already been pestering him for his battle with a ferocious underwater beast.

Dymitry raises his hands in surrender, leaving Jack to swallow another glass.

"The animal looked more frightened of me than I was of it. It was the hunger that laced its eyes and made me go cold. But I knew if I succumbed to fear, my movements would have been immobilized me, and I would have turned into its meal, leaving Dymitry to sit in the boat for days before he would have realized my bones were rotting underwater," Jack says.

"My pal here is the next Hercules, Joe, and his path will lead him to victory."

Joe perks up. "What path?"

Jack interrupts. "Dymitry is talking about the hero's journey; it is the path of a lonely hero who tries to find himself on an unexpected quest. One that

promises adventure and peril, maybe a damsel in distress along the way. Only this path will test his strength from who he was to who he will become."

Joe looks speechless, trying to comprehend, as he has had one too many drinks. He smiles and gives his advice. "It sounds like a long trip to get to this destination. Maybe he should try an airline, instead. He could get there a lot faster, and get a free movie out of it."

Dymitry pats Jack proudly on the shoulder. On cue, Jack chokes on his drink and all the contents inside his mouth splatter.

"Alright, guys. I am calling it a night. It was great catching up with you, Joe." Jack leans in toward Dymitry. His friend's eyes grow wide in knowing now. "Also, Dymitry, learn how to control that tongue of yours, else we will land in trouble."

"Aye, aye captain." Dymitry gives him a mocking salute and gulps, a lump forming in his throat, and watches Jack make his way out of Lorenzo's.

As soon as the night air hits Jack, his forehead furrows. Where was he to spend the night? The thought of heading back home only fills him with the dread of facing barren walls. The house without Alice was no less than a garden without blooming flowers. Instead, Jack makes his way toward the office back at the dock. What better than to let the faint scent of the docks, the subtle reek of fuel from the yachts and fishing boats, and also the distinct stench of fresh fish serenade him?

His hair remains disheveled, legs perched in mid-air as Jack leans back in the worn-out burgundy couch pressed along the white chipped walls of his office. As soon as his sore back makes contact with the plush material, his eyelids, heavy with the hectic week, close without a second thought. His mind, worry stricken, induces vivid nightmares of losing Alice, with the shark mocking his deserted state.

As dawn starts to break, seizing the glum night with the lightness of a pale blue skyline free of clouds, Jack wakes with a jolt. Taking time, his eyes adjust to the mix of cold and hot entering through the only window in his office that is ajar. The pelting of raindrops resonates the entire office with somber drumming, leaving him to peek outside. He moves his hand to rub the sleep away from his eyes, only to yelp in pain. The bruise on his cheek throbs with vivid pain, taking him back to his encounter with Gustavo. Jack collapses back on the couch and is able to see the gray skyline. Clouds are huddled together, letting him know the downpour only means to give an empty threat, much like Gustavo.

Moments pass by before Jack heads to secure a piece of cold meat from the refrigerator in his office. Now, as the piece of meat presses against his hammering pain, he knows he will have to replace it for his friend's company. Dymitry's smirk flashes before him as he picks out another memory under the resonating sound of a thousand raindrops crashing against the roof. How proud had Dymitry been when Jack had recounted his escapade with the great white? It was obvious.

Of course, when Dymitry had retold the story to Joe, bits were fabricated, and Jack knew the story would only be elevated to heighten Jack's fearless persona, as if Alice was to hear it too. However, the greatest story, one that he had been searching for his whole life, is within fingers' grasp, and yet he has no one to share it with.

A groan escapes his lips, remembering how Alice had walked out. Despite having spent a considerable amount of time without the person he knew for years, it wasn't the same without her there.

To have walked away must have hurt her, and knowing how Jack was the reason behind it hurt him more. An apology was needed, but for now, he knew he needed to devise a plan to retrieve the metal he had seen underwater from Cuban waters without attracting attention. Knowing Bob for the little time he had, Jack knew it would not be long before he would have to apprise him of the inconvenient misadventure.

As he broods over the thoughts of reporting the incident to his new em-

ployer, he trudges in his office unannounced. The muttering went unheard by Bob, who holds displeasure on his face like a sergeant on duty.

"Speak of the devil and here he comes. Were you even planning to tell me?"

"Cut me some slack, Bob. I only got back last night. And to be fair, we reached out and couldn't reach you, so we went out to Lorenzo's. And as soon as I open my eyes, you barge into my office."

"Right, I am sorry. I just saw the state of the Triton and assumed you found yourself more trouble? What happened to your face?" Bob's voice took a sharp turn from being apologetic to horror.

Jack shudders as the echoes of the ocean waves bring him under the tides of his tormentors. He shakes his head and, clearing all thoughts of calamity, confides in Bob. Each detail, from his near doom to escaping the death grip multiple times, his retaliation, and his stumbling upon what he believes to be the actual resting place of the U-boat.

Having to ingest all the events of a five-day excursion, Bob stands from the armchair and takes out a cigar from his pocket. The smoke fills the room like a veil of fog keeping the truth at bay. Once the glowing red of the stick perched between his lips diffuses, he crushes the remaining ashes beneath his shoes. Now as he faces Jack, all worry fades. To Jack, the sight is of absolute confusion. *How can Bob not be concerned that his intentions could invoke the wrath of authorities?*

"I gather your main trouble now is how to move the U-boat from Cuban waters into international waters, to avoid it being Cuban property. As everyone knows, if you are to touch their possession, then hell hath no fury."

"Yes, and Gustavo?."

"Right, of course!"

Jack felt relieved in his new friend, a confidant, someone to help, to do the impossible. He pulled out a piece of paper and handed it to Bob.

"What's this?"

"With our recent discovery, and the nautical data we remembered from Dymitry's software, those are the estimated coordinates of the U-Boat. It is still a lot of ocean to cover, but should get us in the vicinity."

"Off the shores of Havana?"

"Yes, and if we can get access to drop down with the Triton, Dymitry and I have come up with a way to drag the U-boat over to international waters. It will require some small expense, though."

Bob shakes his head in agreement while still staring at the paper. "That's easy. I can take care of that."

Jack hesitated. "Bob, I wasn't... I mean you don't have to?"

Bob interrupts. "Nonsense. We have come this far; tell Dymitry to send me a list of supplies, and I will have them delivered to the boat. I will work on a work permit, but will require additional men to be involved."

"What? No! I think we have enough attention on us already. We don't need more people getting involved in this. Next, you know, we will be making national headlines, and the very next day, all three of us will be welcomed with a noose garland."

"Don't be absurd, Jack. You and I both know this is too big for the three of us. So yes, more people will be involved, but don't worry, they can be trusted."

Jack cups his head. Additional men. The mere thought makes him nervous, as it's a broader responsibility and risk, but as Bob said, they have come this far. He looks up to meet Bob, who is patiently waiting for an answer, and nods his head in agreement.

"Give me a couple of days. Don't worry about Gustavo. I will work on that too. Why don't you rest till then, and see a doctor for the bruise?"

Bob gestures toward the violet imprint on Jack's face, indicating the vio-

lence he had to bear. Jack watches Bob leave and silence prevails once more.

Throughout the ride, Jack leans against the windowpane and rehearses his speech, entailing nothing but the sincere apologies he would make to Alice. Rattling against the door, he takes in a sharp breath to embrace Alice's initial disapproval but the sight leaves him irked. The stale air of a closed house hits him, and he lets the door click shut behind him. Each heavy step he takes murmurs isolation. He is only proven right when he clicks on the telephone machine, expecting at least a pathetic excuse of reconciliation to have been left behind. Anger flares within him. Was she not worried about him anymore? The thought of their relationship having sunk causes him to finally evaluate his bottled emotions.

Now as Jack sits alone, the anger no longer concerns him. The only thing that was constant in his life was Alice, and he needed to make things right.

By now the roads are desolate. Hues of yellow shadow the emerald of trees along the way. Families treading down the street are doused in glee, which causes his stomach to churn at the sight. Why was he deprived of the purity of family? But before his thoughts could have wreaked havoc, his car comes to a stop outside his aunt's house.

The curtains are draped carelessly across the white windows. Still, the unmistakable humming seeped from the household, only growing clearer as the roaring of the car's engine dies. Each step Jack takes reminds him of his time as a boy, when he used to cross this very pathway of red bricks. Nostalgia takes over as upon the first ringing of the bell, a woman in her mid-fifties opens the door. The smile that spreads on her lips takes him back in time. How similar was his smile that he flashed the very last time, before he was gone for eternities. He slides his hand in his pocket and forces a smile too.

"Jack, oh, what a pleasure. Come, my boy. I cannot believe you finally decided to pay your Aunt Emma a visit. Danny, come quick. Look who is here."

The gushing comes to an end as Aunt Emma, after leading Jack through her beige hallway lit by warm lights of gold toward the lounge, turns to face

Jack. "You are staying for dinner."

Like an indescribable attraction, Jack is soon joined by his uncle, and the couple flocks around him. While his aunt busies herself in the kitchen, his uncle sets the table, all the while chatting with Jack animatedly about the latest happenings. The time that created a distance between Jack and his father's only sister was bridged by the middle of the evening. Once that happened, the time rolled around that he'd been dreading the most.

Questions regarding him and his current occupation spring much like an unwanted visitor. But knowing his aunt holds no grudge nor dislike toward his life, he enlightens the couple before him once they make their way back to the lounge.

Red wine from his uncle's collection twirls in the spotless round glass cupped in his hand. Jack dodges all questions about Alice, but enjoys the company of family.

"Thank you for the concern, Aunt Emma. But don't you fret your pretty mind, I am fine. It was a small mishap."

"I never understand these small mishaps of yours, Jack. From all the fishermen out there, you and only you seem to be a magnet for trouble."

"Cut the boy some slack, Emma. Did you not see the news recently? The weather is such a disaster these days. Accidents are bound to happen. It does not mean he gives up on his job and sits back at home just to be safe. Am I right, boy?"

"You sure are, Danny."

"I am just worried about him, Danny. He reminds me of his father. He is just like him. Reckless when it comes to himself," Emma trails off, losing her interest in the half-filled glass.

Before the waterworks could have started, which occurred each time Jack paid a visit and the memories of his father came to haunt them, Jack navigates the conversation elsewhere.

"Aunt Emma, Danny, I forgot to tell you the most important part: on my last dive, I encountered a great white."

"You what?" both of them exclaim in unison.

"Yes, it was flashing me its teeth in all their glory."

"Oh God, Jack, are you insane? You could have died."

"But I didn't, Aunt Emma. I sit here alive in front of you. Although the submarine did incur some damage."

"You better hope the insurance pays for it, Jack, else you will soon be in need of new employment."

For most of the night, Jack keeps his aunt and uncle entertained. She recalls how his enthusiasm is just as elevated as his father's was, and how that led him to lose himself to the sea. Jack laughs inwardly at the irony. His father surely had lost himself to the sea. Such was his love and devotion to the waters. Clear or musky, high or low currents, if his father could have traded his limbs for fins, he would surely have. As a child, Jack grew up listening to how Ariel, the mermaid, was a fool. She had the freedom to swim across oceans, not to be perturbed by the tremendous ocean waves, but all she wanted was to touch the ground. And what good did that bring? Per Jack's father, nothing but absolute boredom.

Jack spent the night at his aunt's. To him, the intention was only to revitalize his senses before beginning the next day on a fresher note. He had two crucial tasks at hand. The first was to pacify Alice. Only then would his heart be at ease. He would work with Dymitry in crafting a scheme to help ease his sanity.

Before he could have sat straight in bed and damned the night, the shrilling sound of his cellphone pierces through the silence the house had been encompassed in. Without checking for the caller, he haphazardly receives the call. "Hello?"

"Jack?"

"Alice? Alice, where are you? How are you? Hold on, where are you right now?"

"Calm down, Jack. I am at my brother's."

"Oh."

Silence falls heavy between them. Jack intently listens to Alice's calm breathing. To him, this is a lullaby, soothing his tired soul.

"I hope I didn't disturb you at this point of the night."

"No, no, you didn't. Listen, Alice, can we meet?"

"This is why I called you. I wanted to meet you too, Jack. I miss you. I kind of thought we would have gotten together sooner than this…"

The simple confession, that she wanted to be back together, lifts Jack's spirit. Like a child, he vented everything to Alice. About how he wanted to call, but his foolish pride got in the way. Everything that circulated around her, and how the solitary feelings had made him realize how he needed her beacon.

The call was ended with her asking him to meet her the next morning at St. Augustine Aquarium before class. If previously he was sleepless because of missing her, now the anticipation is what's keeping him up all night.

It was effortless for Jack to bid goodbye to his aunt and uncle in the morning, as they were briefly told how Alice was upset with him, and now he had to make up for him not being at home. With well wishes and butterflies flapping their wings in his stomach, he felt as if he was meeting Alice for the first time.

The emotions coursing through him at the sight of Alice surprised him. He hugged her fiercely, smelling her sweet scent and her warm smile.

"I'm sorry how I acted. I should have been more sympathetic to your needs."

"I am sorry for walking out on you, but whenever times are bad, all I ever

wanted was to be held in your arms and be told everything is going to be all right."

Jack smiles and wraps his arms around Alice and places a feather-like kiss on her cheek. "Alice, everything is going to be all right."

Instead of a response, Alice raises her hands, placing them on both sides of Jack's face, and leans in to seal their lips. Blushing, Jack and Alice leave hand in hand. After dropping her at her college, his phone starts to ring again. Dymitry's groggy voice notifies Jack of how they had a new call come in.

"Hey Jack, we just got a call into Cast A Towing. Someone named Krueger. I guess he is stranded off shore in a Merry Fisher, and is need of our assistance. The HIN number is R-42474. He says that he just dropped anchor because he ran out of gas?"

"You have to be kidding. Who would be that foolish to allow that to happen?"

"Not everyone as both oars in the water, Jack. Anyway, he gave me his coordinates. I'm busy mounting these compressed air tanks onto the Triton, but there is a small motor boat at the dock you can use, if you want to grab some gas and help him out. We can make a few bucks out of it."

Jack is thrown off by the strange request. "That will take a bit. They don't want to call someone closer?"

"I asked that. They said they're fishing, so no rush."

"You see, Dymitry, it's this kind of work that we're always so willing to do for yuppies that Detective Hernandez was making fun of us for."

Well as weird as it sounds, Jack assures Dymitry they'll be able to take care of it. Cast Away Towing hasn't seen its last job yet. With Bob busy pulling strings to weave a net for them to fish out the U-boat from the sea bed, and Dymitry busy getting the Triton ready. Jack uses the opportunity to take the small motor boat, with some extra cans of gas, and leisurely cruise the sea. Besides, getting some fresh air will be good.

A couple of hours later, after finding the stranded boat with the matching HIN number exactly where Dymitry said it would be, there were two men donned in black and red vests waving for help.

Anchoring his small motorboat against the 34-foot Marlin vessel, Jack jumps onboard with an extra gas tank. No words are exchanged as the men scrunch their eyes to keep the sharp sun rays at bay. As Jack walks inside the bridge of the ship, surveying the boat, he is quick to notice the gas bar indicated on the tank is half full. Enough for the captain to steer effortlessly to shore. In addition there is no fishing equipment on board, only some diving equipment and some handheld sea scooters lying on the main deck.

"I don't understand. You guys asked for help...where's Krueger?" Jack trails his voice as a sturdy man walks upstairs from the cabin deck below, while the previous distressed men are now holding pistols pointed at Jack.

"Guten tag, Herr Sterling."

"Boy, am I a magnet for trouble," Jack mumbles, rubbing his forehead.

Jack closes his eyes, waiting for his next set of trials to begin, wondering why his life is always threatening to be capsized.

Chapter VIII

Thule Society

Slowly, the man motions for the men aiming their guns at Jack to lower their weapons. Standing before him is a man dressed in black, with a chiseled jawline and bleach blond hair. He speaks in English with a heavy German accent.

"Allow me to introduce myself, Jack. I am Krueger Dietrich."

The man extends his arm toward Jack, who hesitantly accepts the handshake. Carefully, Jack takes in his surroundings. Seeing the vessel is equipped with only the steer, navigation system, and other necessities on the boat, nothing appears out of the ordinary, except in the lower deck. The door to the cabin is wide open, but no light seems to be shining in, and the windows are tinted more than usual. Despite the room being pitch black, Jack can make out someone sitting in the dark, smoking a cigar, as the orange embers light up intermittently.

"You're probably wondering who we are and why we asked you here?" Krueger states.

Jack scans for an ounce of recognition in any of the three men who surround him, collecting tidbits of information.

Jack jested. "A couple of lonely sailors, looking for a good time? But I've got to tell you guys, I just repaired my relationship, so I don't think it's going to work out."

Krueger gives off a cold stare, failing to find the humor in Jack's comments. "Be careful, Jack. We are not the kind of people you want to mess with."

"Look, I know exactly the kind of people you are."

Krueger and the others look puzzled. "Oh?"

Jack takes in an extended breath and begins. "Yes. You extended your arm, but not before I could see a line tattooed on your arm that looks like it might be part of a Nazi logo. It is only confirmed by your men, who are dressed in black and red colors, similar to that of some Neo-Nazi organizations—only, not one comprised of American white supremacists, but from another region. With the heavy thick German accents and the pride in German firearms you're carrying, my guess is you're descendents of your parents. No one who currently lives in Germany today, but Nazis who had escaped after the war, allowing you to grow up in Argentina. You base your thinking in the resuscitation of false doctrine, seeking vengeance to make your parents proud, because in reality... I don't know? You didn't get enough hugs when you were younger? You might as well call it science fiction, but none of this answers what you want with me?"

Jack notices Krueger looking down at the lower deck toward the mysterious man sitting in the shadows, then turns back around and smiles.

"And who's down there? Your commissar?" Jack tries to head down the stairs, but is immediately stopped by a guard with his gun.

Krueger steps in front of Jack. "You are quite impressive, Jack. Of course, I told my commander that when I saw you at Lorenzo's the other night."

"I really have to find a new hangout," quips Jack.

Krueger starts to fish in the pockets of his white chinos, giving Jack ample

time to rebut himself. Had he paid heed to the crowd around him, Jack knew within the beat of his heart, none of his woes would have begun. Gustavo, and now Krueger, would never have stumbled upon his existence, as he had stumbled upon the Swastika coin.

Jack's train of thought is stopped as Krueger hands him a similar golden circle. Slowly, Jack traces the outline while gulping the lump in his throat. He did not need to turn. He knows Krueger has handed him the very source of his dismay—the very coin that triggered a series of unfortunate events for Jack.

"How did you? Did you take my coin that night?"

Knitting his eyebrows together, Krueger confronts Jack about how he must be mistaking him for another petty thief. "This, to you or any other man, might just be a gold coin, a treasure of worldly price. But to me"— Krueger lifts the coin to let the sunrays make contact with its surface— "it is an heirloom."

Once Krueger is content after having tucked the coin in the furthest end of his pocket, he crosses his arm across his chest.

"Unlike you or other men, I am not a treasure hunter…"

Jack interrupts. "Well, technically I'm not a treasure hunter either."

"SILENCE!" shouts Krueger, and then he continues. "This coin holds far more value to me than anything else in this world. It's the last token I held onto, a token of faith I kept alive with me ever since I was a young child."

A smile breaks out on Krueger's face, wrinkling the corners of his lips. The gleam in his eyes captivates Jack. Having witnessed endless wreckages, Jack knows when a treasure is of more value than meets the eye. At the moment, Jack knows the story Krueger is about to lay on him. It's one of obliterated heritages and buried massacre. He talks of a man named Franz Stangl, a former SS-Commander, one of the true architects of the Holocaust. Throughout the years of the Nazi conquest across Western Europe, all the riches collected were eventually split with all those who served in Hitler's high command. Shares were documented, and based on job performance. After all the gold was loaded onto *U-Boat 2553*, each eligible commander, including Franz Stangl, was personally given one of the swastika gold coins. These would be treated at keys to show that that they were rightful heirs upon the U-Boat's arrival.

Franz Stangl, who perfected the eradication of almost one million Jews, was to personally receive more money than he or his next of kin could spend in their lifetimes. But with the U-Boat lost at sea, all of Franz's hopes and dreams went with it. After the war, the Vatican helped him escape through the ratlines, utilizing some forged documents. Krueger goes on to explain that his father ended up spending his remaining years as a pauper. Scraping and skimping by while he worked on an assembly line for Volkswagen in Brazil. Until 1961, when a Nazi hunter tracked him down, and he was arrested shortly after. Franz was found guilty at the trials in Düsseldorf for his crimes against humanity. They had sentenced him to life, but it was short-lived, as he died six months later due to heart failure. *U-Boat 2553* was supposed to be Franz's retribution; he waited years on that assembly line, hoping that the U-boat would be found one day. Before his arrest, he passed his swastika coin, the one that Jack just laid his eyes on, down to his son Krueger, whose surname is after his mother's.

"Ah, your story is breaking my heart. However, I never found any U-Boat, nor would I give it to you if I did."

"Jack, let's make this easy for both of us. By now, you must have stumbled upon the Thule Society."

Jack narrows his eyes, recalling all that his father had shared with him about the Thule Society. The organization was established shortly after World War I in utmost secrecy. The sole motive of the society was for its members to maintain a reign that catered solely to the Germanic Order.

Krueger pulls up his sleeve and shows the tattoo on his arm of the Nazi

logo, only it is wrapped in a circle. "Its members make a vow that no Jewish or colored blood flows in our veins, or among our ancestors."

"So, I take it DNA tests are forbidden?" Jack mocked.

Krueger again not cracking a smile: "Make jokes, Jack. We are loyal to the Führer's vision of a thousand-year Reich, and will stop at nothing to make that happen. Today there are more of us than the world realizes, and we are sitting in pretty powerful positions. Since 1945 we have been hunting for that treasure, and you, Jack, are the key to us getting what is rightfully ours."

"So, let me get this straight: all you're after is the U-Boat's gold?" asks Jack.

Krueger and the men look at each other with confusion. "Of course. Were you not just listening?"

"Oh, I did, I was just checking." Jack knows the real prize is the Spear of Destiny. If they knew what power it possessed, they would certainly wish to acquire it, but fortunately for him none of them seems to know of its existence. Both Gustavo and Krueger are after the same thing that men's hearts have been chasing through greed since the dawn of time: money. Krueger unfolds his arms and reaches his hands behind his back to retrieve a handgun himself. Slowly, he lifts the barrel and aims it at Jack's heart—one of his hands secured around the trigger and another at the bottom to lock his target. "How about you tell me the coordinates of where you went diving the last time?"

"If there were any doubts in my mind about your sanity, then you gave me all the reasons to affirm that you indeed are demented. All that I came across was the one gold coin that someone stole from me. I do not know where the U-boat rests."

As Jack etches each word of his, Krueger sneers at him, as his brows furrow. "I see this isn't going to work, and we will have to resort to waterboarding."

The authority in Krueger's voice causes sweat to break out along Jack's temples, trickling down his neck. He rummages through his disarrayed thoughts for a pretense to run away. His silence forces Krueger to tilt his head. "Tie him up. Go and grab me a bucket of saltwater and a rag."

Following Krueger's order, a lean man moves toward Jack, leaving Jack to wait for him to cover the distance. Jack fixates his eyes on each step the man takes. All the while, all three guns are aimed at Jack, leaving him to mutter a prayer silently under his breath. Once the man reaches Jack, without sparing a second, Jack ducks before plunging back up and holding the man's extended arm. With one sharp twist, Jack disables the man's grip from his weapon and kicks the gun away from his reach before lifting his knee to kick the man in his groin.

With an out-of-breath yelp, the man falls at Krueger's feet, startling both Krueger and the henchman, who is standing at the back of the room. Taking advantage of the haphazard moment, Jack charges out of the bridge toward the main deck. As fate may have it, Krueger seems to have come prepared for an impromptu dive, assuming he would be retrieving information from Jack, with the diving gear lying on the deck. The yelling from the bridge intensifies, and Krueger leans from the window with his arm extended in Jack's direction. A gunshot erupts, only to end up piercing through the water.

Acting on impulse, Krueger continues to shoot while the other two men run after Jack. He ducks once more to claim the diving gear on the ground, along with picking up a sea scooter. Taking a deep breath in, Jack jumps overboard and with the splash, a layer of white froth forms above the spot from where he dips. Rushing to strap the backpack with the air cylinders on his back, Jack bites on the mouthpiece as a ripple forms and a bullet tears its way inside the water.

Securing the goggles on his eyes, Jack takes note of how one of the men on board is wearing his own gear as well. Jack's eyes are glued on his attacker, his fingers fumbling with the motor of the sea scooter. The bubbles now escaping through the snorkel give away his direction, and soon another ripple behind

him alerts Jack. He snaps his head to notice one of the Germans has dived after him.

Before the German could swim closer to Jack, he flickers the motor once more while flailing his arms to propel himself forward. His strokes grow vicious as the other German jumps in, also on a sea scooter, armed with a knife. Before either of the Germans could get closer, Jack's sea scooter starts and launches him forward, leaving behind a trail of thick opaque saline. Once affirmed, Jack is at least nine feet away from his pursuers. The German on the sea scooter is moving as rapidly as Jack. He clears his head and looks back before maneuvering the sea scooter to a sharp dive. As the German reciprocates Jack's movements, he lifts his scooter to surface above water.

Jack continues to make another sharp turn, swimming to his extreme left, leaving behind a bubble trail that the Germans follow. He notices a smack of jellyfish rising from the depths of the ocean. If he were to slow down now, then he knew he would fall victim to the cruelty of the wannabe Nazis who would eventually pull what information he had about the U-Boat out of him, and they would discover a prize bigger then gold. Yet, if he were to head forth strong, he would be the target of the brutality of the smack. Without another thought, Jack throttles the sea scooter, increasing his speed to head straight into the jellyfish. As soon as his motor thrusts him amidst the floating tentacles, despite having to veer through, his exposed legs become victim to the stings. He clenches his eyes and tightens his grip around the scooter, trusting the machine to carry his burden further. Once the constant slashes against his legs turn into a throbbing sting, his eyelids pry open, and he tilts his head over his shoulder to catch a glimpse of the nearing threat. The sight, however, leaves him perplexed and relieved at the same time.

One of the men pursuing Jack did not manage to surface after crashing into the jellyfish's venomous stinging. Surely, he must have been betrayed by his luck not to have won out against the vicious attack of the smack. Jack knows he could have been in the German's shoes. He could have been the one whose body was being plummeted to the seabed. The speeding and whirling of water pulls Jack out from the undertow, snapping his eyes to the speeding man from above. Unaware of the leverage the German has over him, even as Jack tries to flee by diving back underwater, he is pulled back abruptly. With the blink of an eye and a hold tightened around his collar, the German yanks Jack toward him and lands his free knuckle against his jaw. The sea scooter falls out of Jack's grip, and the two men take a free fall alongside the abyss.

Ignoring and not catching enough breath beforehand, the German swims closer to Jack and lands yet another punch at the same spot. Jack, unprepared, nestles the pounding bruise on his cheek, giving the German enough advantage to strip the breathing apparatus off Jack. Growing conscious of his mistake, Jack tries to kick his attacker back but to no avail— his air is cut off, letting water seep into his lungs. Flailing, Jack attempts to release himself from the cage the German holds him in within his sturdy arms.

He continues to hold Jack tightly while flashing his other hand to his back to retrieve a knife. Seeing the rustic jagged ends of the knife, Jack wriggles free, but his muscles grow weary. His breath hitches while his eyes sweep the hollow mass of water around them, but his mind seems to be numb. Jack's movement is immobilized, and he floats in the hold of the attacker idly. Admitting defeat, Jack closes his eyes and anticipates being jabbed. But the only thing he feels is the roll of the waves.

The previous tranquility of the waves around them is now induced with an invasion, causing goosebumps to rise against his skin. As the tiny hair strands stand erect, they turn to look behind the German, noticing the presence of a beast. The German instantly lets go of Jack's collar, causing the relief to wash over him. With one swift thrust of his hands, Jack propels himself toward the surface. Before he has a chance to register a diversion in tow—not only to escape the German but also the great white shark—the water surrounding him changes color.

Instead of the calming aqua, the hues are tainted with infusing crimson. Jack inhales deeply, filling his lungs to maximum capacity, and dives underwater once more. But now, all he sees is the torso of the German dangling

from the sawtooths of the shark. His heart rate escalates, and fear palpitates through his system, making him turn around frantically to swim away from the sight. Jack knows too well that he is no match for another Bruce. The boat is far enough away that the shark could catch him before he could swim even halfway.

This is the ruin Jack knew about and never intended to revive. While the shark busied itself with gnawing on the fresh feast, he pulls up once more before diving back in and swimming toward the reef behind the shark. As time passes by, he—having ducked his presence behind the assortment of corals—continues to observe the blood diluting against the passing current.

When the horizon of blue once again clears, it gives Jack a seamless view of nothingness calling out to him. He gives away his hiding place. Placing as much burden as possible on his arms until the ache starts to burn within his muscles, he fights the current to reach his boat, that is still next to the German's Marlin vessel. Only another death awaits him as he plunges from the tides. Gasping for air, he shakes his head to move the strands from his forehead, clouding his vision, but soon he wishes he had let his vision remain cloaked for a little longer.

The smirk on Krueger Dietrich's face as he stares down at Jack from his boat with a gun pointed at him soon turns into a thin line. The previous wrinkles around his eyes smooth out, and his eyes freeze, following a line of blood running down the side of his face from a bullet wound to the head that came from afar. While Jack still can't make out who it is, the mysterious man from below the deck earlier starts up the boat's engine and takes off as fast as the vessel can go. With a quick jerking motion, it forces the stiff body of Krueger to be tossed overboard. A splash startles Jack, and it's followed by the similar pool of blood from beneath.

Jack's heart roars louder than before, his muscles burning from swimming so hard. He blinks once and then twice, and then the ocean breeze, sultry and cold, slaps him out of the terror. Without sparing another thought to the mystic howls of death that seem to have claimed three lives, he climbs onto the deck of his boat. The hunger of the ocean would have demanded yet another life had he remained straddling the water. His wrinkled feet touch the hard and cold surface of his boat, sending shivers and reality spiraling up his legs.

Jack allows time for his breath to tame itself from the previous wild chase he had been on, but his eyes come across the fleeting smile of Gustavo Vincenti. A mock salute follows as Gustavo's immaculate yacht passes by Jack.

"NOW YOU OWE ME ONE!" Gustavo yells as he gives a wicked grin at Jack in the water.

Gustavo then looks to his subordinates. "Now after that other vessel. Don't let him get away!"

Soon the roaring of the yacht disappears, trying to chase down the mysterious man, letting the howls of the ocean grow loud and vivid. The temper of the ocean rises, causing turbulent waves to rock the ship momentously. The coin! Realizing how Krueger held the last form of verification of this extravagant hunt, Jack did not bother thinking twice and dived back in the ocean. As fate may have it, he located Krueger's body still sinking, allowing him enough time to reach it. Murmuring a sorry silently, as he did not mean to disrespect the body, Jack successfully extracts the swastika coin from his shirt's upper pocket before swimming back to his boat. All the while, his mind keeps vividly replaying the near sudden death. The uninviting adventure that came knocking on his door seemed to have knocked his senses. Thankful of the sail back home because of its ability to ease the churning tides of his mind, he retreats to the safety and warmth of his apartment, where Alice awaits his arrival. He just has to make a quick stop at Lorenzo's first.

Later that night, Jack opens the door to his home as Alice answers. A smile is perched on her lips as no words are needed. Looking at a roughed up and worn out Jack, she recognizes his somber expression of a rough day, much like the glum breeze engulfing the air. Instead, she prepares a warm bath for

him, hoping for the controlled water to cleanse the saline from his skin and let him breathe. He basks himself in the comforts of solitude with her presence. Like an anchor, she plunges all of the demons tailing Jack to the bay, letting him take a walk back to the shore of his memories.

With a blanket pulled to their chests and her fingers laced with his free hand, he finds strength. This time, her grip around his hand tightens. She starts to close the distance between them, both of their eyes closing and giving in to the cozy atmosphere of their environment. All previous resentment and the hardness of their words gets washed away, their love toward one another rekindling. But before they could reunite, the wailing of the phone jolts them apart.

"Hello?" Jack intently listens to the caller, who starts to pour all of their heart out. By the end, only a groan escapes his lips. "Tomorrow morning? Are you for real, Bob? Ok, see you then."

Jack places the phone back and slumps beside Alice. This time, her lips turn into an "O." He concludes that the ravishing hunger of the sea is begging for more blood before it can satisfy its pelting cruelty, and begins to tell Alice everything.

Chapter IX

U-boat 2553

When the morning sun rose by the pier, anchored on the dock was the *Calypso*, on which everyone was on board plotting over a map. Alice enjoyed getting filled in on everything happening, and finally feeling included. Although Jack had still been semi-emotionless, she was accepting that she couldn't change that. Instead, she vowed to embrace it.

Soon the ashes from Bob's cigar gathered in a pile, as he has been engaged in his plan, and he looks up at the team. "So, Adler Enterprises has a salvage contract with the Cubans. As luck would have it, a large containership leaving off the coast of Havana transporting over 4,000 shipping containers didn't get that far before there was an explosion. The damage was so severe it ended up blowing several cargo containers to the sea. From what little information they have, it appears one of the cargo boxes was filled with fireworks that were undeclared on the ship's manifest. The best part is, it's only a mile off the coordinates where you need to be, Jack."

"You're kidding. What are the odds?" queried Jack.

"The Cubans have asked Adler Enterprises for help. I have arranged a

floating sheerleg with some trusted crew, plus all the necessary paperwork, so we can go clean it up. Told them we would be there by nightfall."

"Seriously Bob, exactly what kind of relationship do you have with Adler?" Jack inquired.

"Look, I hold some leverage over the CEO. I retained it for a rainy day. Willing to cash in my chip, and seek this opportunity to look for your Nazi submarine. However, know we won't have much time, as the Cubans patrol their waters like a shark, using vessels that listen in with sonar for invading subs. With some of their cargo overboard, they will probably be extra cautious against sea pirates from the Caribbean."

Alice speaks up. "I want to ride with Jack in the Triton."

Jack face displays shock and worry. "No way! It's too dangerous, Alice. I just told you about what happened yesterday."

"I don't care, Jack. Let me make that decision. I'm tired of sitting on the sidelines. Either I'm a part of your life, or not."

Jack stands out of his element, frozen without a response. As he'd just gotten Alice back, he didn't want to lose her again. All he could do was give half a smile, nod his head and agree.

Bob and Dymitry look at each other with confusion. "What happened yesterday?" Bob inquired.

Jack sees the smile on Alice's face as she leans into him with excitement; he continues and fills the others in on yesterday's events. They realize that the closer they get to finding the U-Boat, the more dangerous the situation is becoming, with unwanted attention. The gamble they are playing this time has high stakes. While Cuban wreckage provides a great distraction to manually retrieve the Spear and all the bullion, it would take too long and be risky. Also, knowing the rules about salvaged items found in Cuban waters, should they find the U-Boat, they would have no choice but to attempt to drag it over into American waters without getting caught. Bob would be on the floating sheerleg with Adler's crew, working on raising the Cuban cargo containers. At the same time, Dymitry would follow on the *Calypso* while keeping track of all invading patrol boats through the communication system. Jack and Alice could then be in the Triton, pushing the U-Boat to American waters. Dymitry and Jack rig up a device that can help them with that task, without the risk of dragging or tearing it apart from corrosion. From there, Dymitry will then reel up the vessel to the surface so they can search the remains. The plan seemed solid, but even one slight miscalculation could land them all in a Cuban prison for years.

Jack can't help wondering about what to do about Gustavo, as he seems to be drawing in closer. However, this was a fleeting thought, as even Jack knew the inspector's diplomatic immunity has no authority in a region governed by a communist party. Not to mention he was probably still chasing down the German vessel from yesterday. With everything buttoned up and the plan ironed out, they set sail for Cuba's Havana waters.

Nightfall comes, and upon their arrival, out in the ocean lies the inoperable Cuban cargo ship, dimly lit with a limited crew, cleaning up the remaining debris. Dymitry is ushered back to his ship's bridge, while Jack and Alice try to disperse into the mini-submarine. From out of the shadows, the eerie tone of sirens, followed by flashing lights, suddenly immobilizes their movement. Three small border patrol boats, known as Zhuk-class vessels, used for monitoring the ocean waters against piracy, pulls up to the sheerleg.

"Dobriy Vyecher!" is yelled, the common greeting for Russia, as a man in an orange vest jumps overboard armed with an Ak47 and a flashlight. Bob is already standing by to greet him. Jack tries to listen in from the *Calypso,* as their voices are barely audible.

"Good evening, officer," Bob replies, as the Guard is silent after first listening to squawks on his radio, communicated in Russian.

Then, in a heavy accent, he replies back, "Good evening. Assume you are with Alder Enterprises. Do you have all your necessary documentation?"

As if he has been down this road many times, Bob, with such a relaxed charm, hands the guard a folder with all the required papers.

Jack and Alice are about to climb into the Triton when they are also surprised by two guards walking onto their vessel. Bob sees the new intruders on the *Calypso*, but is only interrupted by the first Russian guard, who is meticulously going over his credentials. The guard, transfixed on the paperwork, doesn't even make eye contact with Bob before challenging him. "Why, if you have big boat, do you need small tugboat?"

Before Bob replies, he pulls out and lights his cigar with his silver zippo, then places gently back in his pocket. "Don't suppose you know where I can pick up a couple of these, do you?"

The guard notices it's a Cuban cigar. "Those are still banned in US, no?"

Bob smiles. "When you reach my age, you look at life a little differently."

The guard stares back at Bob with no response.

Bob then goes on to answer his original question. "The sheerleg crane doesn't rotate, so having an additional tugboat makes it easier to pick any smaller cargo."

On board the *Calypso*, Jack is not as confident as Bob, because he knows the fox is in the hen house. The Russian guard's attention draws toward the round blue tarp on the deck of the ship. Just as the solider begins to pull on the tarp, revealing the bright yellow Triton's top, his focus is interrupted by Jack.

"Why are the Russians overseeing a cargo wreckage?" asks Jack has he leans against the tarp, knowing if fully uncovered, it will reveal the specially-designed gadget on the bottom of the mini sub, which he has no excuse for.

The guard is taken aback by Jack's forwardness. "This was no accident. Cargo container was purposely blown up. Being that some of our own cargo was on there, we can't take any chances." He then proceeds to lean into his radio and speak Russian to the other guard, as he is looking at the discovered Triton.

On the sheerleg, the voice comes across the radio, were the other Russian solider turns and looks at Bob. "Why do you have a mini-sub?"

Bob is frustrated. "Exactly *how* do you think we are going to fish these containers out of the sea? We need a set of eyes down there. The approval paperwork is there, but if that isn't good enough, I'll be happy to turn this ship around and go home."

The Russian is silent for a moment. Admiring Bob's moxie, he gives a nod while handing him back his paperwork. "I will let my Kapitan know everything checks out. Stay within the perimeter of the cargo ship. Any of your men travel outside the designated area, they will be arrested immediately. This is your warning. We will be watching."

Bob lets out a puff of smoke from his cigar in a perfect hollow ring, then shakes his head in an agreement. "I understand."

The time has stood still on the *Calypso*, as Jack gulps while the guard is about to pull back the full tarp when he is quickly interrupted by his walkie talkie breaking the silence. A brief conversation back and forth ensues in Russian, resulting in a command for them to leave. With a wave to the other Russian guards, they exit the *Calypso*, keeping the Triton's secrets safe. After the patrol guards are out of sight, Bob gets his men working on finding the missing cargo. Dymitry then goes and hooks up the Triton for a dive.

"Remember Jack, you're tethered to the fiber optic cable, which has a max range of around 7,500 feet. I know you can't dive further than that, but with us now locked in this perimeter, let's hope you don't have to travel any further."

Jack nods and settles in the mini-sub with Alice, as Dymitry shuts the hatch firmly. Without flickering the lights on, Jack speaks into the radio, telling Dymitry to release the winch. Within seconds, Jack and Alice plunge

into absolute darkness. Frightened by the sudden jolt, Alice hastily clutches Jack's wrist.

"Relax, Alice. I won't let anything happen to you, but I'm about to take you to a whole new world."

Alice notices the broken shark tooth wedged in a deep scratch on the bubble. "Should I be worried?"

"Not unless Bruce comes backs to pay us a visit."

Alice raises her brows in worry.

"Teasing. We will be fine!" Jack smiles, shutting the hatch.

Nodding, Alice remains closer to Jack. As promised, when he is sure they are far from the reach of the coastal guards, he switches on the lights of the vessel. The yellow illuminates the scenic view, bringing the aquatic nightlife before them. A gasp escapes Alice's lips, her eyes transfixed on what lay before her scrutiny.

"Oh, Jack…you were right." Alice gasps. "As far as the eye can see, it's a thing of beauty. There are just so many living creatures under here."

"That's why they call it the ocean, sweetheart," Jack remarks, knowing he is winning her over.

Like a child, Alice leans her palm flat against the spotless acrylic orb. Her eyes fixate on the massive hollow of dark and the gentle water, allowing them a seamless flight. To her, the silken movements of the corals against its reef, the colors radiant under the mock sunlight of the submarine, it is all a sight of absolute brilliance. Like a stroll in the park, she is breathing underwater. Fishes, like birds, spread their wings and swish gracefully to plunge their burden forward.

"Jack, I could spend eternity down here!" Alice says like a child, as she is mesmerized by the charm of the ocean.

How effortless, Alice thinks to herself. The rippling water deludes her into believing it offers nothing but peace. But Jack knows the truth of the rickety temper of the water. All the same, it brings Jack smiles, as she is enjoying his natural habitat. The sand-encrusted seabed leaves her senses tantalized. She wants to feel the grains against her skin, wondering if they feel different than the sand on the shore. Her curious mind wonders if the shore is as hot as the one above, due to the sun. Or does it remain unbothered by the weather of their land environment? The submarine passes by ripples, where the iridescent luminance of the moon reflects the seabed, which glistens like stardust. Her eyes capture the radiance of the moon and hues of dark blue. Her olive eyes dance with amusement, captivating Jack's attention as they continue to explore the abyss.

Time passes through the night. Off in the distance, the crack of dawn is veering its head. On board the sheerleg, Bob's men have already found a few of the missing cargo containers and pulled them out of the ocean, using the ship's crane. Bob is apprehensive, and paces back and forth along the boat deck, looking out into the sea for the approximation of where Jack might be. Lifting his hand, he gazes at his watch, paces some more, then picks up his walkie-talkie, communicating over to the *Calypso*. "It's been almost an hour. Any news from Jack?"

The sounds squawk back from Dymitry: *"I'm still with him… He hasn't found anything yet."*

Bob has never been more disappointed in receiving updates. "Well, it's not going to take us much longer here; unfortunately, this may be a bust." He takes his half-smoked cigar and tosses it overboard. Then he leans against the deck's rail, cursing under his breath, only for the silence of the ocean waves to be disrupted once more by the squelch of the radio.

Dymitry's voice gasped with surprise. *"Bob, it's Jack. He thinks he found something? I am patching him through."*

"Hey, Bob!"

"Jack, your making this old man nervous. Tell me you found something,

buddy."

"Maybe? There are some rock ledges about sixty meters north of us. Something metallic is reflecting back."

Dymitry interrupts the communication. *"That's no good, Jack. That's another two hundred feet just to get there, and you're almost out of cable as it is! You need more than that just to move around. Without me breaking our restricted perimeter, I'm going to have to untether you."*

"NO! We can't do that, Dymitry. I need you as my eyes and ears. Bob, we can't just ignore this?"

Bob closes his eyes and takes in a deep breath, feeling the confidence of knowing what the risks are and how he will have to atone for them, but they have come so far. He opens his eyes and gives a holler back.

"I agree. Dymitry, go outside the perimeter and follow Jack. We can't lose communication."

Dymitry knows not to argue. *"You got it!"*

"Make it count, boys." Bob smiles as he walks off to check on his men.

Dymitry pushes the *Calypso's* throttle control forward and sails north out of the permitter, giving the Triton enough cable slack to move forward.

Not long after, the mini-sub pivots between two rock ledges to a wide-open trench, to unknown depths to the earth's core. Jack and Alice's faces are frozen, as if they were looking through a window of time. Jack and Alice peer through the Triton's chilled bubble in amazement, as in front them lies hidden from the world the German iron metal *U-Boat 2553*.

Carefully, Jack nears them toward the now derelict sunken vessel. Unlike its enormous versions, this vessel is smaller in size. Still, the glorious pale green algae rests upon her, covering up parts of the majestic grey steel that made these U-Boats so recognizable. Next to the periscope sits the conning tower, painted on her the symbol that drives chills down our backs, a white swastika logo—now blighted in color, along with the U-Boat, identifier *2553*. The lifeless motion gives way to its dejected state of abandonment. The control room, now solemn, seems to be calling out to its lost voyagers. Jack's imagination is filled with echoes of Nazi German dialected screams for help in the dark water, feeling the pull of the forsaken boat as it is drawn nearer. His hands itch to trail the railing of the surface, to be transported back to the time of its glory. Now the sunken U-boat is just a sight of a mess, a symbolism of power that lost its authority. Toward the rear, the ballast damage lays in the wreckage as it was ripped apart from the US Navy's torpedo. Metal fragments and treasure mixed in with debris sprawl across the ocean bed. Now a plight ringing through the silence of the night, aching his heart.

"This is beautiful, Jack. How can there be beauty in the broken?"

Alice's question leaves Jack startled, despite knowing the answer with the beats of his heart. The scars the vessel incurred run deep along the lines, like a creased forehead depicting its former woes. The bleakness that emerges from within it gives way to the oblivion state of those who now live, unaware of the catastrophe the soldiers must have undergone. *Of course there is beauty in the broken,* Jack muses to himself. After all, the experience that comes with fighting endless battles and demons does have a reward. A reward a soldier only inherits after having lost his life safeguarding the interest of the feudal lords.

Working diligently throughout the night, back on the sheerleg, Bob is overseeing Alder's men attaching the crane to a few of the cargo containers they could find. He is interrupted by an echo that comes across his walkie talkie, in sync with Dymitry's.

"Bob, we found it" shouted Jack.

"That's great news, kid!"

"Uh…not so great," Alice states, causing the old man to go frantic on the other end of the radio system. Alice continues to explain to Bob that Jack has maneuvered the Triton closer to the sunken U-boat, but the vessel is wedged

in a trench..

Jack interjects. "What this means is that we have to raise it even higher, requiring a bit more time with the compressor."

"Man, can things just go smoothly for once?" Dymitry cries.

"Dymitry, how much time do we have on our watch?" Jack replies.

"So far, there's no patrol on my radar. How much time do you reckon is needed, Jack?"

"Hard to say. How about I get to you in a while?"

Ignoring the grunts that follow, much like a crab, the Triton moves about, taking a 360-degree view of the ship. Jack's eyes trailing along the lengths of the eons-old boat. He knows he needs to use some leverage to push the bottom out from the trench, hence he maneuvers to the Triton to the back of the U-boat, where the wreckage of the ballast sits.

"Uh, oh...I take it back, Jack. You might have company. I'm detecting a vessel crossing towards your direction."

"Figures," grumbles Jack.

"What do we do now?" Dymitry snaps.

Panic breaks out amongst them, causing Alice to look around erratically. Jack turns his head around haphazardly.

"Jack," Bob's voice advises as it comes through the acoustic speaker. *"Every sound can be picked up on sonar. You'd better turn everything off and just rest for a couple of minutes if you want to avoid being in the hands of the Cubans, my friend."*

"Or worse, the Russians!" Dymitry adds.

Each second, Jack feels his heart resonating mayday. At the back of his mind, he knows he will have to shut down the machine, but it would mean delaying their exit. Seconds pass, and he feels time stop as his hand makes contact with the machine and he shuts the system off. Pin drop silence engulfs them, leaving him to feel threatened by even the tamed roars of his heart.

Chapter X

Say Yes

ilence ensues and soon, as the thundering of their erratic heartbeats also ceases. The eerie darkness causes Alice to move closer to Jack, causing him to wrap his arm around her protectively. Her breaths fan out against the hollow of his neck. Seconds pass, and she slightly pushes herself away, feeling the heat creep up her neck. The scene around her is no longer of desolation. A glowing blue hue is being emitted from below the trench, casting a halo around the U-boat. She turns around, noticing that the corals emit a similar casting of a halo.

The previous dull browns are now lighted by pale pinks, dull orange, and fluorescent greens and yellows. No longer are they doused in water that seeped cold into their bones, sending shivers up and down their spine. Well, the chills do go down their spine, but only after realizing their position. They are breathing underwater. The casting of blue sprawls as far as their vision allows, ignited by luminous and sultry movements of the coral reefs.

The mischief of the pink reminds Alice of the close proximity she shares with Jack after a long time. Blue from the trenches gnaws at her mind, of the calm around them and of the sentience she brings to Jack. Even when his temper spirals out of control, she can chase his demons away. Each ruffling coral speaks of a secret beyond their comprehension, yet enough to intrigue them to cover the distance between them. When silent, Alice makes out the blobs the corals spoke in, each varying from the other, the highs of ecstasy and the lows of a mundane viewing.

Alice leans against Jack's chest, taking in the trench expanding like a border. Her mind wonders what lies beyond the trenches, and if there is life beneath. Or, if the waters begged to differ, beseeching an alternate reality than what lies here. Indeed, the waters portray another reality of life amidst the sea. What people conceive to be a foe, at the moment, provides them with serenity. The water, despite not drenching them, cleanses their soul. Its purity revitalizes their minds and hearts. Further down, sea vegetation allures their attention of seaweeds, sea kelps, and anemones. The greenery leaves their fingers, wanting to caress their velvety surface.

From between the lips of the trenches, a jellyfish glowing orange floats up, followed by another, and then another. Soon, the few turn numerous. Like floating lamps, illuminating inside the Triton, they glide across, the jellyfish spreading in the vacant waters, encrusting like stars in the massive sky.

Their emitting of orange hues gives way to the intricate architecture of the ridged surface of the reefs, of the hollows and tentacle-like vacuums spread throughout on the stony surface. Lifting their gaze, Jack and Alice realize they are deep within the mystic realm, where another life exists. They are the invaders, brimming with curiosity. At the same time, they pose a threat to aquatic life swimming in silence and disguise. In spite of being unarmed, their strange physique is enough to startle the fish. Like a child startled by a stranger, the Triton scares the crawling orange crabs away along the seabed.

Their eyes trail each movement of the crabs, from their feet scrambling to their continuously opening and closing claws. The critter is armed with scissors to cut any arm threatening its existence. It performs a show of colors, a display of life hidden from the eyes of the universe that lay above. Here, the corals whisper songs to the fish, the jellyfish hum a mystic tune, and the crabs and lobsters scurry away to their oracular hidings. The cold that must

be there does not reach their warm holding. The acrylic pressure hull shields both Alice and Jack from the looming peril, while letting them gaze in awe at the manifesting marvel of nature.

Despite the distance from his world, Jack oddly feels at home. Jack smiles as he runs his fingers gently down Alice's hair, watching her deep in her trance of the sea. To hold her in his arms, he feels his life complete. Together, they continue to gaze at the abundance of tranquil silence, feeling the desire to surface, only to dive back down and float freely with the fish.

Jack muses to himself how strange the human mind is. On land, where the sand fills the gaps between the toes, watching the birds soar and spread their glorious wings, a man yearns to take his own flight. Now underwater, his own muscles long to spread and let the water touch them. His heart desires to swim too, to let his tongue feel the saltiness of the water. Each fleeting second as the Russian vessel nears, Jack and Alice forget space and time. They let their space freeze them. All they hear is the quiet humming of their own heart, now synced with the other. The mellow of daunting water creates an illusion, irking him to forget his present and forever embrace the cavity of the trenches. His eyes trail each movement of the crabs once more, of how they continue to glide across the light sand. However, an unusual speck causes both him and Alice to move closer to the spherical acrylic surface.

"Well, you'll have plenty of gold coins, now."

Scattered across the seabed are several of Hitler's Rubicon gold coins that trail off into the direction from which the U-boat came. Jack's eyes stay fixated on them.

"This explains how I found one under Captain Gibbons' *Fly 460*. Some of these coins must have been carried away by the ocean's current."

With the Triton lights on, Jack can't help noticing other treasures spread about. One that draws his attention is a raw uncut diamond on the ocean floor. Being in the moment, with all that beauty and treasure, and far from reality, Jack wonders if his life would remain serene with just Alice. The more he contemplates the idea, the vibrant specks of color building within the pieces of the uncut stone shine brighter. Within a heartbeat, he finds the answer. His life would entail far more colors than the spectrum a diamond could ever hold. Be it whatever weather, cold or hot, be it a harsh storm, even if he were to drown, he knew his life would have the buoyancy if Alice were by his side. She is his guiding light. With a thrust of his hand, he turns the Triton back on, awakening life around into the mini-sub. Jack maneuvers the mini-sub closer to the sparkling stones, with its small rumble from the engine, and the external lights are glistening onto the ocean floor.

Over on the sheerleg, a Russian ship passes by as Bob's crew is winching up another cargo container they found.

The boat stops as the Kapitan, standing on the deck, looks around and then yells out to Bob, "I was told you had a mini-submarine on board, yet I have NOT seen it?

Bob is standing on the deck, looking back at the Kapitan. "I don't know what to say, except it's dark out? He's down there. He is leading my guys to your cargo containers, and helping strap them on the crane."

The Kapitan gazes down into the ocean again, seeing lights moving under the water, cascading from the diver's helmets. He nods to his bridge deck to take off, then gives a double finger salute back to Bob.

As the Russian vessel takes off, Dymitry's voice breaks the silence through the radio, explaining that the Triton has been turned back on. Bob bellows out, "Jack, is everything okay? Why did you turn on the power back on?" Continuing to worry. "The Cubans?"

Jack smiles and speaks in a relaxed tone as he maneuvers the mini-sub. "They're not Cubans, Bob. They're comrades."

Bob grumbles back, *I know who they are, kid! Now shut that thing down. They were already over here asking questions.*"

Alice's voice also becomes distressed. "Jack, what are you doing?"

"Just hang on," Jack replies in a thrilled demeanor.

Like an alien predator stalking its prey, each sense heightened and the carnivore vigilant, the Triton prowls the seabed. All that Alice clings to is her feeling of fate changing, while Jack clings to another heightened emotion. One of love and never letting go. The previous night, watching her excitement, for her to be sharing his passion, he knew no one else could ever understand him the way she does. She is his beacon, his set of wings, and his reason to come home. Even now, her understanding of his passion increases tenfold.

To Jack, the forbidden treasure before his eyes does not matter. The true treasure he now sees is in the form of the woman in his company. Her smile gleams brighter than any treasure. The twinkling of her olive eyes is far more precious than any emerald. The purity of her soul just surpassed that of the oceans alone. Each second he feels a connection with Alice growing deeper than the true depths of the ocean, one which is still not exploited.

A bland growl comes into their hearing, alerting them that the Russian ship is nearing their position.

Dymitry whispers in range through the transmission, with hopes of not getting caught. *"Jack, you have got to turn the Triton off or the jig is up. From what I can tell they are minutes away."*

All Jack has are a few minutes at his disposal. Minutes for him to muster his courage, gather the stones, answer what calls out to him, and bundle it all together before presenting to Alice. Minutes to alter his life. His eyes snap toward the remote; and without thinking of the consequences, without dwelling on the ifs, he grabs hold of the joystick, propelling the robotic arm to move at his command. Every other man grows alarmed. Panic grips their hearts, including Alice. But Jack is held in a trance, his eyes dilating as he quickly maneuvers the robotic arm to grab hold of a piece of stone that he estimates to be seven carats. Its ingenious hexagon shape makes him reach out for it and, slowly, he brings it near to the clear bubble wall.

"What's wrong with you, Jack? Are you out of your mind?" Dymitry contin-

ues to badger.

Bob can't help himself but chime in. *"You will get everyone caught. What are you doing down there? Repeat, the Russians will be over you guys within a minute and a half. SHUT EVERYTHING DOWN! That's an order, son!"*

Alice, deeply concerned, asks, *"Jack?"*

Jack smiles as he continues to maneuver the controls to the back end of the U-Boat. "A minute and a half. Good, it's all I need."

Jack ignores the agitated cries of Dymitry and Bob, while Alice is frozen to the spot. He gets out of his seat and bends down on one knee while extending his arm toward Alice, and clears his throat. Alice's adrenaline levels heighten as her heart rate goes a-flutter, and massive nervousness sets in. She hides her smile behind her hand.

"Alice, I find myself exploring new territory, for which I am at a loss for words." Jack breathes. "I spent my whole life searching for the unknown, to discover the truth that lies beneath. Whether it was searching for my Dad or hunting lost ships and sunken artifacts, my true treasure has been by my side. I am a sailor lost at sea, looking to the stars for my true North. You are my true North. During tough times, when I was drowning, you were the light that led me."

Above water, moving at haste, is the Zhuk-class Russian ship. Inside, one of the skippers with the Russian crew speaks with the Kapitan.

"Kapitan…" Grabbing the Kapitan's attention, he continues to ask in Russian: "While we don't see any ships, we think we might be picking up a faint machinery noise? Permission to slow our ships speed, for a deeper search?"

The Kapitan looks at the skipper and nods. Just as a vulture circles its dying prey, waiting to strike. The Russian ship starts to slow down and makes a circumference cruise around the targeted area, listening in to its surroundings.

Back in the Triton, Alice is listening to Jack, who's still bent on one knee

as he grabs her hand. "Alice, I want to share with you an adventure of a lifetime, knowing years from now that all that you'll ask is just to be standing there wanting to be held in my arms. If you are willing to go to the ocean's depths with me, I would be a fool to let you go. I can't promise we won't have problems, but know you won't have to face them alone. I promise to laugh with you when times are good, endure with you when times are bad, and to love you fearlessly forever, because everything's going to be all right."

Jack takes in a deep breath and closes his eyes. Slowly, he fills his vision with Alice. She places her palm against her mouth to suppress the sobs threatening to escape.

"Alice, will you do…"

Dymitry explodes. *"JACK, THE SHIP IS HEADING RIGHT FOR—"*

"JACK, IF YOU UTTER ANOTHER WORD, AND DON'T TURN THAT DAMN SUB OFF, THEY WILL HEAR YOU AND BLOW YOU OUT OF THE WATER!" Bob and Dymitry yell in unison, yet their warning goes unheard by Alice and Jack, who are encapsulated in their own space. The secluded vacuum makes both of them smile, tears cascading down Alice's cheek.

Jack continues to profess, "Will you do me the honor and agree to take me as your husband for the rest of your life?"

"You guys, enough playing around! The ship is practically above you!" Dymitry's voice grows erratic.

Alice, in shock, quietly replies, "I…I"

"JUST SAY YES ALREADY, ALICE, I WILL PAY FOR THE WEDDING, PLEASE!" yells Bob.

Alice, aggravated at Bob bellowing through the radio, turns to look around her. The bouquet of corals and the floating lamps in the shape of jellyfish radiate their makeshift floating skyline. This is her fairytale proposal. It isn't traditional by any means: no photographers, no fancy clothes. But she already knows she is the luckiest woman, and the first to have an underwater marriage proposal.

The vibration around them grows dense, alerting all of them that the Russian Zhuk-Class ship has reached them. Bob incessantly chants a "Yes" on her behalf.

"Yes. Of course, yes, I will marry you!" Alice exclaims.

As soon as the words roll from the tip of her tongue, Jack experiences an altered state of mind due to the thrill of the moment, a natural high. He slams his left hand on the power button and cradles his right hand around her curved waist to pull her to him. Within that split second, everything goes black, and sound becomes an ambient vacuum. Surprise laces her gaze, as Jack has never been the romantic type. Darkness conquers their enchanted state, letting the luminosity of the aquatic life dazzle their love from afar. His lips meet the softness of hers, and they move in sync, holding their breath while letting the fire of passion burn on. Jack and Alice lose themselves in a stuporous moment as he holds her in his arms, not moving a muscle, as the soft rumbling of the Russian Ship can be heard right over them.

Onboard the Zhuk-Class ship, the Kapitan reaches out to the skipper. "Anything?"

The bushy eyed skipper shakes his head "no." The Kapitan gives one more nod, commanding the ship to pick up speed and continue on with its regular patrolled course. As the roll of the Russian ship passes over, Jack and Alice run out of breath, they tear apart, letting the glare and rebutting of Bob and Dymitry come through the radio.

"THAT WAS TOO CLOSE! I am amazed at the display of maturity by both of you," Dymitry condemned. *"Anyway, I will leave the lecture for Bob, and let you guys know the ship is out of reach from you guys. So, you should be back on track now."*

Bob jumps on the radio. *"What are you trying to do, give an old man a*

heart attack? Congratulations, by the way, now let's get that U-Boat before the Russians come back, and we can celebrate all around."

"Roger that." Jack smiles.

Jack turns back and switches the machine back on. Slowly, the U-boat triumphantly starts to rise from its fallen state. All of them cheer with glee at the achievement. Alice leans in for another chaste kiss.

"I am so proud of you, Jack." She leans in to give him another kiss.

Dymitry teases, *"And I am so grossed out by the two of you, right now."*

"Now is that anyway a best man should talk?" Jack grins.

"Best man? Well, why didn't you lead with that? Couldn't be happier for the two of you. Congrats Alice for taking the plunge, although you're probably safer down there inside that plastic bubble, surrounded by shark invested Cuban waters then marrying that dawg." Dymitry laughs.

"Alright Dymitry, I say it's about time we see if our gadget works and we try to raise that U-boat!" Jack presses down on what appears to be a makeshift lever. A door opens up below the mini sub. Drifting down is a massive bright red liner hooked up by hose to two oversized air compressor tanks. He carefully maneuvers it toward the U-Boat's open ballast. Using the Triton's mechanical arm, Jack grabs hold of the red liner, slowly inserting into the back of the U-Boat.

"Like stuffing a Thanksgiving turkey," Jack says, then looks at Alice and smiles as his eyes lead to the large orange button on the panel. "Would you do the honors, Mrs. Sterling?"

Alice beams. "I thought you would take my last name?"

A crack of laughter is heard from the radio. *"The adventures of Jack Fernsby, I love it!"* Dymitry continues to chuckle.

Jack looks over at Alice and gives her a look so swift and venomous. "I think we are about to have another fight."

Alice can't help herself but smile back, and hits the orange button. The underwater compressor suddenly kicks in, sending compressed air from the tanks through the hose into the U-Boat, where the massive red liner now rests, only to suddenly be woken to a new life as air inhales into that thin rubber bag, growing immensely with every single breath. Even under the dark waters, a bright red elongated balloon bulges out of any visible openings that the old submarine may have. What was once lost is now found, and what was thought dead has now risen. The bright-colored bladder continues to fill up the sunken vessel, slowly raising the U-Boat inches off the ground. Dirt and debris that laid restless for over fifty years now stirs in motion as the German submarine ascends off the ocean floor. Then, like a bulldozer that has complete accuracy and commands the pushing of dirt around with its blade, the Triton makes its way, pushing the now red-balloon-filled U-Boat out of the trench and toward international waters.

On top of the ocean, the Russian vessel approaches the sheerleg again as the Kapitan is looking at some papers. "According to my manifest, all the cargo containers are accounted for but two? They hold NO real value, so you may call it a night. Spaseeba, which means in American, thank you for your services. I'm sure our government has already taken care of your fees."

"You sure? Give us an hour. I'm sure we can find them." Bob is just trying to buy some more time.

The Kapitan shakes his head. "That will not be necessary. Da sveedaneeya. You can call up your men, with your mini-sub and tear down please."

The Kapitan stares at Bob to give the order. He pulls up the walkie talkie to his lips. "Alright men, time to tear down, let's get out of here."

"HALT!" orders the Russian Kapitan. "Why is that vessel out there? He's past the perimeter." He points at the tugboat off in the distance.

Bob replies in his calm demeanor, "We are wrapping things up, decided to send him home."

The Kapitan continues to stare at the ship. "Then why is he moving so slow?"

Bob looks back over at the *Calypso* off in the distance, then shrugs. "Sight-seeing?" Grabbing his radio, he informs that Kapitan that he will tell him to pick up the speed.

Kapitan gives a wince. "And the mini-sub? It is on there?"

Bob nods in response.

The Russian looks over at Bob. "Don't bother, we will go and check it out for ourselves. We would like to make sure everything is alright," he says in a facetious tone, walking in the bridge of his boat. He then pauses and looks back at Bob. "I trust you and the sheerleg will be leaving now. A good day, sir." The Kaptain proceeds to yell at his crew in Russian, as the Zhuk-class vessel sails off toward the *Calypso*.

The sweat finally starts to assemble upon Bob's brow as he jumps on the radio. "Dymitry, you better tell Jack to hurry. You're about to be knee-deep in a Russian hijacking. The minute they didn't see that sub, they headed your way."

"On it. Operation Yellow Balloon!" Dymitry replies, as he grabs a small air tank and runs out to the blue tarp on the deck of the *Calypso*.

Although Jack's movements are not restricted, the weight of the fragile piece of antique slows his movement, for fear of it crumbling. Much to his dismay, he continues to struggle with moving forward, initiating a throbbing shaking of the vessel.

A dull, yet prominent crackling causes Jack to snap his attention back, and his eyes widen in realization. A part of the U-boat seems to have peeled off due to a minor dragging motion, making him inhale sharply. Alice places her palm flat on his shoulder, easing his tensed muscles.

Dymitry's voice cracks across Jacks radio. *"I know we have to go slow, but a Zhuk ship is headed our way!"*

Jack knows the urgency of the matter, and while not moving at a rapid pace, he is still fleeing the seabed. The rickety sand underneath scrapes the bottom of the U-boat, announcing the theft being conducted in secrecy mutedly. As meticulous as Jack tries to be, he knows the sound will only alert them of their presence, and yet shutting down the air compressor would only send the U-Boat crashing to its fate, producing a sound that would also tip off the Russians.

Once more, Dymitry's radar and systems blare, declaring the ship is getting closer. His voice regains its forlorn tone. Panic surfaces and clutches Jack's heart, making it roar louder in the silence. He increases the throttle.

"I can't stop now, we are close to the border!"

Despite Jack's voice being low and laden with worry, he turns to meet Alice's eyes. Fear burns brighter in them.

Up above, the Russian vessel is approaching; looking through the binoculars, the Kapitan sees a blue tarp covering a ball-shaped object on the deck of the *Calypso*. Dymitry, looking out the window of his bridge, sees the Russian Zhuk-Class ship steadily advancing. Sweat begins to roll down his brow as he knows behind the tarp lies a yellow blown up balloon, made to look like the Triton.

Jumping on the radio, Dymitry calls out, "Come in, Bob! Jack needs more time. The Zhuk is still approaching, and I'm not sure he is falling for operation yellow balloon? Over?" The echo of silence returns. "BOB?!"

Dimitry's voice continues to reverberate as Bob's radio lies abandoned on the ship's deck, as he storms outward. Bob descends into the ocean's pits with a momentous dip, sending ripples across the surface like an Olympian swimmer. After a beat, he resurfaces with a gasp of air and makes his way to a small speedboat he has docked up against the sheerleg. Several crew members peer over to make sure the older man is alright, but their faces are beaming with disbelief.

Bob climbs in and starts up the speedboat, taking off with great haste. Upon his fleeing, he yells back at his crew, "DON'T WORRY ABOUT ME FOLLOW THE *CALYPSO* AND GET BACK TO INTERNATIONAL WATERS, JACK NEEDS YOU!"

The crew can be seen agreeing and setting the sheerleg course for international waters, as fast as their vessel will travel.

While under the sea, Jack and Alice are in panic mode, as they can't stop parts of the German submarine from breaking apart. The back end of the vessel continues to drag along the ocean floor.

"Careful, Jack. We go too fast she will rip apart." Alice shivers as she glances nervously at the U-boat rupture.

"I know, I know. We are almost there. Just another twenty meters!" Jack states out of frustration as he looks down at his nautical gauge. "Dymitry, how are we looking?"

Onboard the *Calypso,* Jacks's voice is temporarily ignored as Dymitry sees the wind blowing off the tarp's corner, revealing the yellow balloon. A bright red flare suddenly shoots up in the sky. Voices travel across the PA speaker's air: "This is the Russian patrol; you are past the designated area, and have not been given clearance to leave. Be prepared to be boarded."

Looking out his bridge window, Dymitry sees the Russian vessel only moments away, giving out a sorrowful sigh. "Well, Jack, we had a good run, but still, it's a long way to go, and we have only a short time to get there." Realizing their lack of options, he says, "I think we need to consider...wait, what is that old man doing?" The query that is evident in Dymitry's voice as he continues to look out as sea only causes Jack to worry.

"WHAT IS IT?" Jack replies through the radio.

"It's Bob. He's in his speed boat, going full throttle toward the Russians."

"What is he going to do, ram them?" asks Jack.

Dymitry shakes his head, as he is in trance. "Not sure?"

Inside the speed boat, locked in autopilot, Bob pulls out some old fireworks he had tucked away under the storage compartment. He notices a giant red and blue cardboard cannon with a wick sticking out, the one with the bright color illustration of the forty-fifth President dressed up like Rambo, and the non-politically-correct title. The "screw your feelings" rocket. A smile widens across Bob's face. Holding onto the cannon's bottom base, he ignites the rocket toward the Zhurk-class ship. "You call that a flare? This is a flare!"

Within seconds, as the Russian ship is only a few feet away from boarding the *Calypso*, a loud sonic boom is heard above the soldiers' heads, only to be followed by the cracking noise of fireworks as the sky lights up with fiery red glimmers that spell out the massive words "TRUMP 2020," then dissipates in the wind. The soldiers who were huddled on the deck, thinking it was a foreign projectile, are quick to stand up in range, sending the alarm to take off after the speedboat.

As the Russian vessel departs, Dymitry gasps in amazement. "He did it! He bought us the time we need. I also see the sheerleg is rapidly approaching. We will follow you to the rendezvous point. Jack, let's take her home!"

Jack now knows he is under no supervision, so he drops the acceleration enough to safely drive the U-boat past the border.

Chapter XI

Pick a Side

Safe over on the international waters, just outside the Cuban's jurisdiction, the *Calypso* is docked by the sheerleg, and Dymitry is on board with the crew setting up the crane.

"Jack, I'm anxious about Bob being picked up, or worse, shot." Alice sighs as she looks out through the spherical orb into the ocean with a face of despair.

In contrast, Jack's focused on maneuvering the Triton around, attaching all the tow cables around the U-Boat to lift it out of the water. "We can't worry about that right now. We need to hoist this vessel up carefully, or we'll pull it apart like a ragdoll. When we're done, we'll see about finding a way of rescuing him."

Dymitry's voice echoes across the radio. *"As much as I hate it too, Jack is right. We can't worry about him now. Let us know when you're ready for us to pull, alright?"*

Silence follows, like a doctor having announced the operation reaching a critical stage. Dymitry grows distressed while Jack and Alice break out in a pool of sweat. To Jack, the U-boat is no less than an infant. He has to cradle it gently. His movements now turn slow, and gingerly he uses the robotic arms of the Triton to grab hold of the thick tow cable and winch of the lift ship. The metal in his grip seems heavy, making him struggle with moving it to near the curved hull of the U-boat.

Every time the chain moves, the rust on it sheds its dust, and the sand rising from the seabed due to the vigorous movement creates a temporary dust storm. He repeats the motion with the spare tow cables and secures their winch around the hull of the U-boat to create a triangle pull formation. Satisfaction courses through his veins, making Jack smile triumphantly before alerting Dymitry to start their second phase of salvation.

"Aye, aye captain."

Dymitry leans closer to his monitor, his eyes narrowing on the camera view, and his fingers curl around the controller to maneuver the movements of the lift ship delicately. The U-boat suddenly jerks forward, making Jack yell in the microphone for Dymitry not to hasten their thirty-minute time frame.

"Remember, Dymitry, slow and steady wins the race," materializes across the speaker.

As told, Dymitry continues to haul the fragile boat, ensuring a seamless movement before it starts to lift. As soon as the front hull starts to ascend, Jack's heart stops beating. His breaths hitch, fearing any second the tow cable will snap and the U-boat will collapse, crumbling back into the ocean in pieces. Even so, Dymitry continues to set a pace for his lift ship, locking in the angle of the winch and a steady speed for the cable to coil. Having little choice but to wait patiently, Jack and Alice lean in their designated seats to watch the sight of the tow with hope and fear.

Having little to do while waiting for the U-boat to rise from its decaying captivity, a sudden motorboat is heard racing in by the sheerleg.

"ITS BOB!" Dymitry's voice echoes on the radio.

Bob climbs up and walks out to the deck, holding a cigar. Clouds of smoke begin to rise and swirl around him, engulfing him in a daze of deluded glory. His mind drifts further down the horizon before him. The rippling moonbeam allures him into a fantasy of an unfathomable fortune waiting to be shared.

Dymitry runs to give him a hug while holding his walkie talkie. "How did you get away? We were worried about you."

Bob smiles. "No need to worry about me. I knew they couldn't catch me in that speedboat, and once I was in international waters, I knew they would turn around."

Alice and Jack are in amazement. Jack says, *"I guess you have some adventure left in you yet?"*

"Yeah just like your proposal. Now get up here and let's open up this baby and celebrate," Bob replies.

"It will take some time. We are strapped underneath it, using the Triton's engine to help lift it with the balloon, so it's not being pulled on. Will be there shortly."

On the sheerleg, Bob is beaming with joy. He lights up a cigar. A familiar voice his heard from behind.

"Ah, burning nicotine helps alleviate the burden of reality. Although at your age, I am not sure if it's wise to be smoking."

The mocking voice startles Bob, causing the half-burnt cigar to escape his iron grip and drown into the ocean. Instantly, he turns on his heels, goosebumps running across his spine. Still, he holds the sweat threatening to form around his forehead at bay upon spotting the grinning on Gustavo's thin lips. Another jolting sound of water, parting to let men dive deeper into the pits of nothingness, catches Bob's attention. A larger ship behind Dymitry's seems to be unloading men geared with scuba equipment. The previous creases on Bob's head are cleared, and his mouth forms into an O shape before fear grips him.

"What…you…how?"

"Calm down, Bob. You don't have to stutter." Gustavo leisurely walks underneath the crane and peeks over the deck, where dozens of cable tows are piercing through the water, lifting something.

"Is that where Sterling is? I'll be collecting my treasure now," Gustavo says.

Half a smirk forms on his face before turning his attention back to his men, who have some of the sheerleg crew at gun point. His gray metallic ship also seems to have given the divers the go ahead, as they suddenly bolt into the water like a bullet from a gun. When reality finally settles within Bob, and he registers the horror unfolding before him, he regains his disheveled spirit. A scowl forms on his lips. His gut gnaws at Gustavo's audacity to be intruding on his mission.

"You know, you're a real son of a bitch."

At the confession, Bob's pulse drops, and he glances at the control house to see whether Dymitry is on the same pages with regard to escaping. Both Bob and Dymitry know of the consequences that are slowly creeping up on them. Seeing how they are outnumbered by the divers, Bob continues to stand in silence at Gustavo's side. Each second starts to weigh heavily. Each second seems to tick by longer. Each breath trickles heat and panic.

For Bob to simply abandon his current position would entitle Gustavo to full control. For Dymitry to barge out of the control station would enable another one of Gustavo's men to seize captainship and fully regain charge of their passage. Dymitry continues to scan his room quietly in the hopes of acquiring a weapon and gaining the upper hand by holding Gustavo captive, but to no avail. The sheerleg barely has an armory, except for a radar system that seems to be sending out disoriented wavelengths as an emergency message to Jack.

Jack, on the other hand, has his eyes fixed on the rising boat, which leaves him oblivious to the stirring storm above the waters. Each signal beseeching its predicament is dilated by the forming bubbles. The water seems to be churning a deeper sense of nausea with each bubble rising around the U-boat. By now, all of his conversation with Alice has subsided, leaving his own eyes to water. He does not dare to blink his eyes for a split second, for fear of a mishap if he was to slacken on his duty. Alas, his worry comes true, as his eyes widen in shock upon bullets piercing through the dense waters.

One after another, the divers only make both Jack and Alice move closer to danger. Their shield of protection is being depleted with each rising moment. Each new diver before him drums havoc louder than his own faint heartbeat. Jack murmurs a denial before it turns into a chant.

"They are trying to shoot at us. Those aren't Bob's men?"

More bubbles escape as the divers plunge deeper into the cavity of the ocean, raising alarm with each fleeting second. The previous signs of aquatic life no longer exist, as all the creatures scurry to safety upon sensing the imminent fate of destruction about to unfurl.

"Jack, look over there."

Alice carefully lifts her slender finger to point up east, and his gaze follows. Some of the divers seem to be turning away, while some are floating still. To Jack, it seems the divers are deliberating on their further actions, until it dawns upon him of the risks that lurk in the waters after a certain depth. All previous dread evaporates from within Jack's mind, his tensed shoulders relaxing for a brief moment. The escaping moment grants him enough time to explain to Alice the reason the divers have retreated. They are currently located below 60 meters, at which point oxygen toxicity kicks in in deep divers, causing tunnel vision, loss of consciousness and seizures.

"So, our knight in shining armor is the depth?" Alice raises her eyebrows, trying to wrap her mind around the unfolding trouble.

A flashing of an idea makes both Alice and Jack yell for Dymitry in unison through the radio system. This is their only hope of guarding the U-boat until the current invasion can be tackled. If Dymitry were to stop the tow cable from winding, Jack would have sufficient time to unhinge the winch from the hull of the antique submarine.

"Dymitry, Dymitry, can you hear me? We need to stop the lift. We have some unexpected visitors. Dymitry?" Jack patiently waits for his friend's voice to emerge from up above, unprepared for the next revelation of horror to be dropped on him.

"He can hear you just fine, Mr. Sterling."

As soon as Gustavo's voice comes across the acoustic speaker, all blood drains from his veins, and his body turns pale. Silence follows, making Gustavo tap on the microphone. A knocking sound fills the silence of Jack's Triton.

"I know you can hear me, Sterling, so I won't waste my time waiting for your answer. I trust you have secured my U-boat carefully. I am eagerly looking forward to meeting you and thanking you in person for all your efforts. All of this would not have been possible without you, and for that, the Vatican is truly grateful."

Jack, frustrated as to what to do, holds down on the communications switch and talks back. "Gustavo, you were right. There is no gold here. She has already been ransacked, so cut a deal..." However, Jack's fabrication in the hopes of filling Gustavo with false knowledge is impeded.

"Save yourself the lies, Sterling." Gustavo takes a deep breath and mumbles incoherently before uttering, *"I've bugged your Triton, so we have been eavesdropping for quite some time. We know you were in Cuba this morning, and even know your new fiancé is with you, too. So, if you value the lives of everyone, I suggest you steady the course and bring up my U-Boat!"* Gustavo sneers.

Gustavo and his men's attention are suddenly distracted by a new group

of invaders boarding the ship.

"What the hell?" they mutter, their current irritability disrupted.

From the waters above, the floating sheerleg is surrounded by more incoming speedboats. The veiling of the massive water is crippled by more drivers cutting through the thick waters like a knife. Jack and Alice train their ears on the gun shot commotion blaring through the radio system.

"What's going on, Jack?"

"It appears someone else has been tipped off ,and has come for the treasure."

"Who?"

"The Thule Society!" *A secret organization of Neo-Nazis.*

"What do we do, Jack?" Exasperation evident in Alice's voice only makes Jack snap at her.

"I'm sorry, but we don't have much choice. Sadly, we may have to just pick a side and hope for the best, even though we won't like either outcome."

"But what about Dymitry and Bob?" Alice says with a worried face, whose glazed eyes begin to accumulate water.

His movements are restricted beyond the acrylic bubble. Knowing how immobile he is at the moment, he taps his foot anxiously in his own prison. His fist by his side itches to repel all the divers plunging into the waters. A flight of a dozen divers emerges before them, causing Jack and Alice's feelings of being trapped to be heightened to an unfolding fight. Instantly, he recalls his own combat from a few days back, how he was left to tackle the German divers. Now he they've been replaced by Gustavo's men.

Distant yells grow prominent. Jack sees the water parting before a limp body falls to their death within the trenches. Only a trail of diffusing crimson floats above before the passing currents wash away the trace of a hideous crime. Alice gasps and places her palm flat against her mouth to suppress her terror. They watch over them as several divers fight it out in the ocean, only to end in bloodshed. All screams of agony go unheard, and the life underwater continues its previous cooing of tranquility.

As the fighting ensues, Jack's eyes flicker toward the rising U-boat, then takes notice of the Triton's depth gauge, which now has reached above the 30-meter level. It no longer matters if the divers can propel themselves further into the water. Their safety net is now gone. Watching the underwater massacre, fear grips his heart tighter. He spots a German diver using a dull glistening knife to slice through yet another one of Gustavo's men. Seeing blood oozing and being washed out simultaneously, the German diver then proceeds to swim above the Triton.

Jack tries to reach Dymitry. His voice grows erratic. "Dymitry, are you there? They are trying to cut the cables! Dymitry!"

The radio goes silent. Jack and Alice look out the plastic acrylic orb and see the Triton's sliced communications cable slowly floating down past them.

Screams from Alice echo as the eerie diver now appears leaning on the outside of acylic bubble. The deep scratch with the chipped shark tooth catches the diver's eye as he begins to thrust his knife into it. Jack and Alice are defenseless. The Triton shakes back and forth. The mysterious diver continues to repeatedly jab his dull glistening knife, catching Jack's eyes, allowing for an abandoned childhood memory to cast its way to existence once more.

Jack is suddenly taken back to the summer of 1998, when his father, William Sterling, had taken him scuba diving in the lake of Gibraltar off the southern coast of Spain. It was only a couple of years after Jack had saved Dymitry's life at Camp Little Bear; this year, however, turned out to be a bit more traumatic for Jack's psyche, and one he would work hard to try to forget. The beginning of the year started with his Mom's persistent headaches and seizures. She was diagnosed with having glioblastoma, an aggressive brain tumor that took her life only three months after being discovered. There was a small funeral, with Jack and his father, Aunt Emma and Danny.

It was hard for Jack to forget, as it was a traditional Florida rainfall. The air was humid, but the sky was grey. Bald-cypress trees blowing in the wind. Everyone was dressed in black attire. To Jack's ears, the priest's voice was murmured, as it was overcome by the tapping of rain on his umbrella. Jack was trying to come to grips with death, which was difficult for a boy of twelve. He refused to believe that when he walked through his front door from school, the echoes of yelling out for his mother would go unanswered. An empty chair now sat abandoned by the dinner table. The memories of her sitting on his bed, saying good night by tucking him in and wrapping the blankets around him extra tight like a burrito. While Jack knew he was too old for that now, what he wouldn't give for one last precious moment of comfort from his mother.

Still grieving himself, William thought it best to take his son on one of his long fishing expeditions to help distract him from the pain. It didn't take Jack long to realize his father's "fishing expeditions" were exploratory underwater treasure hunting adventures. The lake of Gibraltar had been a fascination of William's for quite some time. Jack had heard the tales from his father many times of what possible artifacts lay hidden in those waters, and he couldn't help letting his imagination run wild. They would spend several weeks living on William's boat, which would later become known as *The Falcon*. The days would be spent diving underwater and exploring the world beneath, while the nights would be consumed by lying on the deck of their vessel, staring up at the stars, wondering what worlds extended past the cosmos. William had shared many stories with Jack, like the one about mysterious *U-Boat 2553*, in hopes they would one day find it; however, his attention was focused on something much bigger. Its very existence was believed to be a myth, as it was supposedly lost to the world thousands of years ago by a massive tsunami. The strange part of that conversation Jack will never forget is how his father explained to him that he was on the cusp of finding it, and he couldn't allow for any distractions, as others are getting closer.

"Was Mom or myself a distraction?" Jack asks.

William looks back, realizing what he had said. "NEVER. I will always love both of you. Don't forget that!"

That next day, after a typical dive, like any other, they were making their way back to the ship. They were passing a rock formation they had passed several times before. However, something caught Williams's eye. He gave Jack an underwater signal to wait as he sifted through the coral. Jack's attention was staring at the trench only a few feet away. While he knew he couldn't swim down there before being crushed by the pressure, he couldn't help but gaze upon the thought that just a mile or two down was probably some duetted gold scattered amongst the floor. Jack remembers his Dad telling him that while it is not cost-effective to mine, there is an estimated 20 million tons of gold dispersed throughout the ocean. For a kid, his imaginations would run wild, wanting to find some. With a quick jolt from the edge of the trench, a school of blue stripe snappers darted up and around, startling Jack back a bit. Colorful bright yellow fish who scurry about, hiding from bigger prey, Jack knew reefs were teeming oases of aquatic life that never got dull, as surprises were around every corner.

Jack turned around in amazement, as he saw his father had found an ancient relic, one Jack had never seen before. A round metallic disc with writing consisting of hieroglyphs that wrapped around the circle. Jack would learn later it was some sort of key. The mystery still haunts Jack today, because despite the relic being ancient, the hieroglyphics illuminated blue, almost as if it had some advanced electrical power, which even he knew should have been impossible. Before Jack's eyes could gaze upon it more, another light came into focus from behind his father, which gleamed off another diver; the water was a bit murky, so no one saw him coming. Just as he came into view, he had pulled out a dull glistening knife, which he thrust toward William. Despite Jack's mouth being filled by the scuba regulator, he had let out a suppressed scream of panic as he pointed in fear toward the new visitor's direction. Grabbing William's attention, he was quick to turn around, locking arms and stopping the knife from going into his own wetsuit. Like an under-

water wrestling match, they spiraled and whirled around in circles trying to overcome the other as they inched near the trench. Jack saw his father drop the artifact. As it floated down the gully, he released his grip, trying to grab it; the diver ended up stabbing William with the knife, and the relic disappeared down the trench into the darkness.

Still in buoyancy, Jack's face turns pale in fear. He is suddenly engulfed in bubbles as something swims by him with astonishing speed. As the bubbles cleared, he saw the mysterious diver now floating, as he appeared to have been rendered unconscious. Off in the distance, Jack caught a glimpse of what he could only describe as a large fish's tail disappearing beyond the line of sight... or was it something else? Worried his eyes might be deluding him due to being in a shocked state, reality kicked in as he rushed to his father's aid. Blood began to spew out of William's suit. With the artifact gone, Jack grabbed his father by the waist, helping him swim back to the boat, leaving the mysterious diver to his demise.

On the boat, William tended to his own wounds. The knife blade had pierced his wet suit, but it only grazed his side, leaving only a flesh wound. He doesn't seem to be concerned about what they lost, or the mysterious diver. Instead Jack noticed his father just staring out at sea with a smile on his face. When Jack turned his eyes to focus on what his father was looking at, a rather large splash ripples from the water.

"What was that?" Jack asked.

William looked back at Jack with a smile still beaming on his face and replied, "Just a friend, little skipper, just a friend."

After arriving back to St. Augustine, William's mind seemed to be preoccupied. Jack was just a side thought, and Jack felt it. A few days later, he was told to pack his bags, as his father had to go on another unexpected trip; only he would not be taking the *Falcon*, but sailing with an associate, and Jack would not be able to tag along. Despite the resistance and several attempts to argue his position, that he should go with him, he lost the fight and was forced to pack extra bags, as his father didn't know when he would return.

Upon arrival at Aunt Emma's, William attempted to hug Jack. Still, Jack was so furious he ran to the guest room and slammed the door closed, refusing to say goodbye. All he could hear were the soft words through the oak bedroom door of his father saying, "You will always be my little skipper, and I will be back as soon as I ca. Take care of the boat while I'm gone. I hope you will understand."

Jack refused to reply; minutes passed, his eyes turn blood shot red and slowly filled water, and pain ran down the back of his throat as he held back the tears. He couldn't hold it any longer and opened up the door to say goodbye, but his father had already gone. Aunt Emma, who was in the kitchen in tears, peered at Jack, who was standing by the front door at a loss for words, being in an unemotional state. Uncle Danny got up from his La-Z-Boy; he didn't say a word, just walked up and gave Jack a much-needed hug.

Four months had passed and still no word from William, not even so much as a letter. Summer had faded into fall, the days became shorter, and with less sunlight, the green leaves started to fade into warm pigment colors that blanketed the scenery. Aunt Emma was cooking dinner as usual, while Danny was in the living room reading the local St. Augustine paper, which is considered by today's standards to be old-fashioned, which worked for them. Jack had just gotten home from school and was sitting at the dining room table doing his homework when the doorbell rang. All the sounds in the room fell silent. It was a bit unusual, as they don't get many visitors, especially this time of day. All of Jack's logic and deductions of who was at the door had come to a halt within his mind, as he couldn't bear the result. When Aunt Emma finally opened the door, two police officers stood there, asking if they had by chance heard from William. With the scared look on Emma's face and eyes starting to swell, they already knew the answer for which they were seeking. The officers took their hats off as they were saddened to tell Emma the news of a fishing charter that was recently reported lost at sea by the Galician Government. It appeared that the vessel had reported leaving St.

Augustine, and was supposed to meet up with a diving crew over in Spain; they never reached their final destination, as it was over fourteen weeks ago.

"Again, the Spanish coast guard isn't the best in response time. Our coastguard made a few calls, and is currently searching with a couple of their boats and choppers," they said. There was no tracking system registered for that fishing charter; according to St. Augustine's harbor, the last reported manifest listed one of the crew members as a William Sterling, bearing this address for emergency contacts. While US Coast Guard hoped for the best, the likelihood of them being found was doubtful, given the time frame. The officers gave their condolences and parted ways, informing them that they would report if anything changes. Jack listened to the entire conversation from the other room, guilt growing on his heart for refusing to say goodbye, denial quickly setting in. He refused to believe his father was lost at sea. He was better than that, and no one could lose both parents in a single year. Jack internally would commit himself to spend as long as it took to find him. Aunt Emma had walked in to talk with Jack, sitting at the table, and didn't even know he was shedding tears.

"Jack," said Aunt Emma.

He wiped the tears off his face and went back to his homework. Young Jack refused to acknowledge his Aunt was in the room, as he did not want to talk about it.

"JACK!" Suddenly the voice became familiar, as Alice is screaming his name, as he'd just spaced out on memories of his past. Jack's mind coming back into reality, his eyes focus on the diver who is hanging onto the outside of the acrylic bubble, making an attempt to crack it open in hopes of giving way to the massive water pressure of the vast sea, giving Jack and Alice their last breath. Like the entanglement with Bruce, Jack knew the spherical acrylic pressure hull could withstand any attempt this diver tried to make to break it. However, like an annoying misquito, why let it continue to suck onto you? Jack lurches forward, grabbing the joystick controls for one of the Triton's arms, freeing it from the U-boat.

A hideous crooked smile spreads under the diver's mask, one that had laid dormant in his psyche of evil. He comes to realisation that he's got an underwater drill. He pulls it out from his side belt, only to suddenly be caught off guard by the lack of sudden air that stopped from his regulator. The diver's eyes bulge and his brows furrow, as he begins gasping for air. Dropping the drill, he turns and looks back at his hose connected to his air tank, where the Triton's mechanical arm now pinches it off. Appearing like a wounded seal, the diver shakes and jolts back and forth, using his last breath trying to release his air hose from the sub's deadly grip.

"Jack, will he break free?" Alice inquires in fear.

"Not with that hydraulic arm, nothing can break..." Jack is suddenly interrupted by Alice's screams as a large thump hits the top of the Triton. Jack's eye quickly adjusts, as his familiar acquaintance has returned. The jaws of death of a great white shark instantaneously bite into the diver, ripping him free of the Triton's hydraulic arm and his lower torso.

Both Jack and Alice holler in disbelief as they watch the great white shark carry the upper half of him off into the distance, chewing on his newfound food, savoring every bite.

"Yeah, okay, Bruce could break it free," Jack says with a new panic in his voice.

Knowing that with all the bloodshed from the fighting parties, the sharks have now arrived, and it's an open buffet.

Back on top of the Craig, with the confusion of both Gustavo's men, the original Adler Enterprise crew, and the new Neo-Nazi visitors wearing swastika emblems, it's a fight to survive as the chaos continues. Several men are on deck swinging their hands into each other's faces, and that is soon interrupted by a spray of bullets from both invading parties, leaving the Adler crew defenseless victims of the crossfire. Dymitry manages to escape and make it up to the control room, bolting the doors behind him, but not going unseen. Inside, Dymitry grabs the radio and attempts to communicate down

to the Triton.

"Jack, Alice, can you hear me? Come in."

No response.

"The communication must be down... Jack, if you can hear me, I'm going to try to stop the lift. It's too dangerous…" Dymitry is suddenly interrupted by three Neo-Nazi men shattering the glass before unlatching the bolt and entering. His eyes expand, noticing how each man possesses a dagger firmly clasped in their grip. While Dymitry's heart skips a beat in fear, he seizes the moment to lurch at the man on his left. In one swift movement, Dymitry locks the assailant's hand and twists it behind his back before smashing his head against the steel support beam, rendering him unconscious. The hit causes the other two men to look in his direction, and they quickly advance. Dymitry grasps the dagger as fast as possible from the man on the floor and swerves to his left, dodging one of the assailants. Still, the last man in front of him blocks the door, making Dymitry raise his leg and kick the man in his groin, sending him to the floor. Without hesitating this time, and as the second man turns to look at him with bloodshot red eyes, Dymitry pierces the dagger against the man's chest and runs out on the deck in hopes of making it to the back of the ship to stop the lift.

Before Dymitry lies bodies scattered around the floor. His eyes sweep the area, which is now doused in blood from several crew members from Adler Enterprises, the Neo-Nazi strangers, and some of Gustavo's men. The remaining German tears out of the control room and pulls out a gun from his inner jacket and aims it directly at Dymitry, who sees him and closes his eyes to avoid looking at the face of death. A single gunshot goes off, echoing into the sky, soon followed by the body's sound hitting the ground.

All the divers have plummeted to their demise under the sea, casualties of underwater greed and shark's hunger. Jack and Alice strap themselves in their seats as they see the two hundred-and-fourteen-foot U-boat finally ascending out of the water. What was thought to be dead now breathes life once more, letting fresh air fan its tainted body. Despite the large red balloon stuffed inside the U-Boat that fills its cavity, it is now slowly deflating, the remaining water pouring out of the damaged submarine's hull, along with some remaining sea life that had made this submarine a home for several decades.

Like a slow elevator awaiting that final floor, both the U-boat and Triton rise just above the ship's main deck, slowly being pulled up by the ship's crane. Alice and Jack's faces express despair, as they can see the human carnage lying about the floor. A bloody massacre has taken place, and despite their run-in with death, Jack is thankful Alice wasn't around to be an exposed victim on board this vessel. His only worry now is for his friends.

Soon, the automatic crane swings from the stern to quarter starboard, hanging over the deck's edge before coming to a complete stop, causing both vessels to slowly rock back and forth as the water continues to drip down. There was no crew to greet them, nor anyone to assist them down. They were lucky the crane's lift was in autopilot. Dymitry was exceptional in calculating the exact distance he needed to raise and clear both the U-Boat and Triton, as it is just dangling only a few feet above the deck.

Jack unbuckles his belt and he turns to place a simple kiss on Alice's forehead.

"Stay here until I come and get you, okay?"

"WHAT? NO, JACK! NO! I am not leaving you alone. I'm going with you. Help me out of this thing."

Alice attempts to unbuckle herself, but Jack presses his lips to hers. He slowly untangles her hand from her belt latch. He breaks the kiss, moving back to wipe the lone tear with his thumb that has escaped the corner of her left eye.

"Alice, everything is going to be alright," replies Jack.

Jack hits the compressor shut off valve to allow the red balloon to start

to deflate, then opens the hatch to climb out, shutting it back behind him. The nauseating smell of spilled blood fills Jack's nose to remind him of the catastrophe that has taken place. Jack walks over to the crane's controls and puts the release lever into the locked position, a preventive measure to make sure it doesn't slip and unwind back into the sea. Knowing Jack is located at the back of the ship, hoping everyone has congregated upfront, he proceeds to tread lightly, as he does not know who is hiding in the shadows.

Each footstep closer, he dreads the thought of what has happened to Dymitry and Bob; from the looks of this slaughter, he can't tell if Gustavo triumphed or if they will be following a new Nazi regime. Either outcome is bleak, and they may end up like Alder's crew, innocent victims of gluttony and power. Jack begins to regret even bringing up the coin and looking for the Spear of Destiny; when do artifacts become more valuable when they are kept hidden from the world? Upon the empty walk toward the control room, he spots a set of dead bodies; one of them is face down, as a bullet has pierced right through his chest. Jack turns his body over with the toe of his shoe, spotting a 9mm still clutched in the dead man's palm. Eagerly, Jack grabs hold of his gun for his safety, then checks the chamber to see that it is still loaded. Looking at the deceased soldier and seeing the direction his body landed, the estimated bullet direction, along with his gun position told Jack that this guy was about to fire upon someone before someone else got the better of him. Jack's attention swiftly focuses on another direction as a commotion begins to unfold. Jack continues to advance. In the far distance, his worries instantly disappear, and restraint sets in as he sees both Bob and Dymitry, still alive, standing at the front of the ship being held at gunpoint by Gustavo's subordinates. In front of them, Gustavo is kneeling on top of one of the remaining Neo-Nazi soldiers.

Gustavo's fist lands across the soldiers face with a forceful thrust while his other hand is holding his hair, repeatedly bruising his face with such satisfaction, leaving his fist coated in the assailant's blood.

"I'm not going to ask again, you, Nazi bastard! How did you know we were here?" threatens Gustavo.

The soldier, whose back is currently on the ground, looks over toward Dymitry and Bob's direction. A feeling of pride overwhelms him as he looks back at Gustavo, gives a grin, then speaks up in a broad German accent, "MEIN FÜHRER SAYS…GO TO HELL YOU DIRTY SICILIAN PIG!"

The soldier raises his hand to smash his fist alongside Gustavo's face, but is quickly blocked. With a forceful thrust, Gustavo then smashes his forehead into the solders head. Within a span, Gustavo raises his right fist and then repeatedly propels it into his victim. Having failed to notice that the Neo-Nazi's hand secretly reaches for a small gun tucked inside his boot. In one swift move the soldier hits Gustavo across the head, pulling back the hammer, and now holds him at gunpoint. Gustavo's men are caught off guard, and too slow to react. The barrel pressed to Gustavo's temple makes him gulp in fear.

With the hammer cocked, the soldier then proceeds to tighten his finger and pulls the trigger, causing another gunshot to announce a death. Seconds pass by, and no one moves a muscle. Gustavo's eyes become relieved, realizing he is still alive, as he turns his head toward the collapsing body of the Neo-Nazi soldier. Soon the blood from the bullet hole in the back of his head forms a pool around Gustavo's black Oxfords. Looking up, his men pull their weapons toward Jack, standing there with the barrel of his gun smoking.

"Now we are even, Gustavo." Jack throws down his gun to look over at his friends, checking to see if they are okay as they give back their assurances with simple nods.

Gustavo, looking back down at the dead soldier, realizes that he almost took his life. He screams out of rage, punching the dead man's bleeding face several more times with his fist before dragging him by the hair, only to lift his body in the air and throw it overboard. As if it was a timed event at Sea World, no sooner did the Neo-Nazi's body hit the ocean's top surface layer than multiple sharks emerge out of the water and begin to tear his body to

shreds. Gustavo, enjoying the final result for this unexpected visitor, puts a smile back on his face, and then he proceeds to walk over to where Jack is standing. He pulls out a handkerchief from inside his jacket and begins to wipe off the blood from his hands.

"They were with the Thule Society, looking to get back what was promised to their ancestors. The man on the Marlin vessel the other day was most likely one of their leaders; I take it you did not catch him?" Jack inquires.

Gustavo looks sternly at Jack. "No, he gave us the slip, a mistake that will not happen again, I can assure you. We have to assume they have been listening, much as we were."

Dymitry shakes his head out of frustration. "That's it! When we get back home, I'm fumigating everything…too many bugs."

Gustavo looks back and gives a half a smile, then continues talking with Jack. "Your friend is funny. He was about to take a bullet from one these guys til my men stopped them. See, we work great together. I save you, you save me, we save them, one big happy family. Everyone is now safe."

"What about the innocent crew from this ship? They are all dead now," Bob disappointedly states.

Gustavo looks back at Bob, shrugs his shoulders, and smirks. "It's a casualty of war; I've lost good men today too. But you want to blame anyone, blame yourselves. I warned you Sterling, not to continue on this path. But now we are here. Let's go get my treasure!" He then proceeds to put his flat palms together, rubbing them back and forth as his inner soul succumbs to greed.

"I'm sure this isn't the last we have seen of them?" Jack responds.

A curse escapes Gustavo's lips. Ignoring the warning, he nods his head for Jack to get going, gesturing for his men to lead everyone to the back of the ship, reminding them they maintain control, as they have the weapons.

Their erratic heartbeats and shivering soul wait for the daunting reality.

While the competition for Gustavo comes to an end, Jack knows this is the beginning of another dilemma. Another portal of misfortune seems to have opened, and draws Jack in. A pounding headache erupts against his throbbing temples as he walks in silence toward the stern of the ship, oblivious to the key that is about to unlock another series of bloodshed and an inescapable adventure.

His breath mingles with the stench of sultry ocean breeze and the rotting of blood. His mind turns hazy in fear for Alice's safety, who is patiently waiting for him to return and help her to safety. Realizing how Jack is in far deeper water than before, he condemns himself for having proposed to Alice and putting her through his troubles permanently. Is this his love, and all he could offer her? Alice didn't seem to fully understand his desire behind his work, but she was trying, and that's all he could ask for.

Chapter XII

Enigma

A fiery gasp erupts as water still cascades down the sides of the oblong U-boat, startling everyone on deck. Each set of eyes snap in the direction of the noise, hearts coming to a standstill. The red balloon has deflated. At the moment, animosity and resentment are forgotten.

Unbeknownst to the *U-boat 2553* Elektro, harboring no treasure or a prophecy of eternal dominance, Jack, Gustavo, Bob, and Dymitry all walk toward the boat, captivated in an elusive trance. Gustavo continues to circle the vessel like a predator scrutinizing its prey. The rest of the men only continue to gawk. A shuffling sound from behind brings Jack back to the present, and he turns to notice that Alice has set herself free from the protection of the mini-sub. As soon as she joins them, Jack holds her free hand tightly in his cold one, seeking her warmth. All it takes is for her to look at him, and he blinks his eyes and provides her with an affirmation.

Slowly, the very source responsible for extracting the submarine from its decay surrenders itself to death. Noticing how the balloon is no longer a threat, that it isn't going to explode and unleash a wind strong enough to throw them overboard, Gustavo beckons his men to survey the hole incurred all those years ago along the back of the ship. They use it as a carved passage, conceiving of the hollow to be filled like a cave full of treasure.

However, the perceived cave is full of an empty promise. Water, mist, sea salt, algae, and loosely scattered gold coins are all that welcome Gustavo and his men. He runs a hand through his thick gray hair to push the strands away from his eyes. No promise of wealth, and certainly no source of an immortal power staff lies before their naked eyes.

The echoes of Jack and his companions fill the chilly cold within the submarine, making Gustavo turn in his direction with a scowl.

He lifts his finger, and spits rage toward Jack. "You...you stole all the treasure and the Spear of Destiny before we showed up, didn't you?"

Gustavo continues to take a menacing step toward the entrance of the hole. Jack's eyes roam around the enclosed tunnel-like space, and he takes in all the blown-out meters and levers. Metal bars and pipes run along the circular walls. Rust and bleak char are encrusted, along with traces of solidified oil and algae. Paths of moss and seaweed drape the pipes running along the foot of the vessel.

"Sir, what seems like the former control room and the crew room are clear. There is nothing but water, rust, and broken metal everywhere."

Gustavo's previous snarl returns and he storms in the direction of Jack and Alice, standing beneath the broken hull of the control room. In a swift movement, before Jack can retaliate, Gustavo leaps to grab hold of Alice's wrist firmly. Tugging her toward him, he holds her firmly against his chest and pulls out his gun from beneath his belt before placing it against her temple. His chest roughly rises and collapses, giving all the members in the room enough time to take in the new hostage.

"Let me go..." Alice shrieks, struggling underneath the iron grip of Gus-

tavo's arm.

But he only snakes his hand tighter around her neck and forces the muzzle of the gun further into her temple.

"Gustavo, put the gun away," Bob cries.

"You are insane. Let her go. She has nothing to do with it," Dymitry yells.

While the others yell, Jack maintains his composure and lifts his hand in front to pacify Gustavo. Jack observes Gustavo's paling red face mirroring his. His breath comes out hot, ready to burn the man caging Alice. Alas, Jack knows the consequences all too well if he were to take a step forward.

"I'm insane? I warned you, Jack, against trying to outsmart me. But you paid no heed. Now I give you one last chance. You surrender the Spear of Destiny and the treasure, or I will blow her brains out, and then feed her body to the sharks."

The anger radiating off Gustavo causes heat to rush up his neck. No longer is the ambiance peculiar. Jack is familiar with how often such heated conversations will turn out. Nothing but sheer rage will prevail, defying the remote possibility of a truce. The savagery streaking Gustavo's eyes only grows vivid, and Jack sneers at him. However, Jack fails to see that the fear and anger lurking in his eyes only makes him vulnerable for Gustavo to exploit Alice. She is his greatest strength, and his only kryptonite. Jack notices Alice's slight quiver, and his fist clenches by his side. Gritting his teeth, he finally breaks the silence, but never once glances at Gustavo. His eyes are trained on Alice, who pleads with him in secrecy.

"I can assure you, Gustavo, that I am not a psychotic narcissist wanting to have a holy lance of power beyond my control. I am not power hungry." Jack pauses so he can think. "So how about this: you let Alice go, and I will help you find it. Or you can kill all of us, and you will go back to the Vatican empty-handed, but only if I don't kill you first."

Gustavo's vein running along his neck throbs with anguish and fury. His heart roars louder with wrath. He roughly twists Alice's harm behind her, causing a sharp yelp of pain to erupt from her parched lips. Jack, willing to pound Gustavo, charges forward, but stops immediately as Gustavo places his finger on the trigger. His feet halt and helplessness courses through his veins. He knows it is all his fault for letting her accompany him. His mind starts to delude itself... what if he would have left Alice alone? But to no avail.

"You are in no position to bargain. So I suggest you better get going. Hunt down this U-Boat with those other two pathetic companions of yours."

Gustavo spits in disgust and holds Alice by her wrist. Pointing his gun behind, he motions for his men to recklessly shove Dymitry and Bob in front. Jack offers Dymitry an apologetic smile, and in turn, his friend places his hand on his shoulders for comfort. Dymitry knows the truth better than anyone else of how these things will often go down. After all, he has been with Jack as far back as Camp Little Bear. He knows the bitterness, hardships, obstacles, and the dull exhaustion that comes with such forced adventures. It is the thrill that makes both of them go forward and solve any riddle, no matter how encrypted.

Heaving a sigh, all three of them walk in absolute darkness and silence inward. All of the previous hatches now lay idle. Their hinges no longer function, making their crawl less excruciating. The U-boat appears to have been traveling with just the bare essentials, as the submarine seems to have been stripped away of standard contents. While he knew it was impossible, Jack couldn't help but wonder if sea pirates, or worse, treasure hunters had robbed it. Noticing what once must have been the source of oxygen, now the induction valves, are torn apart by time and covered in sea dust. The foul stench of age and rust overpower them as they venture further in. They move across the electric diesel room to come across blown-out and charred pipes.

Only the last reading of vitals now remains to quench their curiosity. Jack lets his eyes go over all of the various meters as he stops for a second in the control room. Each meter only tugs at his heart, recounting the strenuous fifty-five day journey the U-boat had been making to Bariloche. Its last speed

before it submerged as per the speed meter indicates 7.6 knots. Stuck in the Devils Triangle, as the map above the meter had pinned, a distance of 9,321 miles seemed to be covered in…Jack narrows his eyes to focus on the now smudged number. Unsure if the figure read '839 hours' or '900', he settles for a figure in between.

His eyes move to the other meter beside it, only the red arrow indicates the speed to be above 17 knots. Must have been when the submarine was still on the surface, Jack surmises. With a heavy heart, he moves forward.

A miserable and buried beseechment of help seems to weave amidst them, making Dymitry shudder. While to Jack, the drowned pain and agony is a common sight, for the other two it is heart crippling. Such had been the life of Jack for as long as he could remember. The trio scurry on with their search, but to no avail.

Having struck no luck in this room as well, Jack can't help but think more gold coins were lying on the bottom of the ocean bed in Cuba than what they are seeing inside the U-Boat now. They crawl out to the other hatch and make their way to the rear with oil-tainted thumbprints. Nausea wafts over them with a cold breeze, but their eyes take in a barren and forlorn motor room. The room, despite the oxidation through the course of years, gives a clear view of shattered glass unable to withstand the pressure of misfortune.

Fearing defeat, they finally enter the rear of the submarine to find what everyone seeks—resting their eyes on what has only been up to this time envisioned in their heads with rumors and childhood bedtime stories. Before them lies the outside of the massive vault that the Nazi crewmembers spoke of, taking up a quarter of the entire U-Boat, constructed out of iron but covered in an outer shell of stainless steel. With great success, too, despite the rest of the vessel, this room managed to resist any corrosion, rust, or algae. If the treasure were inside, it surely would have been protected. However, Jack's mind can't help but rush to what was coming next.

The large ten-foot-wide door rests halfway open, as the hinges which were not lined in stainless steel, but iron were rusted shut, forcing the vault door to be stuck in its current position. If this was the last voyage of a sinking U-Boat and a particular door to Hitler's most prized possessions, it being left open could only mean one thing. The treasure is long gone.

While it appears most of the damage was to the outside of the U-Boat, inside, just as Jack had already feared, along the walls of the vault, black fire stains and shrapnel marks indicate the direction of impact from the US torpedo. The impact was in just the right spot, damaging the airtight vault. Taking in too much water, she went down shortly after. Over time the back-up generator, dehumidifier, and pressure sensors were all corroded. The room that took up so much of the German vessel was now empty. The search for the treasure appeared to be worthless, much like the hopes and dreams of the dictator who had once owned them. Had it not been for the submarine's numeric identifier, and the specially constructed room, Jack would have thought he had the wrong U-Boat. There were a couple of straggling gold coins wedged in odd places in the room, which confirmed the U-Boat's true identity, but Gustavo's men were quick to snatch them up.

"STERLING! If you're messing with me, I swear," bellows out Gustavo as he clinches the arms of Alice, who is still held as a hostage.

"Calm down, Gustavo. I just need some time," replies Jack.

"Jack, this can't be. The Spear of Destiny has to be here. Maybe we missed something back in Cuba?" Bob says, perplexed.

"No, there were some small treasure droppings among the debris, but nothing from what is missing of this magnitude."

Ready to turn away, Bob trips over an unseen sight on the floor. Giving out a yell of frustration, he says, "Damn it, I just fell over a metal beam bolted to the floor. Seems like a weird place to put that. What purposes does it serve, but to trip older aged men?"

Dymitry notices another one next to it. Jack crouches on the floor to in-

spect a set of parallel bars. Tarnished yet intact. The bars run neatly along the floor as if bolted to an unrevealed discovery.

"Is this strange, or is there a rear hatch on this thing?" inquires Jack.

"A rear hatch? You mean like a tailboard?" Dymitry asks with a voice brimming with curiosity.

"Seems like it," Jack nods.

Jack leans closer and gently taps to check if the area is hollow. A vacant echo comes, leaving all of them wide-eyed.

"A midget sub!" Jack turns to look at Bob and Dymitry while gaining the attention of Gustavo. "Designed toward the end of the war to attack Allied ships near landing beaches or harbors, midget subs were sometimes used for reconnaissance, but this one was used as a..."

"An escape sub!" Bob chimes in.

"Yes, normally the hatch only opens to fill water in the backroom, in this case the vault, letting the mini-escape sub float out. And then the hatch is closed back to decompress all the water." Jack examines the damage in the side of the vessel, and continues. "With the torpedo hole, the hatch of the U-Boat couldn't work, however, the hole along the ballast side of the submarine was large enough for the midget sub to escape through. The room was already filled with water, so all the escape sub had to do was drive out of here."

"Through the hole?" Gustavo hesitates.

"Yes."

"And the treasure?"

"Well...clearly, Captain Prien didn't go down with his ship," Jack smirks.

"How could all that treasure fit into a midget sub?"

"It couldn't!" Jack pauses. "Not in one trip anyway." Like a detective on a case, Jack starts to move toward the rear. "Notice all these markings around the blast opening. That is not wreckage, but metal on metal scraping against one another. The midget sub was just barely small enough to get through, but there are several of them, showing me that he made several trips."

"So, someone else has had the treasure and been keeping it secret all this time?" asks Gustavo as Jack nods.

"Possibly the Germans?" Bob replies.

Jack thinks out loud. "But then why would the Germans be after it, if they already have it?" He scratches his chin, then continues, "Prien is long dead by now and we have we never heard of any stories of the Holy Lance since Hitler. It might be impossible to find it now?"

Bob sighs after hearing of yet another failure.

Jack's findings leaves Gustavo gritting his teeth more. Indignation creeps up his neck. His grip loosens on Alice's wrist, and she seizes the opportunity to flee to Jack. Slowly, Gustavo lifts his gaze from the hatch and looks at the empty faces of his victims. He has come this far, expecting for a fortune to be waiting for him. And now to bear the thought of his fragmental honor collapsing leaves him breathing out his irritation.

Gustavo moves in to threaten everyone. "If such is the case, and there is nothing for me to yield off this ghost ship, then none of you any longer serve a purpose, only putting the Vatican in danger with what you know." The venomous words cause Jack's brow to furrow. Gustavo locks his eyes with Jack's, his brimming with a vengeance and Jack's burning with caution.

"Don't take it personally. It is necessary to protect the national interest of all nations. I'm truly sorry it has to go down this way."

"I'll bet you are," Bob challenges.

Gustavo nods. "Let these waters be your final resting ground." Gustavo signals to his men. "Bring this redundant lot back out."

As Gustavo walks out, detached clouds of anxiety hover above him. Each one of his men holds a gun before them and points them at Jack, Bob, Dymitry, and Alice before ushering them out the rear. Knowing how they are unequipped to pursue armed combat, they oblige to the orders and steadily cross the hatch. But their minds suffer a turmoil of their own. The word "escape" seems like a far-fetched notion to them.

No longer affected by the motion of the sea, no longer being manipulated by time, and no longer being affected by the carefree horizon above their heads, a flicker of hope resonates before Jack. Ignoring the yell that comes from behind his shoulder, his feet drag him toward the trivial flame waiting to be rekindled by his blistering spark of valor. A box of oddities gives its glimpse, strapped amidst the inner walls of the common way.

Jack conspires to get out of the situation. "Gustavo, hold up. I think I might have something for you?"

Curiosity hazes his mind. Gustavo gives a nod for Jack to check it out, while Jack's friends turn into silent spectators waiting on a prize to be uncovered for all.

His fingers reach through the velvety seaweeds tangled above to feel underneath it, and he tugs on them before disposing of them. The notion is enough to alert Jack that the box was not always on board. Finally, Jack musters the courage and tightens his hold around the box to pluck it off the wall. His first tug is unfruitful, making him knock at the box from above, and a clicking sound echoes. He slides his finger underneath the box and extracts it. Swiping his fingers on it to get rid of the traces of sea salt and impurities, he notices the box was constructed of wood and fits his palm perfectly. Much to his dismay, the box has no latch or lock. With a slight twist, its upper half comes off.

"What is that?" asks Alice, as Bob quickly comes to Jack's side to gawk at the swastika symbol carved on top of another wooden box.

Not knowing how to quench Bob's curiosity, Jack merely shrugs. In si-

lence, they continue to inspect the box. Their breaths start to create an aware-
ness of time passing by, much like the ticking of a clock. Another seaweed
embedded in the middle of the symbol is removed by Jack to uncover a keyhole in the middle of the box.

"I think it's a message box."

Gustavo looks up to Bob and walks closer to them, demanding that Jack
open the box. Having little say over what Gustavo has over them, Jack proceeds to hold the lid. But before he can tug on it, Bob swiftly smacks his
hand.

"Are you insane, boy? You think the Germans will be stupid enough to
leave a message box unguarded?"

"I'm not," Jack remarks.

Dymitry is even more curious. "Wait, you're not saying the box will release poison? Or shoot rockets or something?"

"No, Dymitry. These coffers are known as puzzle boxes. They can be
opened by solving a puzzle; the message is usually encrypted in a crafted
riddle. If unsolved, the box can work as a bomb and explode internally."

Jack's revelation makes Dymitry and Alice take a step back, along with
Gustavo, and he scoffs at him.

"I don't have that much time to waste. Just smash it already," Gustavo
grumbles.

"Um, excuse me? Did you not hear what I just said? You cannot tamper
with the box. It will damage whatever lies inside. You need to solve the riddle!"

Gustavo grabs the box and shakes it against his ear, everyone afraid that
he might destroy whatever is inside. Gustavo throws the wooden coffer back
to Jack, who catches it. "Well, one of you had better and figure it out...and
fast."

Jack's chest moves up and down heavily, and he continues to tame his breath. Closing his eyes, Jack runs his tongue across his now chapped lips. Wondering of an alternate escape, he temporarily resigns his soul to induce peace for his friend's safety sake. "I…I can try to solve the puzzle."

Not one of them bothers to inquire about the how's and if's associated with solving the puzzle. They let Jack take the lead. Years ago, in the company of his father, he was often given the task of solving puzzles. Growing up, the passion for solving mysteries only had led him to Cast Away Tow Services. His occupation came with enough practice for him to crack his mind open to the endless possibilities of a lost vessel, before unstringing a web of an enigmas, which was initially why he was good at his job working for eMarine.

Time passes as Jack twists and turns the box, managing to slide open a corner of it, much to his surprise. A pop follows and opens a lower right-side drawer at the bottom of the box. The sight of vacancy leaves him pulling out the drawer in urgency and annoyance. As if a reward for his impatience, he uncovers yet another hidden wooden compartment with a long wooden peg.

Dymitry breaks the concentrated silence. "Jack, you should totally put Alice's wedding ring in a box like this."

Jack looks up at Alice, remembering the diamond from the Triton. "Alice, the ring?"

Alice smiles. "Don't worry, I have it. Wouldn't forget that."

"We don't have time for this. I'm getting very impatient." Gustavo pulls back his coat and puts his hand on his gun handle.

Jack moves his bloodshot eyes to glare, wanting to bury Gustavo six feet down. But sensing him shooting daggers at the man quiets him down. Jack gets back to the task at hand, of liberating a secret that will lure him toward a path of calamity. He continues to manipulate the box, and pulls the left corner down, revealing a small hole in the back. Furrows form on his forehead and beads of sweat roll down his jaw, dampening the collar of his shirt. He places the small wooden peg from the hidden compartment into the hole, letting one more wooden drawer of significance come forth.

Unlike the last time, Jack's vision is blessed with a metal skeleton key. Greedily, he picks up the key and inserts it in the prominent keyhole, sitting proudly on top of the box. But, failing to turn it, the reticent box mocks his state of misery. He closes his eyes, cursing under his breath, wanting to exert all his powers on it.

Before Jack can destroy the box, Alice senses his rising temper and snatches the box from his hand. With a tender touch, she presses her finger on the keyhole plate to slide it down, giving way for the key to enter its designated lock fully. It turns silkily.

The box finally opens, and their breaths hitch in their throats. For seconds, their hearts refuse to pronounce yet another beat. Panic and agitation defy their sensibility, and Alice picks out an aging roll of paper. A strong stench of flint magnesium causes distaste to spread all over their senses.

As Jack had noted, "It is one of the most astute precautionary measures in case of the box landing into the wrong hands. Had the box been broken as he had demanded before, the magnesium would have caught fire and burnt the very message scribbled in the cigar-like paper." There is however one last box door Jack notes, but the lock uses a combination to open.

"The roll of paper must be the combination? "

"Read it out, Alice."

"It's in German," Jack remarked.

Everyone looks at Gustavo, who only shrugs his shoulders and replies, "Not all Italians speak German."

Bob takes the paper from her, seeing eight columns having nine rows of five digits that were what seemed a random mix of numbers and letters.

His eyes review the digits multiple times, and he runs his hand through his disheveled hair. The words, bold and simple, hold a set of meaning hard to grasp. Each column contradicts the first. Each sentence defies the odds of the latter.

"Some message," Bob says. "It makes no sense."

"It's an enigma…" Jack replies.

He is met with questioning gazes. Jack raises his eyebrows quizzically and Bob puts the paper back down.

"See, during World War II, the Germans used to communicate through coded messages. Unfortunately, we need an Enigma Machine to figure it out."

"There might be one on the ship?" Alice wonders.

Bob is frustrated. "So what? Even if we were to find one, weren't these things impossible to be decoded, Jack?"

Dymitry has been holding his tongue, as he can hardly wait to tell the news. "I can do it!"

Bob chokes on air, his eyes watering, not beliving what he is hearing. "I'm sorry, are you claiming you can crack this code? Did you even find the Enigma Machine? Or are you just rubbing salt on our wounds?"

It was not the response Dymitry was hoping for. "I am not joking. We don't even need to find the Enigma Machine." Dymitry stands straighter, his chest protruding out now and his demeanor turning somber.

"Everyone knows solving mysteries and puzzles and unearthing treasure is Jack's thing. Computers and secret codes, that's mine. You played your part Jack, now it's my turn to do my half."

Dymitry walks back to Bob holding the box, and pulls out his cell phone. "I do however need Wi-Fi. No bars being out at sea. If you let me go back to the *Calypso* and use my laptop?" Gustavo is getting impatient. "I have a satellite phone. You can share my hotspot."

"And the password is?"

"The number four." And then Gustavo whispers out of embarrassment as his lips utter these words. "'Porn use only,' all lower case."

Everyone stares at Gustavo, who snaps back, "Don't judge me!"

Dymitry hits a few keys on his phone. "We designed an app based on the algorithms used by Alan Turing to decipher the Enigma Code."

Within a few more quick strokes the scroll of paper produced the alphanumeric combination that was needed to unlock the drawer of the box. "Done!" Dymitry shouts.

"What the Americans wouldn't pay to have had that back in the war. Just amazing," Bob states.

Jack smiles. "Good job, Dymitry."

Jack carefully unlatches the box, only for a leather brown diary to stumble out. He runs his fingers over the initials engraved at the bottom: "K. H."

After prying open and realizing all of the contents are scribbled in German, Jack spares no time and hands them over to Bob for translation. The old man leisurely flips through the contents. No shame or guilt in disrespecting the privacy of a diary, as it was far from entertaining for them to be divulging in the secrets of the past. Bob reckons that whoever owned the diary made various entries on different dates.

"What does it say?" Gustavo demands, making Bob frown.

He flips to the next page, only to be flipping the rest of the pages erratically as his eyes grow bloodshot red. He looks up to meet the eyes of everyone else before him, but his voice has lost its courage.

"Don't just stand there, Bob. What happened?"

Bob translates and reads the journal out loud.

April 24th, 1945.

Coordinates malfunctioned while passing through Bermuda. Four days ago, the U-Boat was hit by surprise with a US Navy torpedo. The crew abandoned ship, as we were forced to submerge during the attack. I can only hope sub-lieutenant Müller, who was captured by the Allies, intentionally was successful in getting out the word to alert the German forces of our locator beacon that we have now powered. Führer knows the frequency, and I'm confident he will not leave his treasure nor his men to suffer. Unfortunately, we are dragging along the ocean floor; too much water is coming in on the ballast side. I write to you from inside the control room where Captain Prien and I have managed to hold back the water pressure for the time being. U-Boat 2553 is a sturdy vessel, and I'm proud to have served on her. Not sure how much longer we will last, and hope the Kriegsmarine will rescue us soon. Captain Prien refuses to surface, too risky for cargo to fall in the enemy's hands. The Captain is still determined to make it to Argentina. Heil Hitler.—Lieutenant Klaus Herberger.

April 27th.

We have now lost all our power; soon the water will give way as it continues to leak even in the control room slowly. Bariloche is no longer an option. We can no longer wait on the Kriegsmarine. May the Führer have mercy on us and Captain Prien. I have used the oxygen rebreather and went down to opened up the vault. I now see the treasure stored as compared to what the only the gods may hold; however, the real beauty lies in the mini-sub identified as Seehund. We saw it stashed away inside the vault. Luckily, the damage in the rear of the U-Boat is just wide enough for the Seehund to pass through. With only enough room for the two of us. Captain Prien thought it best we only take the Holy Lance, as he knows that is Führer's top priority. We can only hope and pray the Kriegsmarine will find the U-Boat and other treasure before it falls into the Allies' hands. Captain Prien has given me confidence we will find a safe haven and make it back to Europe, as he has done this before. I will leave this journal here, and hopefully, we reach contact. Heil Hitler - Lieutenant Klaus Herberger.

"This is where it gets interesting," Bob notes as he returns to the journal.

May 20th, 1945

Captain Prien and I have discovered a subterranean cenote near the Yucatan Peninsula, completely habitable, where we took refuge. We have rigged out an outside container to the mini-sub, allowing us to make several trips back and forth, collecting the rest of the Gold and treasures. From the looks of the U-Boat, you have not yet made contact. Do hope you plan on doing it soon? I know the locator beacon will not last much longer, five days max? Our new location can be found at 20° 30' 48.474 [lat] 86° 45' 26.568 [long] Will we protect Führer's cargo at all costs and wait for your arrival. — Lieutenant Klaus Herberger.

"Yucatan? That's not too far from where we found the *Fly 460?*" Dymitry asks.

Jack clarifies, "Yes, which would explain why we found the original gold coin there, dropping one or two coins along the way."

"What's a subterranean cenote?" Alice inquires.

"Think of it as a natural sinkhole or pit on the surface, massively deep, yet on the bottom is a pool of water, in this case leading to the ocean," adds Jack.

Bob interjects, "Hold on, Jack, this where it gets bizarre. Klaus writes one last entry."

With a raised eyebrow Alice gets concerned. "Wait, you're saying they lived down there?"

Jack indulges in the possibilities. "Well, I'm sure they eventually made their way to Argentina, probably took up hiding somewhere until they passed away. But most likely they left the treasure there and yes, with the right air maintained in that cave, there could have even been vegetation. They probably lived there for a couple of years."

Gustavo huffs in annoyance. "I don't care! Bob, continue…"

July 15th, 1945.

I estimate? Days start to blend and hard to keep track of? The Führer should

have conquered all of Europe by now. Maybe even Russia, or even made their way to Argentina? Yet the Kriegsmarine have not rescued us? I have checked every time I have made a trip to the U-Boat; it lays as frozen as when she made her final rest. Of course, the beacon is dead; nightmares start to mess with my mind that Müller didn't get the word out? How could Hitler leave his prized passion missing this long? We will continue to remain hidden per Captain Prien's orders. This voyage will be my last trip, as the Seehund is low on diesel. I have now depleted all the fuel from the U-boat and stripped away all necessary elements for survival. Also starting to worry about the Captain, he has refused to come with me the past couple of trips. He continues to guard the Spear of Destiny, although I fear his obsession is growing strong. He never allows it to leave his side. Not sure how much longer I can take. You have the coordinates. Expect to see you soon.

- Klaus

All the while, as Bob, Dymitry, Alice, and Jack converse amidst themselves about the journal and how they should be approaching it, Gustavo realizes his dire need of their assistance. The new coordinates they have discovered are inevitably bound to come with far more formidable and treacherous thorns. As Lieutenant Klaus Herberger noted: "protect Führer's cargo at all costs," could mean more traps and puzzles. Jack seems to have a flair for extracting.

As they all walk back outside of the U-Boat back on to the deck of the Craig, Gustavo clears his throat and forcefully declares for them to take Jack's ship, and they will assist him till the furthest end, if that's what it took. If they uncover the spear of destiny, in return he will spare their lives. Jack realizes he is still being held at gunpoint, and if he were to go against Gustavo's will, then his friends would pay a price for a morbid treasure buried eons ago. Hence, with the safety of his family at heart, Jack hesitantly affirms to Gustavo that he and the rest will embark on the uncertain journey with him, encouraging Gustavo to put away his firearm.

"So, what are you going to do with the U-Boat? You can't just leave her dangling here," inquired Jack.

"True, we don't want people sailing by and asking questions." Gustavo looks at the metal rusted sub, then back at crane's controls, and with one massive kick, he hits the release lever out of the locked position.

Everyone's face burst forth with terror!

"No!" they all screamed in unison. With the crane's release now dislodged, a sight of horror erupted as the sheer weight of the U-Boat and the Triton both go crashing down, breaking apart as they hit the edge of the ship, then tumbling back into the water. The Craig even rocks back and forth, as the massive impact dents the deck of their ship. Gustavo and his men stand back and laugh as everyone else runs up to the deck's edge to see the devastation.

Lying in the water, scattered about, are the broken sections of U-Boat 2553; the years of decay was too much to bear with such a hard impact. The pieces slowly sink back into the sea, which will be its final resting place. Jack and Dymitry notice that the hatch on the Triton was opened; as the ocean water gushes into the cockpit, it too will be buried with memories.

Jack's face is in disbelief. Bob puts his hand on Jack's shoulder. "Sorry, kid."

Dymitry looks down, filled with rage. "I'm going to kick his ass."

Jack grabs Dymitry's arm. "Don't. We're out gunned. This is just material stuff; we have to wait for the right opportunity to present itself."

"Agreed, let's not do anything stupid. Look how many men we lost already," Bob replies.

With Jack still continuing to stare at the ocean, watching everything he had worked for disappear back into the sea, Alice gives Jack a hug. "Sorry for your loss."

Jack smiles. "It's not what you think. I'm just accepting the fact that this was another one of my father's lost artifacts he wanted to find, and there was no sign he had ever been here."

"We all deal with death in different ways, but at some point, you need to come to terms with the fact that…"

Alice pauses and looks back down at the remaining section of the Triton sinking into the ocean, then her heart sinks back.

"No, I'm sorry. If you truly believe he is still out there, then don't stop looking for him."

"COME ON, this isn't a wake, let's go!" Gustavo yells from behind.

With trembling limbs and a promise of freedom, everyone boards onto the *Calypso* with the feeling of brief liberation after coming out of a storm. Jack knows the new path ahead will most likely be filled with far more bloodshed. However, he also knows he is on the verge of discovering God's holy weapon, and feels somewhat responsible for making sure it doesn't fall into the wrong hands and impose impending doom that could crucify humanity all over again.

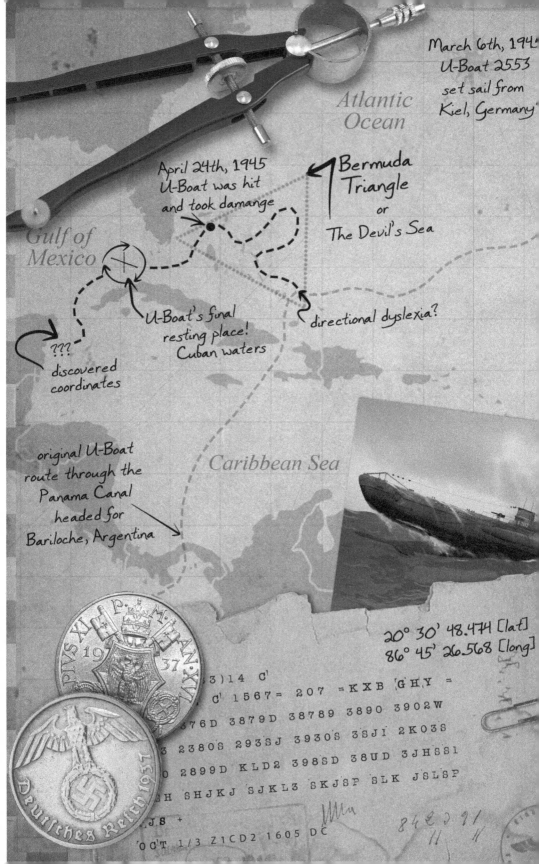

Chapter XIII

Watch the Legs

Much to Jack's astonishment and contentment, he and Dymitry still hold the full control of the navigation of the *Calypso*. The only difference now is of their state – they are being held hostage. Each movement, each breath of theirs is under constant supervision, much like the daunting clouds of gray lingering above them. Their voyage continues in utter silence. After much persuasion, Alice and Dymitry are granted time to rest their heads for a bit, while Jack continues to be the helmsman and steer in the direction of the coordinates they had gotten from the journal.

From his time at sea and after having entered the set of coordinates in the ship's tracking system, their designated location is a conundrum in itself. The coordinates require them to go past part of Hurricane Alley. Encrusted in the northern region of the Atlantic Ocean, Jack's senses heighten. Silence finally falls heavily on top of all of them like a thick comforter. Jack acquaints himself with his disheveled thoughts once more. What more misleading adventure awaits them?

The open sky outside starts to drift from slumber, allowing for a sleepy morning to wake itself up. In spite of darkness looming above the *Calypso*, all of its voyagers remain repressed by the hostility and uncertainty. Be it Bob, Gustavo, or the higher authorities maneuvering Gustavo's strings, their unquenchable thirst for limitless power has set them on a ship to their own catastrophe. Aloof from the peril, each wave crashing against the bottom of the ship holds, and they continue to steer closer and closer to the very waters harboring the power to anchor all of them once and for all.

Jack, on the other hand, grows vigilant of the draught he will soon be diving into. His only wish now is Alice and Dymitry's safety. A burning starts to grow in his throat as he notices the dripping color in the sky, letting him know just how close he has been inching to their destination. Bile and anger grip the lump, and his hands harden around the steering wheel of the ship as the GPS starts to indicate their arrival at the Yucatan Peninsula. He does not want to make the announcement when he knows just how poorly constructed the notion is.

"This is…"

"Stupid?" Gustavo interrupts. "No, Jack. This isn't. For you, maybe, since you will be leaving empty-handed. But be grateful. If that is to happen, you get to walk away free." He throws down a set of scuba gear in front of Jack.

No further announcements are needed, as the grin sprawled on Gustavo's thin lips suffices to break the news like the dawn above. The sun is yet to break free and finally spill the colors into the air. For now, Jack embraces the cold glares of the seething ocean below. His eyes only grow intense upon hearing commotion break out from the hallway, before he starts spitting venom at Gustavo.

"Hey watch it, man," Dymitry growls as one of Gustavo's men roughly shoves him in front of the control room, along with Alice.

"If you're really going to let us free, why are my friends being treated like prisoners?" Jack curses, causing Gustavo to flinch before he finally lifts his arm to gesture for Dymitry and Alice to be set free.

"Listen, Sterling, very carefully. One more tantrum of yours and your friends will be treated as prisoners. I have been bearing with your good-for-nothing attitude, and I am still willing to grant you your freedom, rather than actually holding you captive. So why don't you be a good boy, wear the damn gear, and go find my treasure?"

Jack feels his heart pounding louder once more. His eyes flicker, searching his friends for verification of discomfort. But knowing him well, neither Dymitry nor Alice show any sign of hurt or unease. Jack would not hesitate to leave Gustavo bruised and battered, had they been harmed. The consequences would have come much later, of course, and Jack would have been the one to pay the price in crimson and anguish. He slowly slips on his scuba gear as Alice and Bob cross the room to get on their sets of scuba gear.

Gustavo continues to observe each of their moves as all of the men present in the room start to don their gear on. All but one start, leaving Gustavo to narrow his eyes in Dymitry's direction as he silently shifts from one foot to the other.

"Do you need an special invitation to put on your gear?"

"Oh no, this is completely Jack's area of expertise," Dymitry states flatly, earning Gustavo's escalating irritation.

"This is not a choice, but an order!"

Dymitry crosses his arms. "I'd look like a wounded seal to Jaws down there. AIN'T HAPPENING!"

Dymitry's sudden snapping makes all of them grin widely, except for Gustavo, whose frown deepens. Before the argument between Dymitry and Gustavo can gain velocity, Bob intervenes, explaining to Gustavo how Dymitry has no particular experience with diving. Understanding how his burden of not knowing how to swim could prove hazardous to the whole expedition, Bob will pull Dimitry's weight down there, as an expert diver himself. Gustavo closes the distance between Dymitry and him. His fingers trail under his jacket as pulls out a polished set of handcuffs. In one swift movement, as Dymitry's eyes bulge out of their sockets, one end of the cuff is locked around his wrist, and the other around the steering wheel of the ship.

"HEY?!" Dymitry yells.

"I'm going down with my men; you will be the only one on the boat. I want to make sure you're here when I get back." Gustavo grins.

Dymitry is not finding amusement in Gustavo's antics. "You're taking my friends. Exactly where am I going to go?"

"Nowhere, now."

"What if I have to pee?" asks Dymitry.

"No one is stopping you." Gustavo smiles.

"Come on. That's not necessary?" Jack pounds his fist in his hand, ready for to launch it in Gustavo's face, before Dymitry provides his friend with some much-needed assurance.

"It's alright, Jack. But hurry up and get this Italian d-bag his treasure so we can get out of here."

Once ready, all of them march outward on the deck, willing to face their forced destiny. Gustavo continues to keep a strict watch on all of them. At the back of his mind, he knows well enough that Jack poses no threat. Bob, on the other hand, tells a different story. Jack is deluded by the old man, thinking he's only craving for a harmless crusade. Hence, Bob's generosity has gone unquestioned. But as a man sharing the same intention for their ongoing quest, Gustavo has caught on to the underlying tone of gluttony in Bob's demeanor.

Nonetheless, having known Jack, and how the man was driven on impulse, if he were to discover Bob's hideous truth, he would render both of them useless in the search for an immortal fortune. Gustavo, unwilling to take a risk, and knowing Bob's ability to make his own connections, holds

him captive. All of them line the railings of the *Calypso*, overlooking the agitated tides of the ocean as they whisper a lullaby of everlasting peace. But the peace is masked like a wolf under sheep's skin. Bob can't help notice one of Gustavo's henchmen holding a very large green water-tight bag.

"What's in there?" Bob asks with curiosity.

A secret Gustavo intends to keep. He smiles as he replies, "The end of chaos. Now get going!"

Noticing how no one else is willing to take the first dive into the pits of the sinister, Jack extends his open palm for Alice to grasp. Once her hand is secured in his, they both bite on their mouthpiece and, closing their eyes, dive headfirst. The water cuts through their skulls, and the cold of the water jolts them awake. Bubbles form around them, only increasing as another body pierces through like a bullet. Soon, the rest of them join them in a dive of anything but recreation. Where the water was inked with darkness, a light starts to induce its pigment, washing out all somberness. Despite Jack's long-time journey and drive to finding the Spear of Destiny for his deceased father, he is eager for the mission to come to an end.

Jack continues to spread his limbs like wings in a never-ending flight, and cuts through the heaviness of the undercurrents. The navigation system of the ship might have brought them to the precise location as per the coordinates; still, to hunt for the end of the rope is no less difficult than finding a needle in a haystack. The deeper they pull themselves to the ocean bed, the more it seems to cave in, prolonging their chase. Their energy starts to wear out of their limbs as the pressure turns excessive. Gustavo is on the verge of pulling himself and his men out of the draught when Jack signals for them to remain close.

While no coral reefs are in sight, as the piece of water they are treading is far too gruesome for anyone's amusement, a ditch seems to appear. At first sight, it seems to resemble a mundane parting of the ocean bed—a trench. Only as Jack inches closer, the trench seems to resemble a ditch underwater.

Instead of the type of a furrow, the opening seems like a hatch. Reality dawns on him in the rippling of the water. The first ray of sun bleeding under the tows gives way to a separate flow of water from the ditch.

This must be it. Jack turns to usher the rest behind him with a frantic nod. All previous dread soon gets replaced with euphoria, and like a flock, they continue to swim after Jack further into the ditch. The rugged surface of a slanted wave continues to go down, which gives way like an underwater tunnel. The further they swim, the more the water grows relaxed against their muscles within the tunnel, and the hues of the water regain its aquatic state, rather than a dark threat. Rough walls around them start to show signs of being donned in moss. As it curls further down, Jack comes to an abrupt halt.

His eyes grow hazy as his limbs travel toward the sudden outburst of light from up above, where a halo parts the ocean. Before him rests a mountain, working as a stepladder to the glorified opening above. His movements lose their pace, and now he leisurely roams about the mountain. Slowly, he starts to swim to where the light radiates. The rays dance with the furling wavelets, creating a spectrum of marvel as they stand at the entrance of the cenote.

Seeing the beginning of what could have been an abandoned alley, Gustavo rushes to climb first. Startled, Jack, Alice, and Bob take a cue and spring out to a spectacular sight. Everyone takes off their scuba gear, placing it on the ground to pick up when they leave; they can't help but be mesmerized by what seems to be a 100 ft. ceiling above them, filled with lime and dangling moss. They walk on the new grain of light tan sand and gawk in awe. They are surrounded by what seems to be eons-old work of nature, of water having crashed through and cliffs, breaking to form a secret island tucked in the cavern. The light carpet of sand further leads them to a stony surface above, where another peculiar sight awaits them.

Trees line their surroundings, their silhouettes sheltering the broken and busted cracks of pots laying around. Jack takes off the scuba eyewear as he walks closer to the cliffs. Once near, his eyes focus on various symbols drawn with clay of red and musky green. His fingers trace the hieroglyphics while

he ransacks his mind to find the answer. He knows he has seen such an ancient script long before, but to pinpoint the exact civilization becomes a hard task. He turns around for a brief moment, only to bear the sight of everyone lost in their daze. Carefully, Jack treads further past the trees and along the cliff, where he comes face to face with a symbol that illuminates a bulb above his head.

"The Mayans. This must be one of the sites of the Mayans, Alice."

He turns to face her with a toothy grin, and she reciprocates. For them to have stumbled upon such a site is no less of a treasure. But for the lust-driven hearts surrounding them, the breaking of this revelation only means double the fortune is waiting for them. He removes his eyes from the Kukulkan symbol, a Mayan-feathered deity they used to worship, to Gustavo's reprimanding of his men. He raises his eyebrow at the larger bags the last three divers have with them, because of which they had struggled with their dive.

"Gustavo, I found it." One of his henchmen chimes in, with proudness delacing his tone. He had ventured to the secluded end covered in rocks. At first, the sight resembles nothing more than an avalanche-blocked cave, but as they inspect closely, another miniature submarine seems to have blocked the path.

Gustavo and Bob run in the direction of the man at the rusting black, hiding its identity from all prying eyes. Still, their eyes, scouring for lost riches, seem to have located the Seehund-*U-Boat 2553* mini-submarine, or at least what's left of it, as rust has not been good to it. Only the top hatch seems to be broken off, and the decomposing sides make the Seehund look like swiss cheese, allowing everyone to stare right through it. They are quick to realize it, too, has been ransacked.

Gustavo loses restraint. "I don't understand. We crack that wooden box to find a journal that we deciphered, only to find an already looted sub?"

Jack discards Gustavo's grumbling. He moves along the cliff, his eyes turning up and down to survey their surroundings. Gustavo snaps in Jack's direction, his jaw hardening, and his heart blackening. The whiff of the ocean breeze, damp rocks, and oxidizing metal washes over Jack like a memory. A memory from the past, of one of the tucked away escapades he had with his father. Lost deep in memory lane, Jack absentmindedly continues to walk in silence while the rest are occupied in their own bickering. Mindless to time and space, he envisions the very caves he once plundered with his father in Mexico. The carved and tall walls of cliffs and rock aligned perfectly under the shade of the gigantic leaves.

The further Jack walks, the narrower the passage grows, and stones bite his palms as he leisurely drags his fingers across them. Each step he takes draws him closer to another stench, one he finds hard to distinguish. Here, even the wind refuses to come, and a certain aura of another hidden alley rekindles the dying hope in them. This is not it. His steps find their beat, and he rushes to the front of the sub. Walking underneath it, he comes across to the side the body of the sub was concealing. An entrance constructed from the metal hatch of the submarine now seems to be a bolted door to something more. A cave, perhaps, is holding the secrets they want to unearth.

The steering knob stands firm and proud on it, challenging Jack to tug it. But he knows well that years of being greeted with the sultry breezes had left streaks of rust on it. It is as fragile as porcelain. One slight rattle in the wrong direction could lock the riddle forever, or reward them with what is behind the closed doors. The possession of ultimate knowledge or wealth would be seized by time, until the water would drown them under their anticipation to feel the crisp rays of warmth against their tarnishing surface.

"I think I might have found something of interest."

Jack stands by the foot of the metal latch door, waving at the brawny man engrossed in an argument with Bob. The two quickly break apart, a blush of fear and guilt creeping on their cheeks. Their hushed tones they'd engaged in before are sufficient to raise suspicions. They ignore their previous diversion and briskly walk to Jack. Instead of speaking, he simply moves aside to reveal the door to them.

"Naturally, the door reveals not only a swastika emblem, but also an unusual puzzle dial containing three rings that turn on a compass. If you notice above the cliff, hand-painted in red are some lines and dots. They are clearly used to help solve the puzzle and unlock the latch."

"My, my, Jack. You do have the eyes of a detective," Gustavo mutters out loud, much to his dismay.

His eyes remain glued to the door, and his hands itch to have the hatch blown away. But he knows better now that one irrational and hasty move of his would only send them back home empty-handed. So, he moves aside.

"Now, solve the puzzle, Jack."

Alice places her arm on Jack's and tugs it closer to her. Panic takes her over, and her eyes become the gateway to worry and distress. As much as she is in awe, and proud of Jack, she knows well that the other two men in their company only intend to bring endless woes. To simply have this metal latch door before them open would mean welcoming further misfortune. There is no reward for Alice and Jack. The bonus could be the sparing of their lives, where they would start their *new life* married together. To experience their new beginning is the greatest power they want, but they are bound from achieving it. Jack's unfortunate yet impeccable ability of disclosure and deciphering has led him to untangle yet another delicate web.

He sighs, and his gaze drops for a brief moment before he looks back at Alice. His eyes burdened with guilt and shame. But before his voice can find the words, she places her arms around Jack. "Everything is going to be alright." She then leans in to place her lips on his, filling him with energy and love—a simple kiss, yet eloquent enough to pour her heart out to him. The kiss conveys how she is glad to be by his side rather than to be worrying alone for his safety.

They break apart when Bob clears his throat and Gustavo takes his gun out and places it against Bob's temple. Bob struggles as he tries to wriggle free from Gustavo's firm grip on his arm, but the man only digs his nails deeper into his wrist. The barrel of the gun is forced further into his temple, making Bob go motionless and his body turn pale.

"Waste another second on that mushy shit and Bob will be the first to embrace death. You are not here on a honeymoon, Jack." Gustavo cringes.

"You continue to force me once more, and you can do this yourself, Gustavo." Jack continues to provoke has he moves toward Gustavo, grabbing him by his jacket, leaving his men to raise their weapons in their direction. The previous eerie comfort evaporates the cenote, leaving room for the smog of tension and agitation to rise. All of their suppressed frustration starts to bolt through their veins. The radiating anger causes goosebumps to rise before them until their trance of vexation is broken by the sudden spreading of gray clouds above. Their source of natural light getting disrupted reminds them of the gravity of the situation and of the time they have slipping away.

"GET YOUR DAMN HANDS OFF OF ME! I am warning you, Sterling!" Gustavo curses.

"Jack, Jack. Look at me." Alice tugs Jack by his arm, unfazed by the threat that was cast her way. She holds his face between her palms. "I am here with you. Let's not do anything stupid. Let's just think of this as one of those Sunday puzzles, and together we will solve it, alright?"

Jack realizes Alice is right, and he is unarmed, and his ego would only lead to the bloodshed of all those he cares about. Shaking the irritation off him, Jack lets go of Gustavo and turns back to the door while Bob remains hostage. All of his men now have circled them, their guns each pointing at both Jack and Alice. Deep down in his heart, as much as Jack despises Gustavo, he too wants to savor his achievement. He has come this far and wants to relish his victory. To simply return knowing he had jeopardized his life all on a hoax, on a delirious man's whim, will have depleted him from the very motivation that drives him to work. To indulge in the secrets of the world will provide him with memories that he will forever reminisce in his heart. Dots and lines are drawn with red against the rickety surface of the cliff wall

above what he deems to be three rings engraved within them, leaving him to explain it to Alice.

"Ok, so now we know that the dots are used to represent 1 and the lines each denote five." Jack states as he stares at the markings.

"Great, so this means that the set of this one line and three dots above and the floating one is nine. What about the rings, Jack?" Alice asks.

"Only one way to find out."

Jack places his finger in the first ring and presses it, rotating it once. When nothing happens, he proceeds to press the second ring, causing it to move twice, along with the third ring once. His eyebrows knit together in confusion as he presses the third ring, and it rotates thrice along with the first ring once.

"How is this supposed to work, Jack?"

"I don't know? Maybe you are supposed to move it nine times."

Jack turns to face the rings once more and presses the first ring all over again. However, as the ring presses hard into the metal latch this time, the ground beneath them quivers. Next to the water inlet where the Seehund rests, disruption on the surface of the water causes one of Gustavo's men to walk closer to the edge.

Unaware of what is about to surface, he peeks to locate the source of the disruption. The momentous peace shatters as a porous slinging arm of purple breaks free from the captivity of water, with the suction of a light blue web along with it, revealing a giant pacific octopus, over thirty feet in length.

Bob yells out, "OH MY GOD, IT'S THE KRAKEN!"

Not seeing what was going on, Jack turns around in mid-sentence in reply. "Bob, that's Scandinavian folklore, you don't really believe…HOLY CRAP! ALICE, RUN!"

Instilling a ruckus, one of Gustavo's men screams at the top of his lungs.

His shrilling agony causes Alice to cover her ears in the hopes of blocking the pain-filled screaming for mercy. But the giant octopus's tentacle seems to have hold of him. As the tentacle snakes tighter around the man's ribs, another cracking of bones mixed with throbbing misery fills their senses before the man falls limp in the creature's hold and is pulled underwater. Horror fills their sight. Jack and Alice inch closer to the locked door. They notice one of the tentacles has a chain wrapped around it coming from the water. As if it was the cave's pet.

Another ruckus breaks out, and Jack turns over his shoulder to witness all the octopus tentacles to be reaching out and quenching its thirst for life. The remaining four men of Gustavo lift their weapons, filling the atmosphere with constant and dull firing, while Bob and Gustavo run further away from the sight.

"JACK! GET THAT DAMN DOOR OPEN!" Bob yells in fear.

Jack is quick to reply. "On it!"

Jack hurriedly follows the combination and presses the second and the third ring in the hopes of them moving to make nine. But the door remains intact. He presses the combination again, and presses the first ring once and the third ring twice. But even as the rings move nine times, the door remains intact.

"Hurry, Jack. The Kraken seems to be slamming men to create a beat of its own." Alice's panic-filled voice makes Jack look over his shoulder again, noticing how two more men were now in the octopus' grip while he bashes them repeatedly against the rickety cliff.

"I'm trying, Alice," Jack adds. "Certainly, saying 'open sesame' won't work. The combination seems wrong."

"CUT ITS ARM, BOB!" Gustavo's alarming voice causes Jack to look over to where both Gustavo and Bob are hiding behind enormous boulders, armed with some rusty axes.

"Whatever you do Bob, DO NOT CUT the arm with the chain. I think it's the only thing keeping it contained!" Jack says.

"Roger that!" Bob reassures.

Glad tiding, Jack wonders to himself, and thanks the Mayans for leaving behind the axes that Gustavo and Bob are desperately waving in midair in the hopes of chopping the limbs off the ghastly creature. He focuses his attention back to Alice standing by the latch.

"See, there is a gap between the floating dot and the three dots below."

"Just do it, Jack, don't explain it." Alice frets as she turns to watch the horror behind her and sees one of the men whose previous screaming was filling the scene with horror now muted due to blood profusely oozing from his forehead. Eyes closed, her heart plummets to her chest.

Jack talks to himself, "No, you see, the gap denotes twenty. They forgot to draw the circle resembling twenty in their math, and let the floating cap denote it instead. So, the line equals five, plus the three dots directly above it leaving it to be eight. The floating gap makes it twenty, hence twenty-eight. Another multiplication of theirs is that the one above means the amount below is multiplied with it.

"Yes, twenty-eight is the answer!" Jack's exclamation goes unheard as a beastly yelp of pain shoots through the environment.

Both of them turn to notice how Bob has rather triumphantly sliced an end off one of the limbs of the octopus. A pool of blood starts to flow from it, leaving it deranged for vengeance. Its attack grows vicious, leaving Bob to climb a cliff with his ax in the hopes of freeing the other suffocating man in the octopus' death grip.

Jack, turning back, starts to churn the rings once more. His fingers battle to press the third ring eight times, in the hopes of them turning the mechanism four clicks each round until it clicks twenty-four times. Bob and Gustavo's screaming grows erratic, along with the thundering of the octopus as they cut off two more of its tentacles. Haphazardly, Jack presses the second ring, waiting for the mechanism to turn thrice, as another limb falls off behind him, causing a splash that drenches Bob in fluid and seawater.

Once his count is over, Jack presses the last ring—the first one. A splash of water erupts, causing the water to rise and collapse, and drenches them all to wake them up from the nightmare they are living. A harsh yet dull screeching cleaves through, as the chain attached to one of the tentacles pulls what's left of the Kraken creature back down to the bottomless ocean pit at immense speed. Panting, Bob and Gustavo walk over to where Jack and Alice now stand before a frayed and significant swastika logo. The fierce eagle before them glides away, revealing a naked chamber. Only when the rays from the open reflect on the yellowed pile does it regain life.

Their eyes behold a hollow opening of charcoal illuminated by the gleaming pile of gold coins. Luring them toward it means their demise by the hidden traps set to eliminate the greedy souls wandering its way. Jack remains rooted to his spot, watching closely to see if the rest follow heed. All but one. One of Gustavo's men loses himself to the glistening call of greed, as his heart desires the eternal wealth before him. The yellow aura of gold at the far end of the dark and elongated passage before him pulls his feet in its direction, and his heart loses to a trance unbreakable.

Jack's voice reaches his ears as he makes a wild dash, much to their shock. A simple cry of "STOP" fails to save the man from plunging forward. The moment freezes, causing Jack's heart to hitch in his throat, and his blood runs cold. Gustavo's man slowly turns to face Jack with a frown, as if stating his displeasure to be stopped from acquiring a trivial share of the treasure. Alas, another quivering, much like an earthquake, causes all of them to jump back before the ground gives way to pathways. Crumbling, the illusion of a solid ground breaks free, revealing the carpeted spikes placed carefully in the morbid blue below.

The blood seems to taint the calm water, as the man's body pierces through the rustic wooden spikes. Jack falls on his knees, and Alice moves closer to

his trembling frame. Gustavo and Bob, on the other hand, are left conflicted on their next sacrifice to make in the hopes of avoiding the traps and attaining their possession.

Chapter XIV

I Was Lost,
but Now I Am Found

G ustavo looks around and asks Bob to check if there is another way.

Bob is quick to reply. "Well, there always is, Gustavo. One just needs the patience to figure it out, else all your men will die at the hands of greed."

Bob's remark leaves Gustavo curling his fist, but adjourning the matter, sensing his priority is to figure a safe passage into the cavern.

"Jack, you got this, right?" Alice whispers into his ear, cradling his head in the hopes of comforting him. But all she feels underneath her fingertips is the hectic palpitating of his heart.

"I am sorry, Alice. You were right all this time. I was big-headed. Had I listened to you, you would have been safe from this mess," frets Jack as he tests the remaining ground that forms a path above the spears.

Alice ignores the pain lacing Jack's voice. Instead, she gently lifts his face to meet his gaze. Interlinking their hands and tightening her hold around his palm, she gives him a tug to pull him to his feet before marching toward the entrance of the cave.

"Together we can figure this out and go back home, alright? We have a wedding we have to plan, right?"

All previous drudgery and the storm of inviting death have now vanished. Before them now only lay a short stretch of an obstacle. The perceivable solid ground filled with spears is ready to pierce through flesh, sending its rust to aggravate the pain and blood that follows after incurring misery. They let their hands remain linked together as if seeking guidance from the bond they share while their eyes scrutinize the barren and permeable damp walls of dark brown and moss.

The ceiling, with jagged cones dangling from up above, resembling the very spikes that lie in the water, threaten to collapse at any second. Their goal lies before them, dimly lit by torches at the other end. Alice snaps out of her daze as Jack pulls her toward the left of the cavern entrance.

"Bob…" Jack lifts his hand to gesture for Bob and Gustavo to follow after them. Soon, all of the men trail after Jack blindly as he comes to a halt at the foot of the hazardous lake within the cavern. "Look over there." Jack points to a slanted and narrow slate of rock along the wall that connects the entrance to their destination. All pairs of eyes take in the pathway Jack brings to light before them. They turn to face him with raised eyebrows.

Jack takes another look, then says, "This is the only way to get across to the inside of the cavern."

"But that path is as good as the spiked water. We slip, we fall into this very lake of death," Gustavo argues, his voice raising to a high octave, leaving Bob to intervene.

"You do alot of complaining for the head of NCB. I will go first."

Bob pushes past a snarling Gustavo, nodding at Jack. He fills his lungs with a concoction of courage and fabricated hope before nearing himself to the foot of the water opening. His fingers graze across the rough surface of the bespoke walls of the cavern, vindicating him to try and tighten his hold on its rickety surface. The slight darkness still leaves his heart muddled with thoughts. One wrong move and all that he has worked hard for would be ruined. He leans in closer and whispers a secret, soliciting the cave's mercy to let him pass.

Bob closes his eyes and reopens them to take in the conspiring darkness around him. This is not the time to fear the monster that resided deep within the cavity of the cave. He rebukes his thoughts and takes a leap of faith. While the walls barely give him permission to tread its ground, he clings onto dear life with the aid of the jagged comb dangling from above.

Bob swings his hand to the other tooth of the comb-like stone above and slides his feet closer to the joining rung. He repeats the gesture with his other hand, and then the first, creating a drift, as if a child on a monkey bar. The rest watch him closely, their hearts bursting with a wave of valor. They follow after him. Jack helps Alice first, and then places himself close behind her. He secures his right arm from the side of her waist and under her right arm, working as a net if Alice were to miss a step.

Gustavo and his men perch their bags on their shoulders and repeat the set of motions before them, causing a seamless flight of eager treasure hunters, filled with exhilaration and trepidation. They all have their eyes on the treasure that awaits him. Nonetheless, the riches of the world and the ultimate power they perceive is far from their grasp and understanding. Well, for everyone but Jack. His eyes focus on Alice and her safety.

Bob's face lights up with glee upon his feet hitting the stability of safer ground. He turns to look at Gustavo with mockery dancing in his eyes. All of his wrinkles and frowns are created by the warmth and light of the three torches perched on the walls of the inner cavern. Gustavo's men drop their bags to take in their surroundings, leaving him to venture further within the cavern and onto the right.

Their eyes dilate, and their mouths hang agape at the blaring intensity of the room filled with a mound of gold and other gleaming stones. Stones of

atrocious prices in their world. Alice twirls, her eyes lingering on the walls at the further end of the cave, with a drapery of apathy regarding Gustavo's men. Their minds echo for them to fill their pockets with a fair share to trade for the price of the dreadful flight they have taken.

The red and the white swastika symbol of the flags hanging loosely on the wall are just as tarnished as one would expect. Time has aged them, but its breezes, harboring the power of oxidation, failed to tarnish the reputation of the treasure. Jack walks closer to the gold coins, picking one up and noticing both the swastika logo and the Holy See on the other side, tossing it to Gustavo.

"Here is your dirty laundry, but the coins don't matter anymore, do they Gustavo? You want the Spear," Jack condemns.

Gustavo looks at the coin, then tosses it aside. "And you want to get out of here alive, so I suggest you find it, Sterling."

Jack looks around and notices a poking edge of a square. Curiosity maneuvers the movements of his hand, and he absent-mindedly pulls the aged brown to reveal a frame with a painting of *The Raising of Lazarus*.

"Is that *The Raising of Lazarus?*" Bob asks, bewildered as he reaches out to trace the oil on canvas underneath his fingertips.

Alice walks closer and inspects the piece for herself. She takes in the still vibrant red of the cloth draped over Jesus. Indeed, the one and only, by Peter Paul Ruben.

"It was stolen from the Friendrichshain Flak Tower Repository in Berlin. I faintly recall articles lying around my grandfather's office. Missing inventory number 783. Should of figured it was on U-Boat," Jack adds while inspecting the painting.

He gently places the frame back on the ground to fully comprehend the pile of gold coins.

This is not the only frame within the ground of the assortment of treasure.

Other paintings of Michelangelo rest there too. To any other soul, it would look like the riches were abandoned.

"I don't see my Spear? Look through the rubble and find it." Gustavo rolls out the order to one of his men and turns his attention to the other two. "Make sure the buffoons don't try anything funny."

Jack steps before Alice protectively as two of Gustavo's men hold the barrels of their guns in the direction of Jack, Alice, and Bob.

Jack's jaw clenches, but he remains firm in his position, and helplessly watches the man rummaging through the treasure, tossing aside what they deem as junk.

"He looks like a raccoon going through garbage," Bob chuckles.

Jack closely focuses on each piece lifted from the lump of treasure by Gustavo. From the larger stones of rubies and sapphires to the varying gold coins. He knows the smaller ones are the lost and forlorn treasures of the Maya. Whereas the larger ones possess an aura of arrogance and dominance to them.

With each fleeting second, Gustavo's heart starts to pound worry and anger. Irritated, he seals the air-tight bag filled with his share of each sample from the bare treasure and stuffs it in his inner coat pocket. He turns on his heels to look at Jack accusingly once more. To Gustavo, it seems each of his newer woes are dented by Jack, who is confused as to how he had started to seek comfort in the convenience of blaming someone else for his own failures.

"IT'S NOT HERE! Where is the spear, Sterling?"

"Excuse me?" Jack replies.

Gustavo throws down the treasure out of frustration, a sign he is not in the right mind set, walks over, and puts his face in front of Jack's. He begins to slow his words, as if he is talking to a three-year-old. "Where...Is...The... Spear?"

"No, no, I got your question the first time. But I am not the keeper or guardian of it. I don't know where it is?" Jack mocks.

Gustavo takes his index finger and thrashes it against Jacks chest. "That's because you have had it this whole time, ADMIT IT!"

"Gustavo, how delirious can you be?" Jack argues as he crosses his arms across his chest to block Gustavo's finger-pointing.

Gustavo goes on to regale Jack, hurling irrational theories of how Jack ensured this was all staged, while Dymitry would have had ample time to travel to the real coordinates and yield the treasure for himself.

Gustavo's outrage only allocates Alice enough time on her watch to go under the radar. As discretely as possible, she walks to the steps they had overlooked in the presence of the gold coin piles. Now as she inches closer, another two torches are hoisted on the wall, giving way to stone-carved altar. *Like a scene out of a movie,* she thinks to herself as she takes in the eerie sight of a skeleton lying idle next to it, dressed in cobwebs.

Tilting her head, Alice takes in the faded khaki-green uniform. The now black silver buttons are intact and aligned perfectly against the thick fabric. The stench of age and once rotten flesh fills her senses as she stares at the dead man. Seconds turn into moments, and she feels a pull toward the skeleton, making her take a step back as her eyes widen. She turns to look back at the altar.

Jack walks up behind her. "Alice, are you ok?"

Concern is evident in his eyes. He holds his hands in hers.

"Yeah, I am fine, Jack. Look at what I found. Notice the badge on the uniform: KH. It's Lieutenant Klaus Herberger."

Jack's face goes pale in disbelief. "You're kidding. He just spent the rest of his life here, guarding a Holy relic, never knowing the Germans lost the war. Talk about not letting go."

Alice looks up at Jack with concern. "I understand it's hard to let something go, that we cherish so dear."

Jack is quick to realize Alice's statement isn't about Klaus, but himself and his own obsessions he had with his father's loss. Jack's quiet for a moment, then looks over at Klaus again, changing the subject. "Well, would you look at that? It's an enigma machine lying next to him." As Jack lifts up the machine, another diary is lying underneath.

Jack picks the leather diary up and ruffles through the pages to take note of the entries in German.

Alice walks over and looks inside the diary that Jack is thumbing through.

"Did he leave us more clues?"

Jack has a perplexed expression on his face as he further examines the diary.

"No Alice, actually Klaus must have been doing some light reading, because this diary isn't from him. It's a journal from Adolf."

"ADOLF?" Alice blurts out.

Jack continues to flip through the diary until he gets to the center of the book. "Well, Adolf Driesch. His first name is Hans. Clearly, he is a scientist."

"Why do you say that?" asks Alice.

Jack continues to examine the middle of the book. "Despite what appears to be German scientific formulas, attached inside to what I thought was a bookmark, is actually a small hermetically sealed glass strip. Only it looks like inside is someone's hair, pulled right from the roots?"

"Hair?" responds a now grossed out Alice.

"Yeah, but it's in German. Hey Bob, could you look..." but before the words could roll off his tongue and ask for a translation, Gustavo swiftly plucks the diary from Jack's grip.

"I will be taking care of that, thank you, Mr. Sterling." Gustavo proceeds to pull back out the air-tight bag in his jacket pocket, securing the scientific journal with the rest of his personal treasures, then turns back to look at Jack.

"Now what?" Gustavo's voice trails after taking note of the silent skeleton in their company. "That's disgusting. Who is that?"

Jack and Bob shake their head in frustration. "Lieutenant Klaus, and I was hoping to find something in that book, since his other one had led us here," Jack demands.

"You don't need to waste time reading; you need to look for another secret passageway," Gustavo asserts as he looks around the room with his hand on his gun, just to remind everyone he is in charge.

Bob walks over to Jack. "I hate saying it, but he does have a point? We are, after all, looking for the earth's one and only source of cosmic power. Do you think these Germans would be foolish to simply leave the very spear amidst this mound of treasure?"

Bob's words ring clearly in Jack's mind. All of this is perceived as worthless for the very man who had provoked Jack to take up this quest. Then it dawns on him. Jack gazes at the skeleton of Klaus, taking note of the direction of the face. It seems to him as if before his demise, the man was staring at the altar.

"The altar must be it." He makes the announcement to himself and rushes to the sides of the stone-carved altar.

The right side of the altar comes clean, leaving Jack to assess the left side. There he discovers three glyphs carved out of wood and embedded along the concrete surface of the altar. One seems round in nature, with flames around it, the other resembles a globe, and the third resembles a horseshoe. Within the flicker of a moment, he knows these symbols rendered Hitler's power. He gently taps on the wood to feel if space is hollow, but his knock only feels dense. This confirms that something more complex rests behind the captivity of the wooden glyphs.

Jack lifts his gaze around from the square altar, taking note of a smaller hole clean in the middle. Its diameter would have sufficed to pass a solid object, ruling out the possibility of burning incense or gold as part of a ritual, as most ancient civilizations did.

"I don't understand. This is definitely for a liquid, but why?" Jack's question lingers mid-air, giving Alice the opportunity to blurt out her set of knowledge.

"Didn't people used to burn liquid in olden times for worshipping, or often for hiding things? Maybe, if there is an opening to light it up, then it means Gustavo was right about another passage?"

"Don't give that man any credit," Jack mocks. He shifts his attention to the dark gray and brownstone altar in front.

He bends on his knees and takes one last glance over his shoulder. Sees Gustavo and his men are standing armed. Their bags are already half-filled with the treasure.

"Grave robbers."

He shakes his head, then holds the corners with both hands and slides them down to look for a secret button to press. But as suspected by Alice, a minute opening was sculpted on the bottom of the slate surface.

Alice nods at Jack as he looks up to meet her gaze. Time seems to have stopped for them as their minds ransack their new captivity in the hopes of securing all the materials to ignite a fire. While fires are only capable of burning and crippling existence into ashes, he hopes for this fire to extinguish his blight and clear a pathway out of their persistent dilemma.

Alice crosses the steps and goes down from the altar to investigate the rest of their surroundings. Here, the cavern seems to have smaller openings, acting as makeshift lockers. Only they miss a hatch in enclosing them, and now they remain vulnerable to being violated by anyone. She furrows her

eyebrows and strains her eyes to see clearer in the dark in the hopes of finding anything flammable. The first two openings along the narrow wall of the cavern come clean, leaving her to turn back and return to the altar.

Alice has almost given up, and with a somber face starts to make her way back to the altar. However, fate has other plans for her. Just when she gave up on her search to find a way back home, to hold together the last bit of thread that could pull her out, along the left wall as she exits the smaller inner cavern, she notices a boring red canister resting. Her troubled thoughts disappear as she lifts the canister and rushes back to Jack with a smile on her face.

Seeing the red that projects a warning, Jack and Alice ignore the warning of the plastic in their hands. He takes the canister carefully from her grip and places the black nozzle to fit into the hole. Like a key, the nozzle fits in the hole, and he starts to pour out the contents.

"Why is it red, Jack?" Alice questions.

Bob steps up and faces Alice's bemused face. The frown disappears as Bob steps forth.

"It must be red mercury. The Nazis were a fan of this mixture, as it held the massive power to eradicate humanity from its root. Explains so much why they were so desperate to preserve the Spear of Destiny for themselves."

Jack holds back the canister from spilling more of its horrendous truth in the hole, his eyes widening in horror.

"Bob, if this is mercury chrome, then the whole place can *blow up*."

"Well, then...I say don't make it do that!" Bob smiles, then drops his voice, leaving Jack to look at Alice with horror. He knows the consequences well enough. If such was the case and they proceed with torching the devil's liquid, even their bones would dissolve, and their existences would be wiped out of memory.

Just as the thought of abandoning everything comes into mind, Gustavo takes his position behind Alice and aims his pistol at her head. His face holds no emotion. The cold in his eyes is enough to state his willingness in pressing the trigger against her head. By now, Jack is well versed in his own muscles' tightening and his jaw hardening each time Gustavo turns ludicrous. The rest of the canister is emptied, all the while Jack keeps his eyes on Gustavo.

"You never had any intentions of letting us go, did you?" Jack rages.

"You are smart enough to know the answer to that, Sterling. I also know that you will still help me, despite the outcome. You can't help it. Because like me, you want to see it, touch it, know that it's real, knowing you have come so far and you're this close. We are not all that different, you and I, only I want to profit from it, that's all."

"We are nothing alike!"

Neither of the men is afraid of the other, and they both know it. Hence, this creates a threat that they have tucked in the deepest parts of their hearts. Jack knows as well as Gustavo that if either of them is to even tweak their terms, then the consequences will result in a bloodbath. The very grounds they are standing on would turn into land once more tainted with life and death, greed and wickedness, and yes, Jack is driven to find the Spear.

Anger sparks through him, and Jack throws the now lifeless canister mercilessly by the skeleton. Jumping from the steps of the altar, he walks back to the forewall of the cavern and extracts the torches before returning to the altar. With one thrust, he spews the torch at the bottom of the altar. Thick gray smoke starts to rise the bottom slate of the concrete, and with a click, the wooden glyphs on the side glide themselves to the front.

All of their eyes snap and widen at the sudden activity. Now before Jack is the wooden board with controls entailing the power to unleash yet another adversity onto them. His heart sinks as he realizes what he has done. Bile rises to the back of his throat. The highest temperature the mercury could tolerate is 120°C. A temperature that now denotes death. He realizes he is the one that lit this ticking bomb, and the thought alone makes him curse under his breath.

What kind of a man was he? His thoughts turn cynical as the wooden glyphs ridicule his presence. He knows before him now lie the wires of a ticking bomb, and one wrong move could result in an explosion of destruction. Jack closes his eyes and twists the first symbol of the sun clockwise, in the hopes of resembling Hitler's swastika symbol. While the other religious swastikas denote a movement counter-clockwise, turning the gear clockwise causes a dull and strenuous movement of gears to come to life. As a gear seems to have shifted under the wooden holding on the altar, the material starts to grow hot and rise above.

Jack stands back. "The temperature has risen. It is at least 100°C now!"

Even Gustavo is getting nervous as he gives Jack a stern warning. "Be careful, Sterling. 20°C more and you will lose everything."

Ignoring Gustavo's warning, hesitantly, Jack lifts his finger from the first glyph and glides across the globe. He lets his finger rest for a little while longer on the glyph, uncertain of what the aftermath will be after this moment. He does not have much liberty left anyway.

Alice's tear-filled eyes filled his vision when he proposed to her. Recalling her answer, his lips quirk upward, and his hand turns the glyph clockwise yet again. His movement seems to have triggered irritation within the red mercury, as small bubbles start to form. His breath hitches in his throat as he realizes he has the last 5°C on his watch to meddle with. His mind comes to a halt, and the last gear before him turns blurry. All he knows is that it was a horseshoe, representing luck. He laughs humorlessly to himself at the irony of luck.

To Jack, luck has been no less than a fable. There is nothing to it. It is a hoax, a bluff, a void to fill feeble hearts with an illusion. To him, he always had to work hard in his life. Even then, he was never treated right. And then again there were times when he would fall asleep to the only thought in his mind – maybe luck ran dry, as people claimed. Maybe all the silent tears he shed had washed away his luck. Whatever the case, he is faced with the very thing he despises—luck.

The cavern has turned silent, and its eerie cold spreads all over them. No one dares to move a muscle, not even Gustavo, as he knows this could be his last breath. Their life flashes before them as Jack surrenders the weight of his hand onto the last glyph. The upside-down horseshoe rests beneath his palm. He mutters an apology under his breath before turning it to the right twice.

Time seems to have paused. Their hearts all forget how to breathe, how to race, and how to churn blood to keep their limbs responsive. Even the air seems startled and frozen around them. If only Jack could dissolve the time, turn it back. To when Dymitry was on *The Falcon*, Bob is drinking his Macallan, and Alice buried herself in her books. Only he knows his own desires to find the Spear would have put him right back to this very moment. Time never paused for anyone, and he is no exception.

It is only a matter of minutes, or seconds if they have yet to pass, and Jack prepares himself to feel a split second of pain. Then it would all be over. His endless trials, his unfilled promises, and his dreams that would never get a chance to breathe. All of it would be over soon. Like a nightmare, all of it would be forgotten, along with their identities.

Seconds start to fall heavy and outstretched themselves, but none of them break out of their trance. Only when the ground beneath Jack's feet quivers does he break out of the haze and take a step back. The altar starts to tremble violently, sending rumbles to fall before the entire piece collapses into the ground. Clouds of debris rise, making him cough and swing his hand back and forth to clear the polluted air. After the debris and rumbles of the altar settle, he peeks down. He turns to look over his shoulder, groaning.

"You have to be kidding. Looks like another tunnel and another swim, Bob," Jack describes.

Before Jack, hidden inside the now busted altar, is a set of makeshift stone crafted stairs leading to an underground tunnel where another small pool of dark water rests. While exhausted of the never-ending maze Jack is encom-

passed in, he is relieved to have made it alive. One by one, they climb down the stairs into the altar revealed before, with Gustavo and his four last henchmen in the rear, with one of his men is still carrying the strange large bag.

When they reach where the stairs and meet the water, as almost routine now, they dive in, following the dense flow that leads them down a small tunnel. His heart drums wild in his chest as he feels the cold of the water against him as tiny light cascades off the torches on the wall, driven by endless eagerness and curiosity.

Jack's gut knows just where the tunnel is to lead them, the treasure that everyone seeks, only at what cost? Instead of speaking up now, he lets the current of the water carry them, and for Gustavo to see for himself. Just as expected, their swim allows them to come ashore into a narrow tunnel, and darkness blinds them temporarily before they hear a croaking wheeze.

Chapter XV

Gunther

Startled as their footsteps echo in the narrow tunnel, Jack and Alice, along with the rest, carefully retreat on the newfound ground. The deeper they delve, the dimly lit surroundings start to clear. Like a stormy skyline getting rid of the daunting gray clouds, they are able to make out the narrow concave walls. Apart from the vicious stalactites working as open blinds, they are layered on top of one another to form pockets that open up to the ground surrounding another subterranean lake.

The ceiling here is far lower than all the caves they had to stumble upon thus far, leaving them in wonderment about the treasure that could be buried here. They continue to walk inward, around the edge of the lake, bending their heads to avoid getting stuck in the dangling swords hanging from the ceiling. The further they barge in, the louder a grunting sound grows. Blood drains out of their bodies, and cold encapsulates them, their eyes freeze onto the sight of a hunched creature.

No one dares budge their muscles, and time refuses to take another step. Their heartbeats only seize as the deformed creature, with its hunched back of pale skin slowly turns to face them. A beheaded green fish is tucked securely in the bony hands of the creature. Its skin now becomes clearer in the

single torch lighting the cave. The fish slips from his dagger-like fingernails. Eyes of black widen like a deer caught in headlights. As the decaying fish falls on the ground, the creature wipes his blood-stained mouth with the back of his molding and dirty brown hands.

Jack's eyes travel up and down the creature, taking in his 5.5ft frame. The creature's torso is revealed, exposing a gill-like formation along his ribs. His legs are slender, and his feet enlarged like flippers. Alice gulps the lump in her throat, realizing the creature seems half-human, half-aquatic. The creature's thin lips quirk upward, his black eyes now crinkling and his flat nose scrunched, revealing his set of yellowing teeth. Gustavo presses his lips together tightly in displeasure at the scene, as he notices streaks of flesh and blood in the creature's jagged teeth. Even from the flicker of a smile flashed their way, they know the creature's teeth are razor sharp.

The creature straightens his posture, wiping clean his slim hands against his now tethered and aged dark green pants. Once he seems content to have gotten rid of the life of the fish in his hands, the creature proceeds to comb back his mop-like dark brown strands to reveal the receding line across his paling forehead.

Panic grips Alice's heart, and she stumbles. Before she can slip onto a bed of rocks and a broken surface, Jack leaps to scoop her in her arms, and earns applause from the creature before them. All of their eyes snap in the direction of the echoing claps, instilling terror and shock in them. Nothing matters in time or space. No words seem to fit. Gustavo and Bob open and close their mouths repeatedly as they watch the creature crawl on his fists to the left of the cave and climb onto one of the sleeping quarters like a monkey. Only when he climbs back down, the creature is no longer treading the ground like a primate, but striding before them loud and proud, with a gleaming stick firmly grasped in his hands.

His chest heaves up and down steadily now, his black eyes like the night sky holding a gleam of proudness. If the discovery of the creature previously muddled the group, they were now numb at the sight of what is in the creature's hand. What they only imagined from rumors built up from childhood fantasies. That Gollum-looking creature is holding a spear, but not any standard spear. It is the Holy Lance of the Divine that now emits an arctic green glow around it. Each second they stare at the spear in the creature's hold, they feel its flaring blue seep ice in their hearts and soul.

"Guten…Tag!" His words fall slow and heavy, as the they formed in the back of the hideous creature's throat.

When none of them provide their identity, their minds struggle to grasp the bizarre unfurling situation. The creature narrows his eyes at their intrusive presence.

Bob is in total disbelief, recognizing the German accent and the World War II tattered clothes.

"OH MY GOD, IT'S GUNTHER!" Bob shivers as the creature creeps closer.

"Captain Prien? Don't be silly. How is that possible?" Alice wonders.

Jack gets a bad feeling about this, and pushes Alice behind him. "Maybe it's like the biblical story of the centurion soldier Longinus? He became the protector of the spear, and by biblical accounts, he lived for hundreds of years."

Gustavo chimes in, "But he didn't look like a *fracking* fish face. That is just repulsive."

Jack, unsure of the reasoning, continues, "Well, maybe he adapted to his environment or something." Jack pauses as he stares at the creature. "I mean, you spend seventy-five years in a cave, some evolutionary adaptation might occur? I don't know. There isn't really a study guide on this sort of thing."

In one swift jump, Gunther lands before them, making Alice and Gustavo's men shriek.

Gunther flinches and turns to face them with a scowl, mustering up

sounds from his throat. "Wer...bist...du?"

Gunther's massive grip tightens around the radiating spear, and he growls at them and repeats himself.

"Wer...bist...DU?!"

Jack hollers. "Bob! Translation, please?"

Bob exchanges glances with Jack, seeking his permission to intervene and break the silence.

"Well, it's a bit groggery, but it wants to know who we are," Bob replies.

Bob then steps in front, his face void of all emotions. Gunther grows amused, noticing how Bob now seems fearless, as opposed to his previous stance of trembling.

"Let me tell him who we are," Bob translates into German. "Ich bin Bob, das sind Jack, Alice und Gustavo."

Amusement laces Gunther's voice as he turns to look at Gustavo and his men, with a wicked grin on his face.

Gustavo is left to look back and forth at all the faces, his head slightly quivering. He beckons his men to remain armed as he spits in disgust, *"What the hell are you?"*

But all he is met with is a humorless laugh erupting from Gunther. His laughter seizes, and he stops in front of them. Creasing his forehead, Gunther uses his free right hand to pluck out a fishbone from between his teeth. Sheepishly smiling at them, he flicks the fishbone in Gustavo's direction and wipes his hand across his greasy hair.

"Es...ist...so...lange...her? Wo...ist...mein...Führer,..er...hat...den... Krieg...gewonnen,..nicht...wahr?" the creature croaked.

Bob slowly translates, "He says 'It's been a long time. He wants to know where is Hitler. He won the war, didn't he?'"

Jack turns to Bob, his words a bare whisper as Gunther walks closer to Gustavo's man, sniffing at them like a beast searching for prey.

"Be careful how you answer that question, Bob," pleads Jack.

Gunther notices how all of their eyes are locked on the Spear, making him pull it close to his chest.

Jack realizes the threat that lingers in Gunther's words. He knows any word could trigger the wrath of the creature. Unprepared for what Gunther was capable of, he jumps in to distract the conversation.

"Listen, everyone, there is only one way in or out of this lower den. Yet we had to destroy the entrance from outside it to get in? I don't think Gunther chose to stay here all these years; I think Lieutenant Klaus trapped him here. He wasn't protecting the Spear from the World; he was protecting the World from him," explains Jack.

Gunther hears the word "Klaus" and grits his teeth and cups his head to block out his memories, but the pain throbs against his temple, and he shrieks a hideous sound that confirms Jacks deduction.

All pairs of eyes in the room grow weary of the sudden change in the demeanor of Gunther. They know he is hinting at something more, but what?

A venomous sound rolls off the creatures tongue.

"Bist...du...nicht...ein...des...Dirtten...Reiches?"

"Jack, he now wants to know if we are a part of the Third Reich?" Bob hesitantly replies, as he fears what could come next.

Gustavo, impatient as ever, jumps in front of the creature and reaches his hand out. "Forget it! I'll do it! Yes, we are with Hitler and the Third Reich, now give me the damn Spear and I'll make sure he gets it!"

Bob tries to plead with Gustavo.

"Listen to me: you don't want to say that."

Gustavo gets frustrated and points his gun toward Bob, but not breaking contact with the Gunther creature. "TRANSLATE IT!"

The creature has no reaction to Gustavo pulling a gun out against Bob. Instead, he listens as Bob translates in German what Gustavo said.

The creature chokes as his eyes widen, then small laughs start slowly rising into a monstrous bolstering chuckle.

"Der…Speer…ist…nicht…mehr…Hitlers…zu…nehmen,..er…wird.. bald…kommen,…braucht…ihn…für…die..letzte…heilige…Schlacht,.. die…hier…auf…Erden..stattfinden…wird."

Bob is bewildered as he transcribes. "The spear is no longer Hitler's to take. He will be coming for it soon. He needs it for the last Holy Battle that will take place here on earth."

"Holy Battle? What's he talking about?" questions Alice.

Jack is now transfixed on the creature and his destiny. "Michael, the Archangel." Jack continues to explain, "Remember, he is holding the Holy Lance in Revelations. The last Holy Battle is the biblical account of the slaying of the dragon…Lucifer. *End all evil in the world!* It would appear Gunther believes Michael is going to use the Spear of Destiny to do it. Maybe that is the Holy Lance's purpose all along?"

The creature looks up with his dark eyes, glaring at Alice as if an animal in heat. He begins to wipe away the saliva dripping from his yellow teeth. Only hideous images could be going through his imagination right about now. The creature turns his head toward Bob, only this time, his speech has improved, with no hesitations.

"Sein neuer Meister hat ihn aufgefordert, den Speer bis zu seiner Ankunft zu beschützen. Baut er gerade seine Armee auf?"

"His new master has called upon him to protect the spear until his arrival. He is building his army as we speak?" translates Bob.

Jack's face marvels at the revelation. "It is not Michael who is Gunther's new master." Jack pauses for effect. "It's Lucifer. He wants the Spear for himself!"

Gustavo is not amused, and is getting frustrated on account of this creature.

"Archangels, Holy wars on earth, end of times. I HAVE HEARD ENOUGH! This thing is crazy from isolation, and I am not listening to this religious mumbo jumbo.

"Coming from the man who protects the Pope," mocked Jack.

Gustavo yells back, "WATCH IT, STERLING. I'm done playing games."

Jack tries to intervene and make Gustavo see they are no longer dealing with the peril of nature. Instead, before them stands a spirit of sheer evil and wickedness. Demons are inside of him, whether he wants to believe it or not. And Gunther is the one with power, and they are all helpless. Jack knows if this was to be resolved, if they wished to leave alive, then something else has to be done.

Gustavo, on the other hand, is unwilling to listen to Jack anymore. He grows blind by the lingering power in the cavern, and starts to take another step toward Gunther.

"Alright you disgusting piece of crap, showtime is over. Hand over the spear."

Jack grabs Gustavo by the arm. "Stop being an idiot. You will get us all killed! There was a reason Klaus had trapped him in here."

Gustavo whips out his gun, smacking Jack across the face, gashing his head and sending him down to the ground. Gustavo pulls back the hammer while pointing the weapon at Jack. Alice runs over to Jack's side. The creatures just studies the Italian man.

"SHUT UP! You will get what's coming to you soon enough, YOU ALL

WILL!" shouts Gustavo.

The pale face creature's smile grows wide as he braces for Gustavo to step his way. He nods to himself as he relives the revelation once again. Gunther is the protector, the guard of the Holy Lance. The leaders of the past like Führer only wanted the Spear for power, and Gunther now has that power.

In a raspy voice, the creature doesn't hold back. "Der gute Gunther hat keinen Fisch mehr und hungerte nach frischem Fleisch."

Alice, wiping the blood off Jack's forehead. He is getting nervous. "Okay, Bob, I know he just referred to himself as a third person, but what did he say?"

Bob hesitates. "Umm…Well, Gunther is tired of fish, and he is starved for some fresh meat?"

Jack's feet are paralyzed as he watches Gunther's nails emerge out of his skin like daggers, and his fingers tighten around the Spear of Destiny.

Gustavo smiles as he peers down the eyes of this beast. "He is nothing but a damn wild animal."

Gustavo turns his gun away from Jack and onto Gunther while reaching out with his other hand. "Last chance. Give me the spear or…."

Before he can finish the sentence, a piercing scream is echoed through the cavern, followed by a gunshot that misses Gunther. The hideous creature pulls back his jaw like a python, unleashing a row of sharp teeth that proceed forward as he lunges forth, biting Gustavo's two left fingers clear off the bone, the blood of anguish pouring out.

"FANCULO! THAT'S IT, LOCK AND LOAD PEOPLE, I WANT THAT SPEAR!" Gustavo hollers as he rips off his own shirt sleeve and wraps it around his left hand.

Gustavo and his men stuff ammo in their guns, aiming the barrels and opening fire at Gunther.

Chapter XVI

It's Mine

"NO!"

ack screams, but his voice pales in comparison to the loud cracks and rings of bullets flying, trying to hit the fish-like creature, who appears to be dodging them as he leaps back and forth behind the rocks. Within a split second, a roar erupts, causing the stalactites above them to shiver with fear. This is just the beginning of another nightmare. Bob, Alice, and Jack take cover behind a large boulder.

Panic and horror shoot through the cavern as Gunther's eyes widen. His voice fills the eerie atmosphere with terror, seeping alarm within all the men. While they can't seem to hit the hideous beast, the touch of cold metal under their fingertips provides their pounding hearts with assurance.

The inconsistent rising and collapsing of their chests resemble the stormy turmoil brewing within Gunther's own corrupted heart. His hold tightens around the Spear. His eyes narrow into a threatening glare. The hollow in Gunther's black eyes is enough to haul Jack back to his past. Peril swirls amidst the menacing glares of Gunther as he sweeps his tongue across his parched lips. Jack knows at the moment they are all his prey. This is his reign, and Gunther fears not even death. What could be worse than a soul not in-

timidated by their own demise? No one. Jack knows that while to Gustavo this was all a game he intended to win, for Gunther it was protecting his self-constructed sanctuary.

Jack knows he has to warn Gustavo of how his impulsive decision could cast a shadow of catastrophe over them. Only he is naïve to the current circumstances. One after another, a series of gunshots start to make the rounds, letting Gustavo and his men work as a barricade, so they can barge after Gunther. Jack, along with Alice, ducks and runs in the opposite direction of the unfurling calamity. Watching Gunther continue to leap from the rock before them to the back and take another leap to the rock slightly above onto his right, Bob backs away from the scene. He decides to justify his gunshots only if Gustavo is to fail, much like Jack.

"Why won't you die? " Gustavo demands as he makes a dash after Gunther, who is now climbing the makeshift rock beds on the cavern wall to their right. Without glancing back once or being perturbed by the vibration of the gunshots, Gunther continues with his ascent. Disgust fills Gustavo, and Gunther from up above takes in the bird's eye view. There are a total of five men firing at him. Gunther takes in his position with blinking eyes, as Gustavo's hostility only elevates.

Gunther sneers, recognizing the man standing toward the left and by the foot of the water, who had led the invaders to him. He dove from above. Gunther spreads his arms, revealing a set of skin from underneath his arms interlinked to his torso that allows him a seamless flight. With a humorless cackle, Gunther tackles the man on the ground as he lands on top of him. Only a short bellow escapes the man filled with a vibrating woe of horror as Gunther digs his nails around the man's neck and presses them in. Blood splatters on Gunther's face as he starts to rip the man's neck in half, throwing it mercilessly in the water. Wiping the blood off his face, he roars back at Gustavo's men, who show no fear.

The lion like sound bellowing through the cavern jolts Gustavo to reality. He has unleashed a demon beast that was once sealed by time. It is Gustavo's undoing. Nonetheless, watching his man be ripped apart like cotton candy filled on a stick caused Gustavo's muscles to tense. He looks at his own left-hand, bleeding. He trails his eyes on Gunther's, that are now searching for his next victim. No emotion, no sentience of life reflects in the pool of black savagery of Gunther. He seems completely unfazed by each bullet piercing the air and firing his way.

"FIRE, DAMN YOU! WHY ARE YOU STOPPING?!" Gustavo yells above his lungs as he watches Gunther tread in their direction, backing them against the cavern wall. Gustavo knows if Gunther were to take another step, he would lose.

A silent whisper of chaos radiates around them. The creature is a threat sufficient to dwindle their courage. How is Jack to survive and salvage Alice with him when he is surrounded by beings willing to crucify the other just to save their own skin? Gone was the valor within Bob too that had led him till this point. Jack has no choice but to run over and confront Gustavo and plead for him to stop. Bob joins him, hoping he may be of assistance so they can get out of this alive, both of them warning Alice to stay behind the boulder.

On the other side of the cavern, the cracked ground screams of devastation and the atrociousness of Gunther. Each bullet show is in vain, and Gustavo knows this too. His team is unmatched and unequipped, for they unleashed the beast that Klaus had been keeping locked up for so many years. By now, the men start to tremble in defeat as the creature devours them one by one, hiding in the shadows, and moving at superhuman speed and strength. The air, once filled with heavy bullets, is now overtaken by screams, until there is nothing but silence. The creature leaps out of the dark shadows from above, landing in front of the last remaining soldier. He throws his gun down in a truce, only widening Gunther's crooked smile.

The creature turns to face the man as his steps pick up their pace. The man only backs up faster. The man helplessly looks around him, his eyes begging for mercy. His eyes shriek for the help of his friends, yet no one dares

intervene. They all value their lives, and he knows his time has come, seizing all voices within him as the last glimpse of his mother's smile comes into his eyes. Without issuing any further warning, Gunther bends his knees before hoisting himself in midair and lurching toward the man. The man, barely able to shield himself by placing his hands before him, becomes a victim to being stabbed by the Spear in his abdomen, over and over, while Gunther bares his teeth into the crook of his neck.

Alice closes her eyes and blocks her ears, while all the others simply dart their attention to find even the most trivial opening of an escape from the nightmare. Shrieks escape and resonate, echoing pain and a life lost in the hopes of seeing dawn one last time. Gunther rips back a piece of flesh from the man's neck before biting in again and devouring the once unwilted life, fresh meat causing him to utter words of delight that roll off his tongue.

"Das schmeckt gut!"

Gunther places his hand under his chin, wiping away some dangling human tissue while feigning to pick his next target, even though he has already made up his mind. His beating heart longs to touch and taste that of a female. With the spear in hand, he dodges the ricochet of bullets as he leaps his way over, landing on the boulder above Alice, only to be met with shrill screams as she looks upon the face of death.

"GUNTHER, NO!" Jack yells with a threatening voice, but panic has seeped cold into his heart.

Jack starts to storm in Alice's direction, as he is a few steps behind her. However, before he could cover the distance and as she turns on her heels to run away from Gunther and toward the lake, the creature springs himself onto her back.

"JACK!" Alice screams as she feels Gunther's nails pierce her skin.

Jack yells in anger toward the creature as his feet pick up speed, trying to reach her. "ALICE!"

Alice reaches the shore of the lake as Gunther remains unfazed, and swiftly places the tip of the Spear in her abdomen. His movement is enough to freeze all of them in their spots. Her body starts to go cold under his hold. The mist of the water seems afraid to take another breath, and the rippling comes to a halt. Time seems to have frozen at the twist of fate. The pressure of the Spear's tip starts to intensify as Gunther presses it inward, caught off guard as Jack tackles him to the ground, knocking Alice into the shallow edge of the lake, wincing in pain. Her hand reaches the newly received wound, noticing how half of the Lance is inserted in her body, and dark red blood drenches the hem of her shirt. Jack rushes to her and swoops her in his arms.

Bob seizes the opportunity and grabs hold of Gunther.

"Damn you, Gunther!" screams Bob.

For an elderly gentleman, he is quick to run behind the creature, seizing the opportunity, and grab hold of him. He twists Gunther's arms back and presses his free arm around his neck in the hopes of suffocating him. Each time Bob presses his arm around Gunther, his eyes take in the pool of sweat forming on Alice's paling body. But his attention is brought back to Gunther, resisting Bob with his relentless kicks to attain freedom.

Jack jumps in the shallow water, lifting Alice in his lap. "Alice, Alice, oh God, I am so sorry. I am so, so sorry, Alice." Her eyes flutter and beads of tears and excruciating pain cascade down her cheeks.

Jack's eyes turn watery red as he watches Alice. Her eyes stare back at him. Alice wheezes and firmly presses her hand on the wound near the left of her abdomen. For a brief moment, Jack's heart plummets to the ground as the fear of waking up without her steps into his mind. He shakes his head to get rid of the traitorous thoughts. How can he be thinking of losing this woman and lowering her into the ground, when he wanted to wait for her at the altar? Looking at the Spear still plunged in her abdomen, he holds on even tighter. "Please hang on, hon. I'll try to get this out."

Alice closes her eyes as Jack assures her and gingerly grabs hold of the Spear. Each time he tries to swivel the metal, she winces. Tears and blood start to flow profusely from her. The threat of losing her increases with each drop of blood that she loses. It starts to wear on him, leaving him with little choice but to slowly extract the Spear from her stomach.

Gunther, on the other hand, digs his teeth into Bob's forearm, making him retreat as a yell escapes from him. A set of blue marks forms on Bob's arm, making him stare at Gunther, distraught. Not allocating Bob the requisite time for him to recover, Gunther turns back to face him and lowers his head to meet his gut. Gunther effortlessly lifts Bob's burly physique above his bony frame and throws him against the rocks next to Gustavo. Bob's holler is muffled as he huffs against the ground and clutches his ribs. Now disoriented, Bob looks up and notices Gustavo taking off his overcoat, and throwing down all his possessions, including the airtight bag of treasure. He takes off running toward the one large bag his men had brought in but left foolishly by the cavern's entrance. Despite Bob being in pain, he crawls over and reaches in Gustavo's bag, and pulls out the scientific journal they had found on Klaus and places it in his back pocket.

Alice's screams reverberate off the cavern walls as Jack plucks out the Spear permeated with her blood. Gunther begins to charge after the Spear like a bull. Gunther's footsteps echo heavily, making Jack leave her on the shoreline. He straightens his posture and clasps the Spear firmly in his hand taking a strong defensive stance, as a surge of electricity jolts through his veins. Gunther notices the flash of paling blue in Jack's eyes, making him drop his gaze, realizing the Spear is in Jack's hold now.

Aloof to Jack's nature, the man only craves the simplest notions of life. Gunther advances toward Jack. Jack's fist only curls tighter around what he deems to be metal, the source of savagery and evil as he too runs in Gunther's direction. The scene widens as the two come barreling toward each other against the bank of the shoreline. All of Jack's previous ferociousness and bravery appears to have surged back as he runs toward the savage beast like two freight trains about to collide. Overpowering Gunther with a brief appearance of superhuman strength, he plows into him, sending them both into the water. From a hollow humidity, the sudden vacuum awakens Jack and Gunther. Jack knows Gunther only wants the Spear. It is, after all, the very object that can bestow every soul with immense power. Even when such power came with a hefty cost, castrating the freedom of a person, dictators and dark souls were still drawn to it like negative and positive energy. But such souls forget that the fire entails the ability to burn their wings and cripple their liberty.

Gunther has already paid a cost of a lifetime, and now all he wants is to hold onto his last anchor of hope – while he waits for his new master. With both of them now underwater, the creature thrusts his limbs to inch himself closer, but Jack only swims backwards. Fury starts to stir the water around Gunther. What Jack has failed to comprehend is his own need to resurface to fill his lungs with fresh air, whereas Gunther needs no such source. To him, submerged in water is just the same as being on ground. It is one of the physical evolutions he had acquired after submitting himself to a life of absolute isolation. Having failed to realize this in the haphazard state, Jack swims back up to draw a long breath in, leaving Gunther to take advantage. Gunther pulls Jack down by his feet and bares his nails to forcefully pry the Spear from Jack.

A series of bubbles erupts around Jack, filling his mouth with water that he has to hold back, to prevent from drowning. Quivering, he shrugs Gunther off from his leg, using his free leg to kick Gunther on his head repeatedly. One after another, Jack's heart starts to throb with a dull ache. Each hit starts to develop a reason for him to continue assaulting Gunther. First came Alice, how she had to take the plunge for him. His next hit dedicates itself to Bob, who had tried to peel Gunther off from them. Then a final blow for his father, and the years of frustration for having been robbed of a normal childhood. But soon as Gunther starts to hesitate, Jack's violence increases, and with one powerful kick on Gunther's forehead, Jack frees himself.

Closing his eyes and still holding the Holy Lance, Jack rushes back to the surface in hopes to reach Alice in time. Crawling onto the shore, he is quick to realize, from being disoriented with his underwater battle, that he is now on the far edge of the lake, the opposite side of Alice. Such as a scene from a horror film, as Jack stands up to run after her, Gunther's hand thrusts out of the lake, grabbing hold of Jack's leg, digging his nails in, immobilizing him temporarily. Gunther rises slowly out of the lake, lifting Jack above his head. Jack is overturned briefly, and takes the chance and stabs the Spear into Gunther, just before he is thrown back into the lake like a rag-doll.

Gunther pauses for a moment, thinking victory is his; he finds he too is now short of breath as he looks down, only to see the Spear of Destiny has been pierced straight through his chest. Panting, Gunther collapses on his limbs and starts to crawl on the shore as dark liquid drips from the wound along the middle of his torso. Jack has lost by a fingerbreadth. One more inch upward and Jack would have triumphantly annihilated Gunther's curse. Having failed to do so amplifies Gunther's wrath, and without hesitating, he pulls the Lance out of his chest. At that very moment, Gustavo has returned and drops his bag, as a newfound pleasure is filling his heart. Gunther traces his finger on the jiggered edge of the Spear smeared in his blood and flesh, picking off a stray worm and throwing it back in the water.

Gunther turns to face the intruders who have wreaked chaos ever since their arrival. He had expected an easy defeat of his enemies, as he had done so in the past. Still, they had faced his repulsion headstrong, and were still pulling themselves together in the untangling battlefield. In spite of their courage, every battlefield has its end. Each termination was necessary for the battle to conclude itself, and he did not want to be the one crucified. He tames his breaths.

On the other hand, Jack finally manages to resurface. His posture is just the same. He climbs out of the lake on his palms and knees, heaving and panting loudly. His breaths are ragged, and his lungs burn. Alice is still where he had left her. Only now she collapses back on the ground upon seeing him safe and sound.

Having had enough of the carnage that resulted in the bloodbath, Gustavo, with a wicked grin, bends over to pull out of his mysterious bag "the end of chaos," as he calls it. Gustavo's weapon of mass destruction is a rocket-propelled grenade launcher blessed by the pope that allows him to put an end to the madness for good. Although deep within his heart the secret lurked, the secret of his own intentions, a secret that is far more gruesome than the fate Gunther had suffered. Bob observes his movements. Carefully, Gustavo lifts the burden of the RPG, halting Bob's step. It is evident that the mania that came from all of the events leading up to this moment had played their part in obstructing their sanity. Still, Gustavo seems to be crossing all lines by pulling out a rocket launcher that harbors the power to turn the cavern into all their graves. The world outside would remain unknowing of the unfolding that took place in the deepest recesses of the ocean.

Bob struggles to yell for Gustavo to stop, but he knows he is too late. The weapon is loaded and aimed in the direction of Gunther, who is standing by the other side of the lake. Bob's breaths come to a stop. His body going numb just as Jack realizes what is going on. Gustavo carefully places the launcher's barrel above his shoulder, his right eye closing as he locks his target of Gunther. Jack's eyes flicker over to Alice, noticing how her face is pallid. But the walls of the cavern start to shiver and cry as a boisterous explosion is heard taking an enormous hit. With the utmost force of a hurricane, the blast flings Jack back into the lake as the projectile slams into and engulfs Gunther.

The ground begins to quiver, as all of the stalactites shake, and the combustion of the fireball explosion roars, sending even more pieces of earth and shattered rocks to crumble. Seconds pass, and finally the assault settles within the cavern. In the hopes of showing its distressed state, the cave cedes. No longer does the cave will itself to provide shelter to its assailant. Bob runs over to Alice's side, seeking shelter underneath the wall that is folded. He knows even nature's bunkbed will soon collapse over them to punish them for Gustavo's heinous act.

Like a tremor, the cave shakes, letting Gustavo stand still. He laughs menacingly, distracted by the power. Rocks of meager stature to considerable ones in size start to crack and rain above them.

Gustavo, despite the mayhem up till now, clears his eyes and coughs. All that remains where Gunther once stood is the Spear glistening from a rock ledge just above the lake. His heart flips, and the glowing Spear of Destiny holds Gustavo in a trance, somehow pulling his feet in its direction. The closer Gustavo inches, the more eager he grows to taste the exhilaration of the power the Holy Lance would bring. Gustavo ignores the beating from the stone cracking above, and bends over to grasp the Spear amid the rubble.

Just as Jack comes back out of the water, he takes note of Gustavo. As the rocks continue to fall, Gustavo seems deaf to his surroundings. Venom drifts to his mind, as he can feel the Spear calling out to him like the Greek mythological Siren, whose song lured nearby sailors to their death. Despite Gustavo missing two fingers and fresh blood dripping down the Spear staff, he closes his eyes and feels the power seeping into his bones and rejuvenating his evil thoughts. He holds the Holy Lance up high in the air, with a crazed look about him, laughing and claiming his reign to have begun.

"It's mine, all mine. I feel the power flowing through my veins, making me a god among men."

Alice and Bob seem to disappear in the background as Gustavo's image holding the Spear takes center stage. Jack watches in horror as rage boils in his blood and begins to swim toward him; however, his anger is not shared alone.

Out of the darkness, with his skin severely burned, and eyelids practically melted, the hairless creature emerges from behind as he pounces onto Gustavo's back.

Gunther roars out a monstrous growl as he takes what's left of his razor-sharp nails and digs them deep into Gustavo's eyes, rendering him sightless. He drops the Spear into the water below.

Gustavo screams in desperation rather than confidence as he struggles to get the creature off his back. Only as they are both met with the fate of the ceiling of the cave finally giving way, as massive chunks of rock plummet down upon them sending them, and the rocky ledge they were standing on to the depths of the subterranean lake.

Jack swims over, looking through the rubble still settling in the murky lake, trying to find the treasure that was once in his grasp.

A familiar voice is overheard through the sounds of the continuous rubble falling from above.

"Jack, Bob is hurt. Come help me, please!" cries Alice.

Jack looks over and sees Bob lying on the ground, where rocks have fallen on top of his lower body. Alice, who can barely stand on her own, is trying to lift the rocks off him.

Jack can't help himself, but turns back and continues to look into the water. The Spear is laying there somewhere, free from evil, and so close to the touch. If he can retrieve it he believes all will be right in the world again.

Bob cries in agony, and Alice pleads in tears.

"Jack, PLEASE!"

The words are almost muddled, blanketed by the splashes of falling rocks from above. Jack looks back at Alice and nods.

"I WILL BE THERE IN A SECOND! HOLD ON!"

Jack continues to dive under the water, lifting up rocks, as he knows that if he doesn't get the Spear it will be lost forever. Coming up for air one more time, he hears Alice cry once more, but her voice getting faint.

"COME ON, WHERE IS IT?" he yells, as the sound of his frustration gets lost in the falling debris.

Jack starts to give up to go to help his friends when he sees green light glow in some underwater rocks by the ledge.

Jack is too close to turn away. He grips the rock face as tight as possible as it attempts to roll over and take him with it. He holds his hand out for the Spear, only to find it lodged under a boulder.

It still manages to glisten and glow, even covered in murky water debris. The Holy Lance is now in Jack's finger grasp, and he continues to push and shove, but can't free it from the weight of the fallen rock. A louder crack echoes off the cavern walls as mountainous stones start to fall from above.

Just then, he notices Alice's cries have stopped. He looks around for Bob, and he sees him grasping his leg, but Alice is nowhere in sight.

"Jack, Alice!" Bob yells in pain.

Jack finally gives up and runs over to Bob, looking for any sign of Alice. Slipping, sliding, and clutching at anything that offers him grip, the world in which he exists is giving way, and now his only hope is they can all get out alive.

"Where is she? Where is Alice, Bob?"

"Behind that rock. She tried to go after you but passed out, Jack. Grab her and get out of here. You don't have much time!"

"But Bob, what about you and the Spear? I saw it. It's just by that large boulder sticking out of the water."

"DON'T BE A DAMN FOOL! Forget the Spear and me! My leg is broke Jack, just save the woman you love. That is all that matters."

Jacks eyes start to well. "I can't just leave you."

"GO!"

Before Bob can say any more, Jack knows Bob is right, and only risks slowing them down, as he can't carry both of them. He runs over to Alice. As Jack lifts her, she remains unconscious. He takes her in his arms, making his way for the cavern entrance. Looking back around, he can no longer see Bob in his sight as rocks continue to fall, creating a dust of wreckage.

Through the continued falling debris, he manages to make his way up the makeshift stairs, outside the tomb, down the spike trailed path and through the metal hatch. He grabs a couple of scuba gears that were left behind, placing one on Alice's face, who appears not to be waking up. Thoughts of now losing her consume all of Jack's worries, replacing all thought of the Spear.

"Hold on hon, we are almost home."

Jack holds on to Alice, jumping into the inlet of water containing the underwater tunnel, which leads out of the cenote. The cave pelts its ceiling in the hopes of scurrying all of their bodies away. Through the dark tunnel, a single ray of light underwater leads the way. Leg still burning from the creature's piercing, Jack can't imagine the pain Alice must be going through. He wraps his arms even tighter around her, continuing to swim even faster.

Her wounds are fresh and deep, the gush exuding blood relentlessly in a trail behind them. Just in time, they escape the cenote entrance before it collapses, taking everyone and the Spear with it.

Chapter XVII

A Narrow Escape

ack cradles Alice as he swims back to the ship. His heart yearns to fill his lungs with the sultry ocean breeze, his eyes with the limitless vision of a sorrowful blue. All of this experience with her was to accompany him till his last breath. Even under the water he could feel her body going cold under his touch, making him shiver with fright. He does not want to lose her.

As Jack hooks his right arm around her. His own pace is slow. It is a stroke forward for them, only to be pushed back by the force of the morose currents. Their only guiding light is the transcending color of the ocean. Jack knows the trail of blood Alice is leaving can only attract unwanted hungry guests, but he can't let that worry him. The further Jack thrusts himself, with Alice fighting for her life, their reward comes from them putting a safer distance between themselves and the now crippling sight. One that is not bound to weave itself into history. No ink, no thread was to remain where now Gustavo, Gunther, and Bob, along with the other men were to rest. Their graves are to remain concealed forever, trapped with the Spear. With time and the varying flow of the current, he is certain that no one would need to figure out the GPS coordinates to uncover an excruciating quest.

Every now and then, as Jack exerts pressure on her limbs, the stirring motivation found Alice's body goes further limp under his hold. She rests her head back as it bobbles in water, with her body slowly decompressing while Jack swims up higher. He chants to himself, hoping she can hear his wordless prayers for her for her to remain by his side. Like a changing burst of energy, as he glances back one last time, he notices how far he has swum from the site of a heart-wrenching experience he will someday pen down. Now the dull hues of the aqua light blare into where he is moving, shedding light on the reefs as they come into view. He knows the gruff walls of the cave and the porous trenches are now forever engraved as a remembrance within each beat of his heart.

Jack heaves a sigh of relief upon spotting the transient and rippling shadow of the boat above, calling out for him to brew another wave of energy within him and cover the distance. He tugs Alice closer to his side, realizing how her body has started to weigh a little more. Upon resurfacing, he throws off their masks as she coughs loudly, mumbling nonsense, and a rush of relief overcomes Jack.

"We're going home, baby. Stay with me!"

Catching a second wind, he takes in the sight of salvation. The sight of life, of gleaming green mixed with ocean blue, resurrects her. The intensifying motion of the waves pulls them closer to safety. Of course, the battle is harder. As much as he craves a stronger pair of arms to put an end to his struggle, he has to be Alice's pier, her harbor, and her shore.

Jack is the rescuer. He has always been the one. Maybe this is why, deep down in his heart, he secretly hopes to be rescued too, someday. Of course, Alice is the one to have rescued him. He sees that now, and guilt consumes him for grasping at the Spear for as long as he did while Alice cried for his help.

From him drowning in desolation, from the overwhelming hauls of the water that reminded him of a home he never had, with her he has it all. The

gray blur of the solemn water surrounds him. The first hit of fresh and crisp air reminds him of how badly he craves freedom, and now he has finally attained it. His eyes drift to where the boat's ladders welcome him aboard, commencing another excruciating challenge for him.

To simply lift Alice is out of the question. The pressure of being tugged would only tear her bleeding wound. The calm that came upon sighting the boat soon evaporates, and the eerie wind around them starts to turn chilly, biting into their bones.

"Alice, hon, can you hear me?" Jack whispers into Alice's ear, only for her to loosely lace her arms around his torso like a garland. "Alice, hey, don't fall asleep on me. Come on, we arrived back at the boat. I need you awake."

"Mmm." Alice's reply is weak.

The saltwater burns his eyes, and he's unsure if it's the surrounding depths or his own tears. Alice has witnessed far too much bloodshed. The innocent lives lost. Jack moves them closer to the ladder, and he grips onto the half-cold, half-scorching metal.

It is a rather strange occurrence for the temperature to be contradicting itself, but then again the whole momentum has been unconventional. The highs and lows they have undergone are far more surreal; the only bliss comes as they see a familiar face appear into view from the top of the boat, holding a gun for protection.

"Jack, Alice? Oh my God, you guys are alive! Jack, you are not going to believe what I discovered about my laptop," Dymitry exclaims.

"Dymitry, it's going to have to wait. We're going to need your medical expertise. Alice is hurt, wounded by the Spear," Jack replies.

"Of course, I'm so sorry, hurry, give me her hands!" Dymitry exclaims as he lays a black handgun to the side and bends over to grab Alice.

Dymitry is swift to sense how critical the situation is. "Push her up from there as I pull, so we can try not to strain her wound."

The cloth soaked in drying merlot, sinks his heart. All of the questions that were making the rounds in his head, gnawing at his ever-growing distress and provoking his curiosity could wait. He knows he can always bombard Jack with his thousand questions later. For now, he has to get Alice to safety, warm her up, and pull out their extensive first-aid kit which he had ransacked in their absence out of sheer boredom to tend to her wound.

Ensuring Alice is resting on the sofa bed in the main cabin of the ship, Dymitry starts to tend to her wounds. Jack is left to follow Dymitry's set of commands and rummage through a cabinet in the hopes of finding a set of clean and dried towels to absorb all the numbing aches from their bodies. Jack leans back against the small kitchen countertop as he throws a towel in Dymitry's direction opposite to him. He silently watches Dymitry mutter an apology repeatedly while cleaning her wound with saline and rubbing alcohol before he begins the harshest process: to sew the three-inch slash on her lower abdomen. Jack immediately closes his eyes, holding onto her hand, praying she will recover. Getting to the point of doing all they can, they sit with her and allow fate to take its course.

Jack looks up at Dymitry with curiosity. "How did you even get rid of the handcuffs? Last I remember, you were shackled to your death in case we were never to return." Jack folds his arms across his chest and starts to heat water in the microwave for a fresh cup of coffee.

"Jack, do you really believe I was letting myself be chained? There was no way I was letting you guys drown with a bunch of maniacs."

Jack's lip stretches, making him reminisce the simplest feel of a smile. His friend had outdone himself. Jack's heart flutters with life again. Then, with a soft whisper, the sound of Alice fills the room from behind them.

"You need to take care of Jack, Dymitry," Alice says in her weakened state.

Jack's leg is still bleeding down to his ankle from Gunther's grip, leaving him a permanent souvenir that he will talk about for years to come. He turns around and see's Alice's eyes and face radiating a smile back at Jack.

"Alice, you're awake. Don't worry about me, sweetie," expresses Jack.

Alice jerks up in fright. "What about Bob?"

"Shh." Jack settles her down. "No worries, just rest."

He feels bad lying to her, but he needed to calm her down, knowing she is barely out of shock, and this is a critical time for her right now.

Dymitry moves back and examines the fresh stretch of black zigzags on a glowing blush of skin on Alice's torso. Dymitry abandons the needle and hands her a couple of painkillers.

"That should do it for now. Alice, you will need to rest, save your energy. We need it to make it to shore."

Alice is fast to fall a sleep, her chest rising and falling. But that doesn't stop Dymitry from talking.

"Take care and sleep, okay? Hopefully, by the time you wake up, we will be back home."

Jack leans in and places a kiss on her forehead. His lips linger for a little longer. "Dymitry, let's get going."

"What about the Bob and the others?"

Jack shakes his head.

"And the Spear?"

"Gone forever."

Dymitry just nods in understanding, wipes his hands one more time for good measure, and gets behind the wheel and starts to set a course to land. Dymitry doesn't have the heart to break the news to his friend, of how he feared the wound might be far deeper than what Jack had perceived.

But, on the other hand, Alice surprises Dymitry. Her breathing is far better than what it should be, considering she was mauled with a Spear.

Dejected, both the men look out the boat's window. Off in the distance, falling cliffs replace the spot where there once was an underwater cenote, disrupting the tranquility of the scene before them. *What a lie,* Jack thinks to himself. The waters he had tethered up till date, but he knows better now. These waters only hide the monstrosity that lies beneath. Still, his mind is irked to go beyond and seek more. His eyes are trained on the site they had managed to come out alive from. Each passing second, his mind travels back to Bob, how he had crumbled with the stone cavern that had trapped him. Gunther would become another legend or myth to be added among the rumors of Longinus, Khan or Hitler.

The burden his heart had been carrying up to this point finally finds the escape. His skin tingles with all the unshed emotions, his throat wanting to burst and let the agony shrill the atmosphere. In spite of this, off in the distances he silently watches the last tip of the cliff collapse and drown before him. It processes slowly, however the claws of time threaten to rip his heart apart. His thoughts are only broken when her sobbing turns hysterical. Alice too had been watching the scene of dissolving wreckage from where she lay. She closes her eyes as her body trembles from shock.

Jack, drinking his coffee, chokes back a tear. His sorrow comes to a halt seconds later, as before they could take off they hear a knock under the boat, and then loud splashing from the back of the vessel. Frantic and alarmed, Jack and Dymitry run to take in the sight. Confusion sprawls all over them, and their foreheads furrow at the distant sight of an old man pulling off his scuba mask and coming out of the water and onto the ship. The creases are replaced by smirks, leaving Dymitry to announce to the silence in the room.

"The old man's alive!" Dymitry gasped.

Their hearts rejoice seeing Bob, who noticed everyone's faces were so pale. Placing a hand on his chest, Bob tames his breath as his heart threatens to burst. One of his legs is bleeding and mangled, but he stands with confidence and ease on the other. Once his breath relaxes and he readjusts to his surroundings, he looks at Dymitry and Jack quizzically.

"Not too old to kick your butt, Dymitry!" Bob chuckles.

Still not one of them batted an eye, making Bob roll his eyes.

"Okay children, relax. I am not a ghost. Just manage to escape at the last possible moment," Bob replies.

Bob beckons toward himself before exasperation takes over and he walks to the couch at the back of the bridge room of the ship, slumping down, seeing Alice lay in a weak and frail state.

"How are you doing, dear?" As Bob consoles her, he pushes some hair out of her face.

Alice opens her eyes, and upon seeing Bob, she smiles and falls back to sleep.

Bob gets up to open a cabinet and pulls out a cigar and lighter from where he last left them, then walks over to Jack, who is looking out at sea to where there once was a rocky cliff, as Dymitry is busy sailing them closer to shore.

Bob pulls a cigar and lights it up. "I see you boys have tended to her wounds."

Jack can't help himself as he continues to stare at Bob, as so many thoughts are passing through his mind.

"Bob, I don't understand. How did you escape? I thought your leg was broken."

"A miracle really, with all the shaking, the boulder gave way, and I was able to free my leg. I quickly realized it wasn't broke, and I hobbled out of there." Bob pauses and gives a good puff, soaking in the Cuban fermented peppery harsh leaves, and continues. "The reality is I wasn't that far from you. I saw the two of you off in the distance, but didn't want to bother you, as I knew you needed to concentrate on getting back here safe."

Jack is confused. "And what of the Spear?"

Bob, feeling annoyed, blows a pillar of smoke in Jack's face. "And what about it, Jack? Another second and I would have been right there with that Spear, lost to the ocean forever." Bob pauses for a moment, then shakes his head. "For moment, Alice and I didn't know if that Spear had consumed your head, or whether you were going to come back and save us."

Jack shrugs. "Of course, forgive me, I'm so sorry. I'm just glad you're safe. I don't know what came over me. I just felt transfixed?"

Bob, feeling Jack's struggle, puts his hand on his shoulder. "Forget about it, kid. The important thing is we all made it out alive." Bob goes on smoking. "Just look at the Spear as something that has to have its own destiny. Just take pride and joy in knowing that anyone who goes looking for it will never find it buried under all that landmass under the ocean. The legend of the Spear of Destiny officially ends with Gunther."

Jack finds comfort in Bob's words, and looks back at the ocean. "You know, I didn't think to take any treasure for myself. Well, except for that rock Alice has. Not that I would actually keep any of it, as it really all belongs in a museum."

"Of course you didn't." Dymitry rolls his eyes in response of knowing his friend all too well, especially the boy scout badge he proudly wears on his shoulder.

Bob huffs in good tidings, and begins to pull out of his pocket dozens of Raubgold coins that bear both the seals that he looted from the treasure pile in the cavern. Placing them all in Jack's hands.

"Then this will give you relief. The days of the Vatican's secrecy is over."

Jacks examines the gold coins in his hands, and smiles.

With all the knowledge Bob had locked away in his heart, he feels his soul lighten. He is glad that he has a pair of listening ears to share the fearsome secret of the Spear with. He knows neither of these would ever disclose the information to a third soul. He knows without needing him to say it, that all three of them understand the secret location of the Spear is critical, nor

would they mention it when explaining how they found the gold coins on *U-Boat 2553*. As far as Bob was concerned, he was happy if everyone goes on believing it is still sitting in the Vatican. And the three of them would tuck it away in a confidential file in their minds to eventually forget as a once monumental hunt of theirs.

Jack looks at the swastika coins in his hands and gives them back to Bob. "For your troubles and your expenses."

Dymitry blurts out in frustration, "Jack?"

Bob doesn't know what to say. "But…but Jack… I thought you needed these?"

Jack goes on to confess an act to the both them that he had done before stepping foot on this ambiguous adventure. Of course, his actions had consequences, yet Jack is a meticulous man. He had reached out to Lorenzo and given him a letter stamped with Jack's own seal, only to be broken by the right person. The letter entailed anything but good. The letter bore no good wishes, but only spoke words of utmost importance and had an urgency, detailing the dark history and years of the Vatican's coverup. They were the unheard woes of all those who had lost their lives in the path of a selfish agenda put forth by Pope Pius. It was his hope to rebuild a better tomorrow, from those who lost so much. He also provided physical proof of the evidence that they covered up to show their wrongdoings.

"Are you saying that you gave Lorenzo the Vatican coin you got off Krueger?" Bob trails as he scratches his head in half worry, half fury.

Jack continues to explain how crucial it was for the Vatican to be exposed. They could have been framed, or even worse as he had hunched, they could have been found dead, killed by Gustavo. As Jack continues to elaborate on his pure intentions, Bob understands.

"And who is Lorenzo giving it to?" asks Bob.

"He has someone in the senate he is going to hand it off to, to try to get an international hearing going, and develop some press out of it," Jack insists.

Bob chuckles as to what Jack has done as he glances in Alice's direction, who has by now drifted off to deep sleep. Even their loud banter does not make her stir or complain. Her sight fills Jack with a sense of contentment and bliss. Deep down, Jack knows he could never measure what he lost in the Spear with what he has gained.

Life is undoubtedly odd. It never works just the way Jack wants. It is a roller coaster ride. On the other hand, he always perceives life through a different lens, one in which views are infinite and the possibilities are endless. There are no limits to his passion and wants. With Alice by his side, he has discovered an entirely new world. A galaxy with contrasting stars and life. The whole descent had been exhilarating, filled with anticipation and excitement to take up the different twists and turns that waited for the taken.

What brings Jack more joy is the very fact of no nasty soul ever reaching the holy thing. The Spear is far too pure to be tainted with tragedy repeatedly. Now he is surer than ever. When his house blossoms and his and Alice's children run around wild and free, Jack will forever seal this life of his. He will forever bid goodbye to the ghastly winds and the silent waters and sit down after dinner to pen down his adventures. The book of his life will be his diary, memoir, and legacy that he will leave behind for his children.

"Jack, do you think you will ever return to the sea?" Bob asks, glancing at the setting sun on the horizon.

The orange in the flamingo sky seems to have settled its nerves. The air around them is calm, far more than when they had set foot. Jack thinks to himself, but maintains a worried look.

Instead of replying, Jack only turns to face Alice and watch her face at rest. His mind travels to another enticing possibility, suddenly brightening in his thoughts, causing Bob and Dymitry to inch closer to him.

"Yes, there is other treasure out there I would like to discover...but it's a

lot harder now. What with *The Falcon* being blown up, with Dymitry's software gone, my Triton on its last leg?"

"Bro, I can re-write the code," counters Dymitry with words of encouragement.

Bob nods in agreement.

"Oh, I know you can, Dymitry. Don't get me wrong Bob, the *Calypso* has been a beautiful ship, and you have been awful kind in loaning it to us... but I think Cast Away Towing has to be docked for a while." Jack is hesitant.

Hearing Jack give his excuses, Bob gasps.

"You sound like a fish, flopping around blabbering out of the water." Shaking his head at them foolishly, he retreats to the other room.

Dymitry whispers to Jack.

"Now you've gone and pissed the old man off, and me too. What am I suppose to do now?"

As Jack shrugs his shoulders, Bob walks back in chuckles where he once had secured his vintage dark brown leather briefcase bag before the mishap had begun. Opening the straps, he takes out a set of rectangular, thick white checkbooks. Shaking his head, he continues to ink the page before tearing a paper and putting it before Jack for him to grasp.

"So, you won't take the gold, so how about you three take my money!" Bob smiles.

Jack's eyes narrow on the piece of paper Bob now waves in front of him. Perplexed, Jack looks over at Dymitry, as if soliciting his permission. He nudges for him to at least discover what it states. It is not as if they had not perceived the paper to be a bank check. They were still intrigued at the amount prescribed, and for its intended usage. The check, much to his surprise as he chokes on air, is drafted to him: TEN MILLION DOLLARS. He looks back and forth, from the amount to Bob and back to the amount.

Words fall short.

Bob further elaborates, "Don't look so shocked. I am only giving you this amount because I know you will use it to its rightful purpose. I know you will never disappoint me, Jack. I do not say this to burden you with expectations, but because it is something I love, too. Only I have the money, and you have the energy. Through you, I too will get to witness one of the many marvels. A wonder of the world that not many tourists can see."

"You're…you're…" Jack stutters for the first time in his life. The words are there in his mind. Only they are clouded with disbelief.

"Robert Adler for Adler Enterprises," Dymitry finishes.

Dymitry continues, "I didn't know there was a real face behind the name. Dude, is this why we never knew your last name?"

"Unlike other billionaires, I like to keep a very low profile, let one of my other CEO's take the limelight. It's better for business," Bob replies.

Jack is still looking at the check, then back at Bob. "So, this boat?"

"She's really mine. Figured you'd treat me differently if you had known the truth. I just wanted to feel like part of the crew, and you did that, Jack. So, let me part you with one last gift: the *Calypso*. She is all yours; we will consider it part of our new venture together. I can have my attorneys put all the necessary paperwork together when we get back."

Jack is unsure of what to say. "I don't know what to say. You're a man of mystery Bob or Mr. Alder?"

Bob takes a puff of his cigar and agrees. "Exactly."

Dymitry is still in money shock. "I'm sorry, did you say 'billionaire?' With a 'B,' right?"

Bob shakes his head and looks at his feet, sheepishly, and scratches his head. "Well, now that you have established that, I hope it changes nothing between us. This is just my offer to Jack, and my willingness to be his busi-

ness partner in this adventure he thought of. So, what do you say, Jack?"

Jack looks at his friends for support one last time before their smirks grow contagious, and he catches one too. Dymitry looks back at Jack, who is shaking his head yes to agree while he mouths the letter *B* from his lips. In turn, Jack extends his arm forward for Bob to clutch, affirming the beginning of something more.

Chapter XVIII

A Hero's Journey

ob's lips quirk upward in a smile. This is a new beginning for Jack, while another opportunity for Bob to indulge in the results Jack will solely yield. For Bob, the amount is meager. For Jack, Alice and Dymitry, it is a hefty amount that entails the ability to alter the course of their lives.

Unable to move, Alice lays quietly. She listens to Jack, Dymitry, and Bob reunite in the distance and smiles. Deep down within her soul, she is overwhelmed with relief, knowing their turbulent relationship has finally anchored. She is simply happy that he has found himself. The waters are where Jack truly belongs. Unlike the poison he had swallowed in life after the disappearance of his father, and all the accusations that had arisen from dust, it had forced him to hide behind a mask of a feigned smile. Jack's heart now filled with joy, he walks over to look out the window, at the open sea.

The golden streaks of a dipping sun start to fade within the careless spread of heavy grey clouds moving in. The sound of rolling thunder echoes in the distance as it aimlessly calls out for its companion. With a few negative flashes traveling down, the charged ground gives out a loud clasp as it reaches up to the heavens. Now for that brief moment in time when the two touch, love

has filled the air with electrifying bolts that light up the sky, mesmerizing the child in all of them. A dance mother nature has done for thousands of years as it begins to rain.

Jack puts the check in his pocket and turns to check on Alice, so he can give her the good news that their lives are about to take a significant change. At first glance she's lying unnaturally still. Her head is turned away from them, and Jack kneels by her side. He puts his arms around her, squeezing best he can. "Alice, everything is going to be all right." They are the words he knows will comfort her.

Jack holds her in his arms and she slowly looks up at him, giving off a blissful smile, as the rain calmly taps on the boat's glass. She begins to gently close her eyes, fighting for this moment to last forever.

Bob gestures to Dymitry, and they leave the space to give Jack some privacy.

Jack and Alice continue to listen to the tranquil rainfall as he holds her for a brief moment of silence.

Jack leans up and continues to talk with her. "I need you to get better, hon. I know I talked about how I can't wait to start our adventurous life together when, in fact, it's already begun." He brushes his fingertips along her arms, her body still and frigid.

"Alice?" Jack gasps..

She's still.

"Dymitry! Come quick!" Jack yells.

Dymitry flounders next to Jack, panicked by his tone. With all the emotions running through him, he's not sure if he's hallucinating or in a dream. "Dear God."

Bob remains speechless as Dymitry gazes down at Alice's still body and knows exactly what's wrong.

She's dead.

Dymitry is no doctor, but having the knowledge of a paramedic, he knows the wound was far too deep. The stitches would have turned into a memoir, one that not even time would be able to erase. Some wounds, not even time heals. This is one of those. A bad nightmare forever etched on them.

Jack's eyes well with tears. He lurches for Alice and begins CPR. He grasps for anything and yells incoherent commands at Dymitry.

Dymitry stands next to his friend and watches Jack perform CPR on Alice. After long minutes, Jack is panting.

"Come on, Alice. Come on, hon. Come back to me," he urges.

When Jack collapses on Alice's corpse, Dymitry pulls him away. "She's gone, Jack."

"Do something, Dymitry. You're just standing there!" Jack shoves Dymitry off himself.

Bob grabs Jack by the shoulders and shakes him. "Stop it. I'm sorry son, but you need to let her go."

Dymitry manages to take the blanket to cover Alice's body as Jack's emotions spiral into unknown territories. From a catatonic state, to talking himself and laughing, Jack is going insane.

Jack doesn't fight the demons creeping into his soul. He welcomes them in hopes it will dull the pain.

Guilt. That's all he is able to feel as he replays events in his head, denying the truth laid out in front of him. He walks out onto the deck. His heart is in pain that is filled with remorse. By now, the rain has slowed down, as if it was joining him in sorrow, tears descending down.

Leaning against the deck rail, Jack is lost deep in his thoughts when Bob walks next to him. Together silence is shared as they both look out to the sea, blanketed by the rain.

Bob encourages him before his memories could fill him with regret. "Grieve the way you need to, Jack. I'm sorry about Alice." He embraces the peppery taste of his dried leaf Havana.

"How am I going to survive this, Bob?" Jack hints.

"Just know the love you had with Alice was stronger than death. Now, love can't stop death from happing, nothing can. But no matter how hard death tries, it can't separate people from the love they had. It can't take away our memories, or our feelings, either. It can only bring us pain to those we lost, but in time pain can heal. In the end, life is stronger than death." Bob pauses. "Or something like that, I can't remember. I saw it once in some gift shop," Bob says with half of a smile.

Bob takes another puff of his cigar, then continues. "The point is kid, she would have wanted you to go on living. With each new day will come new adventures. Discovering answers to the universe that both time and history had lost. Sharing those new memories alongside the old ones, with the people you love. The reality is death came knocking on her door the minute that creature stabbed her with the Spear, and as sad as that is, that was fate, and it was unavoidable. Now you can go on and feel sorry for yourself and come up with a million other possibilities of what you could have done to avoid this outcome, or you can allow love to overcome death. Alice will always remain alive in your heart in both remembrance and in spirit, as long as you continue to love her, and get stronger with each passing day. You will overcome Alice's death."

Jack is lost for words. All that Bob said is true, and a small bit of pressure is removed off Jack's chest. Is this not how his life is? Each time he comes across a challenge, it is only lived till the next day. It is a new ruling each time, each time he faces new challenges. A brand new day, a brand new start.

With Alice having no next of kin, and that brief moment in time she shared in the Triton, stating how she said she could spend an eternity in the ocean, the three decided it best to bury her at sea.

Despite the red tape of full body sea burials, Bob made a few calls to get government approval, along with an official death certificate based on Dymity's medical care and input. Jack placed the diamond rock in her pocket, kissed her on the forehead. Then they wrapped her up in a blanket and lowered her body into the water.

"She would want to be with you, Jack, and she'll know to find you on the waters," Dymitry says.

Jack nods and watches Alice's sweet face disappear into the ocean's depths.

Jack then began to imagine Alice with her playful smile painted on her lips, her child-like innocence, and the times they shared and the dreams they had.

"I am sorry, Alice," Jack whispers as they all take a moment of silence.

Jack looks down as the remembrance of her washes over him. Like tidal waves, his heart is drenched all over again with resentment. He knows he must keep her alive, wake up to a new day, and would like her always to be with him. Looking over at Bob, he breaks the silence with a statement. "I have one last request for our new business venture."

Bob looks at Jack with curiosity, but also relieved that he is going to continue the adventure. "What is it, Jack?"

"When you fill out the registration for *Calypso*, I would like you to rename her...*Alice*."

Bob looks up a Jack with a heartfelt respect. "Done. She would have loved that, Jack."

Dymitry's face marvels at the thought and shakes his head in agreement.

A week later they make it back home. Jack seeks shelter in the cloaking of night and lets the stars shine down hope on him. Jack is the first to board the ship with his arms outstretched to help the others, wishing it were Alice's hand he were catching. Each person climbing down finally fills their lungs

and senses with comfort. Of all that they have undergone over the course of a few weeks, they know its scars are there to stay. Not even a lifetime would be enough to undo the trauma incurred. Still, they are blessed more than others who were on the same unfortunate journey.

Jack, Dymitry, and Bob are graced with a chance to start their lives over. Taking pride in the starlight night, Jack declares he will be visiting his Aunt Emma, since he had taken off without bidding goodbye, and now without Alice. Dymitry and Bob too take on their separate paths for the night, each occupied with an urgent matter to tend to. Dymitry had left his own family without a word. Watching death breathing down his neck, he does not want to miss the chance to see their smiles. Bob plays the card of being an established and renowned entrepreneur, and the fact that all the time away from work he has led to some catching up to do.

As Bob drives off, Jack and Dymitry are about to get into their cars, when Jack recalls what Dymitry had said a week ago.

"Dymitry, you said you discovered something about your laptop?"

"Oh, yes, almost forgot! While you guys were exploring in the cenote, I took the free time to take apart what was left of my Mac. I wanted to see if I could salvage anything on the hard-drive."

"And were you able to rescue any data?" Jack is excited for his friend.

Dymitry's brows furrow and his face grows pale with confusion. "No, that's just it. Nothing was on there!"

"Oh, sorry. Well, it was damaged pretty bad. At least you tried."

"No, you are not understanding. The hard-drive was blank. Not even the remnants of an operating system existed, as if it was a *new* hard-drive waiting to be formatted.

Jack's eyes light up as another mystery emerges. "What! Are you sure?"

"Dude, I know what a damaged drive looks like, and it gets weirder. My

MacBook was a standard off the shelf laptop that came with eight gigabytes of memory, which this one had. There was even residue where my Millennium Falcon sticker was on the outside of the charred case."

"Okay?"

"Jack, I manually upgraded my Mac to sixteen gigs the night before the accident."

"So, you are saying…"

"While it may look exactly like mine, it is *not my laptop*, Jack!"

Jack stands in silent thought.

Dymitry begs the question. "Not only was Gustavo spying on us, but he did blow up the boat, and switched Macs. It appears our prosciutto friend had a bigger plan than just the Spear?"

"Doesn't seem like his style; in any event, he is dead. The question now is, who has he given it to?"

Jack and Dymitry agree this will have to be looked into in the days ahead. Having some money in their pocket, they will be able to help find the answers they are looking for, but for tonight they agree to get some much-needed rest and part ways.

Jack's drive is short-lived. He lets the town's breeze serenade him. He soaks in the tranquility of a desolate road as Aunt Emma's lighted house comes into view. Seconds turn into a minute, leaving him to turn on his heels to return. The pale hues are filled with color and blood as Uncle Danny's wrinkles ease around his skin as he stretches his lips to grin at them.

"Jack, I am glad to see you."

"I am glad to see you too, Uncle Danny. Though you look a little worn out. Aunt Emma not giving enough of her amazing coffee?" Jack tries to say with a smile. Not to let grief consume him. It was hard enough sharing the news while at sea, keeping any and all details minimal. All they know is that

Alice is gone.

"You are one to say that, Jack. Seems like you haven't had a shower in ages. As for your Aunt Emma, let me warn you…" There was more he wanted to say, perhaps about Alice, but he trailed off.

Before Uncle Danny could finish and provide Jack with an early warning to give him the time and let him come up with an excuse to pacify his aunt, she barges in on them. Her red-rimmed eyes are dry, but it's obvious she's been crying. The men freeze as Aunt Emma is bewildered to see streaks of dirt across Jack's face. Part of his hair has begun to form dreadlocks, and he is wearing saline-stained clothes.

"Good, lord, this child has a death wish." Aunt Emma's eyes are trained on him, filled with endless questions she is ready to hurl. However, she refrains herself and turns to face her husband. "Danny, show him to the spare bathroom and arrange for a change of clothes."

After having the satisfaction of scrubbing away dirt, grime, grease, and bittersweet memories of the adventure lived, Jack makes it to the dining room table just in time. A feast is sprawled before them all, steam escaping from the porcelain dishes. The warm lights of the chandelier bloom the room with joy and the simplest blessing of having a family to share the meal with. Even before sitting, Jack had whispered his grace under his breath. His eyes were no longer numb with remorse or guilt, but they now gleam with excitement to share news of sheer delight with his family.

In the beginning, a hankering to know where Jack had disappeared to lingered until it grew heavy and Aunt Emma could not deny her curiosity. She drops her cutlery. A clinking erupts, breaking all of them from their animate munching. Mouths full, Uncle Danny and Aunt Emma reoccupy themselves and continue stuffing their mouths with the baked asparagus and chicken. Jack is left with no choice but to swallow the lump in his throat before food could pass. Sheepishly, he turns to face his aunt.

"It is not what you are thinking, Aunt Emma."

"Then delight me, Jack. Were you not out there on one of your whimsical expeditions?"

"Well, when you put it that way, it was neither whimsical nor an expedition." Jack opens his mouth to find the words, but upon failing, he closes his mouth. For a few seconds, he continues to repeat the gesture.

"Just let it be," Danny objects as he eats his dinner.

"I am sorry, Danny, if I am concerned for my nephew. But this is not good. He is ruining his life and risking it. And he took Alice with him, and look where she ended up! It all makes sense now."

Jack ignores the jab, although he wanted to yell. But it was true...despite the hand of fate, allowing the hideous creature to even exist and stab Alice with the Spear, was Jack's fault. Jack was the reason she had died. Like Bob said, other outcomes started floating in his head. Wondering if he had chosen her over the Spear at that very moment, would there have been enough time, or maybe he didn't need to solve the puzzle that opened the hatch, or better yet, he should have stayed mad at her, and she would have never gone with him to Cuba. Surly any of these were better alternative choices. Then she would be sitting across the table with him today. He cringes at the thoughts as his heart pounds with a bitter venom that would have only poisoned his mind with Alice's wrecking memories, floating away into the sea.

Jack eats in silence. His aunt and uncle try to make small talk, but he is on autopilot, just meandering through the motions, letting muscle memory guide him.

For better or worse was yet to be known, but Aunt Emma quickly leaves the room. Minutes later, she returns with a torn open letter and slides it toward Jack. Her demeanor is no longer hostile or jovial. It is guarded. Her eyes are soft, and unspoken words twirl in them, as if begging him to give it a chance. His own wall starts to build up and his jaw tightens.

"I didn't read what's written inside. It just came yesterday. But the hand-

writing seems familiar. It's addressed to 'Little Skipper.'"

Hearing those words, *Little Skipper,* Jack's obsessed thoughts of Alice disperse. Jack takes the letter from her, his body turning cold. Jack's thoughts betray him and he battles his own doubts. Deliberating on bearing yet another pain, he hurriedly pulls the letter out to affirm the sender's name. Sure enough, the initials "W.S." are written in cursive. The ticking of the clock in the room dissolves, and he grows numb to his surroundings. Confusion and anger rise within him. There is only one person that called him "Little Skipper." Is someone meddling with his mind? More than ever, Jack hopes for the letter to harbor any clue of what has happened. Without wasting another breath, and with trembling hands, he lets his eyes peruse the words scribbled.

Hey Little Skipper,

My thoughts are jumbled, and I apologize for the flow of this being so messy. What can I say? I am writing to my son after eons, and finally telling him that I'm alive and well. I'm deeply sorry for the secret I have kept from you all these years, and can only hope you will come to forgive me. Things are not always like they seem. I had my reasons. Ones that I cannot write in this letter. So, I will keep this short and brief, as you have never really left my side.

Firstly, tell your Aunt Emma thank you for taking such great care of you. And you are lucky to have found a gem like Alice, and I am sorry for your loss. Dymitry, having cared for you all this time, especially after my disappearance, can never be measured with any world treasure. And for Danny to have fulfilled the duties of a father in my absence makes me wonder that even I might not have been such a great father.

Wish I could have been there to tell the world you are my son. However, you have to understand the gravity of my situation. But after what you experienced recently, I hope you can understand that what I discovered is even greater than than the Spear.

However, you're in grave danger for what's ahead. I cannot share via any electronic communication device, as I fear I have already been compromised. Jack, I need to see you. Attached are my coordinates. Look forward to finally seeing you soon. 35.9982° N, 5.6879° W.

William Sterling

Jacks eyes well with tears of joy. "My father's alive, Aunt Emma, he is alive!" He hands them the letter.

Danny and Emma's jaws drop in shock.

"That can't be?" Danny questions as Emma can't help but ask, "Where has he been?

"Sounds like he is in trouble. Should we call the police?" replies Emma.

She is interrupted by Danny. "No, I think he just wants to keep it between him and Jack."

Folding the letter back, Jack hurriedly borrows Uncle Danny's cell phone and enters the set of coordinates in the browser. The words come before him: *Strait of Gibraltar.*

He ransacks his mind as he desperately tries to pull the last string of memories associated with Gibraltar. "Did he really find it? Can it be true?"

"Did he really find what, Jack?" Emma asks.

Exasperated, Jack starts to rub his fingers on his forehead. The room is doused in silence. He is given the time to regain his composure. Alas, how is he to answer their silent questions when he himself is unsure?

Maybe the letter is a hoax, or a trap to lure him in. But the handwriting, he knows it is of his father. And how it is his habit to keep things curt when important. Nonetheless, Jack fights the urge for the irking doubts to frustrate his peace. Then it strikes him. His eyes widen. To further clarify his doubts, he once more relies on technology and confirms his thoughts are true. Feeling his heart plummet to his feet, he meets his aunt's already glossing eyes.

"Jack, you're making me nervous. What did your father find, and where has he been all these years?"

"The Lost City of Atlantis," Jack hesitates.

Blood and life drains from Aunt Emma as her face flickers from Jack to Danny's. A look of determination is fixated on Jack's face. What Bob had graced him with hinted that maybe this is fate. Maybe, this is his destiny. Who is he to deny his help to another Sterling? Maybe under the pretext of an adventure, Jack can finally demand answers from his father.

The excitement of the discovery is enough to keep Jack awake all night. His mind is busy planning a possible trip in his near future, to find his stranded father. How the journey of life had taken a full turn. The room is silent, notebooks open and spread out on his side of the bed as he types feverishly on the laptop his uncle had given him for that purpose.

Jack couldn't help but think back to what the southern fire marshall had said: 'When one door closes, another one opens.' Jack realizes a new day is upon him, where his adventure isn't ending, but only beginning.

***

Night has fallen once again upon the quaint city of St. Augustine. All that's visible below the blanket of twilight stars is the slow tide that oscillates inside the majestic wharf, sleeping to the sound of the harboring boats swaying in a gentle rockabye motion. Absolute silence seems to echo the ocean pier's life, only disrupted by a luminous light moving across the dock, hiding the obscure man behind the shadows, who we have come to know as Bob. Stopping for a brief second, he ever so subtly turns on his heels on the creaking panel of the pier and shines his light on the fading green board. The words in white seem to be rusted and depicting the state of the worn-out owners. CAST AWAY TOW. He shakes his head and turns to face the sight before him, his eyes as dark as night. With hurried steps, he scrambles closer to the tugboat *Calypso,* which will soon be named *Alice,* which now stands in silence, engulfed in slumber. The scuba gear is put on quickly. The eyes flutter closed, only to open to embrace himself for the surge of power he is about to indulge in.

Without sparing another thought, Bob lets the cold splashing of water make contact with his skin. His injured leg is bashed up and sprained, but he doesn't care. His senses awaken at the cold biting through the gear. The current of the water pleads with Bob to reconsider his notion. How is a man to refuse the power that would place him atop the world? How does a soul long for death when it has tasted immortality? His eyes are locked and his heart in the trance of his mind, enabling Bob to swim below and under the hull of the vessel.

Darkness fills his face and he shifts to switch on the flashlight secured on his head. Soon the musky water is illuminated, giving Bob a clear view of the secret underwater hatch in the middle of the hull. He begins to press the water-resistant keys that light up upon his touch. Entering his secret code, the elongated doors begin to slide open as the green aura of light spills out into the sea. Glee and ecstasy drive him to extract the very piece of metal he had secured only a week ago. Before him lies the Spear of Destiny. Now resting in his hand, despite being underwater, a jolt of electricity pierces through his veins, briefly sending his eyes a flashing red. His fingers burn under the touch, and for a moment he deliberates if he should discard it, growing oblivious to its power, and what he has seen. But he is just a man who yearns to be something more than a mere mortal, and his heart is bewitched by gluttony. He swims over to where the Triton is clasped along the side of the *Calypso*. Bob starts thinking to himself as he climbs out of the dock, with the Spear in hand, that he knows it was no accident he met Jack in that bar. Despite Bob's acting performance, he knew the story of the Spear.

Bob talks to himself. "Thanks Jack…but you know what they say: keep your friends close, but your enemies closer."

Switching off the light on his forehead, a familiar dark Denali is waiting for Bob on the dock. The driver, James, opens the door, handing him a set of new clothes. He puts the Spear of Destiny into a long custom Pelican case that seals with a cryptic digital lock. A foreboding sound, carrying a thick German accent spews from inside the vehicle. All that can be seen is the tip

of glowing orange embers from the head of a cigar. He smokes it not out of addiction, but a sense of his identity, in control.

"Job well done; does he suspect anything?" the mysterious voice replies.

Bob pulls off his shirt, revealing a swastika symbol on his upper right shoulder.

"No!" Bob mentions as he continues to get dressed.

"I thought the point of blowing up his precious *Falcon* was to steal the software. Why do you insist on keeping Mr. Sterling alive?"

"You wanted the software, not me. You were on that boat with Krueger. He can think on his feet, and help get us what we need."

The mysterious man continues to inhale slowly as a few ashes drop off onto the vehicle's floor. Then he slowly points out, "He better come through. We lost a lot of good men during that fight."

"Well, they were supposed to finish Gustavo off; instead, I had to risk my neck in that cavern." As Bob gets irritated, he throws his wetsuit to the ground.

James walks by and picks it up.

"In the end, it all worked out," the mysterious man replies.

Bob shakes his head. "Did the hair check out?"

A puff of smoke bellows again from the darkness.

"Yes…it's Hitler's."

Bob then smiles. "And the journal?"

"My men have started breaking it down, but Driesch's formulas are quite complex with what we are trying to do."

"Well, cloning worked for you," assures Bob.

Out of the shadows, the figure leans forward into the moonlight cascading down into the Denali. As if the reflection of a mirror is present, an exact replica of Robert Adler is sitting there smoking the cigar while holding a glass of Macallan whisky and staring back at him.

"I didn't rise from the dead," Robert Adler replies in his slow German dialect as he embraces the peppery taste of his dried leaf Havana.

"Well, like I said, Jack will find the last two artifacts we need for the Führer's resurrection, then he can be disposed of." An evil grin of excitement flashes across Bob's face as he climbs into the Denali.

Robert nods in agreement as he blows a perfect halo ring of grey smoke that twirls out of the vehicle's door just as Bob shuts it closed.

The stealth black Denali drives off into the twilight, disappearing into the shade of darkness, leaving only the sound of waves crashing against the wooden dock, among the stillness of the night.

Continue the Adventure

UnderWaterBookSeries
JackSterlingAdventures
Jacks_DeepDives

To sign up for *Jack Sterling* Fan Club:
visit www.jacksterlingadventures.com